PERFECTLY POLISHED

KEENEY BUILDS

BOOK TWO

LYNNE HANCOCK PEARSON

ISBN: 979-8-9853527-7-1

Published by All That Editing LLC

This story takes place on the ancestral lands of the Coast Salish. I honor, with gratitude, the land, and its people.

Editing by: wordsmithalchemy.weebly.com

Proofreading & formatting by: TAFKAM

Cover art by: Designwheelgraphics.com

Visit the author at www.lynnehancockpearson.com

For Matt,
Thank you for always being in my corner.

CHAPTER 1

Thirteen Months Ago....
Forty-five minutes.

Fiona Han discreetly turned off the alarm on her smart watch. It wasn't that she was having a bad time, these were nice people. But they were people who knew far too much about her, and she was ready for this day to be over. With a small smile, she said, "I called an Uber. Hilary, thanks for inviting me. I'll talk to you tomorrow."

"I'll drive you home."

Fiona blinked and stared at Tomas Alvarado. "Umm… thanks, but I'm fine." She waved her phone at him and put it into her purse.

He stood and looked down at her. "I'll drive you home."

Eep!

She did not want to make a scene. He didn't give off an axe-murderer vibe, and her friends were grinning at her like he was perfectly safe, but the rough-edged man who never seemed to smile, unnerved her.

Marcia Ortiz, a woman in her sixties, and best friend to Fiona's mother-in-law Iris, touched her hand. "You'll be fine," she murmured. "You'll be safe with Tomas."

Really? Fiona wasn't so sure. She rose on wobbly legs, tucked her purse under her arm, and accompanied Tomas to the stairs leading from Hilary's deck to the driveway. She glanced back at Marcia, who winked at her.

Eep!

Descending the stairs, she was aware of the man behind her. It seemed that, for the past two weeks, Tomas had been at her back without saying a word. Reaching the driveway, she faced three white pick-up trucks bearing the logo for Keeney Building Supplies, the company Iris owned. With a hand to her elbow, Tomas guided her to the one in the middle, distinguishable from the others by the rosary hanging from the rearview mirror, and opened the passenger door. Fiona eyed the distance up to the seat of the truck, then down at her pencil skirt and heels. Then she was *up*. Tomas placed her gently on the seat and reached around to buckle the seat belt.

"I'm not a child!" She glared up at him.

He met her eyes fully for the very first time. "I know you're not." He closed the door and walked around the hood of the truck.

Walk was the wrong word. Tomas prowled like a predator. Did that make her his prey?

He climbed behind the wheel, his presence sucking up all the air in the truck. Fiona wanted to open the window, to breathe, perhaps to crawl out.

Placing a large hand on the back of her seat, he ignored her as he turned to back out of the driveway. She could smell him. Woodsy, with a trace of lime underneath. If she turned her head ever so slightly, she could brush up against his hand and rub his scent all over her. Where had that thought come from? *It must be the wine.* She shook her head and stared forward.

"I live on Dunlop Street," she told him.

"I know." Tomas met her eyes in the rearview mirror. "I changed the locks on your doors last week."

"Right," she said in a small voice. To keep the douche canoe of her soon-to-be ex-husband out of her house. Suddenly, she widened her eyes. "I haven't paid you yet! I'm so sorry, I forgot all about it. I can write you a check when we get to the house. It's just—"

His eyes sliced to her. "It's taken care of."

"Oh." Tomas worked for her mother-in-law. Iris must have had him do it. "Thank you."

He drove in silence.

Not knowing how to converse with someone who clearly didn't like to talk, she leaned her head back and closed her eyes.

She awoke to see Tomas scouring the word "cunt" off her garage door.

Fiona threw herself from the truck, stumbling as she hit the ground. Righting herself, she flew around the hood of the truck. Tomas whirled and grimaced.

"Ohmygod. Ohmygod. Ohmygod," she chanted, pacing back and forth in front of the garage. Scrawled in dripping red paint, each capital letter was at least two feet high.

Eddie.

He'd chosen a public and humiliating way to get back at her.

Tomas dropped a scrub brush and moved closer to Fiona, stepping between her and the offensive word. He pulled her hands away from her face and squeezed them. "Babe. Go inside. I'm going to get some paint and take care of this."

The setting sun full in his face highlighted the ticking muscle in his jaw. The angry slash of his eyebrows mirrored the angry slash of his mouth, but his eyes were full of concern.

"You can't…. Where will you…." She was unable to form a coherent thought, let alone a complete sentence.

He squeezed her hands again, bringing her attention back to him. "I've got this." He released one hand, led her around the truck to retrieve her clutch, and fished out her keys. Still holding her hand, he guided her to the front door, unlocked it, and led her inside. Closing the door, he pressed her back against it and said, "Stay here."

He waited for her to nod, then moved quickly through the house. When he returned and said, "All clear," Fiona relaxed. Once again, Tomas took her hand. He led her to the living room, gently pushed her onto the couch, and sank onto the coffee table facing her. His gaze roamed her face, and Fiona took in a deep breath and squared her shoulders, feeling slightly less wobbly.

"I'll be back as soon as I can. Lock the doors behind me and try to relax." He gently unclenched her hands from around her purse, opened it up, and pulled out her phone. "Add me to your contacts. I don't think you'll need to, but call me—don't text—*call* me if you get scared."

Tears welled in her eyes. She tried to blink them away, but one escaped, and he wiped it away with a calloused thumb. His eyebrows rose in a silent question which she answered with a quick nod, then he got up and moved to the door. She locked the door behind him and headed to the kitchen to find the wine.

*H*is truck's headlights illuminated Fiona when he pulled into the driveway an hour later. She turned away from the garage door and squinted into the bright lights. Standing barefoot, her beige pencil skirt wrinkled and spattered, black hair escaping her chignon, she wove slightly.

Tomas swore softly as he got out of the truck. A frightened Fiona he was expecting. A drunken, disheveled, grinning Fiona he was not. Polite Fiona with perfect posture aroused him. Fiona with messy hair, smeared makeup, and smelling like spilled wine, undid him.

"Hey," she said brightly. As if standing in her driveway in the dark painting over obscene words was a normal part of her day. For she had painted over the word. Or, more accurately, she had painted within and around the word, adding dots, splashes, rays, and swirls, until the ugly word had become…beautiful.

"Nail polish?"

A small table stood to the side, covered with bottles of polish in an array of colors.

Fiona shrugged, the movement causing her to sway. "It's what was available." On unsteady legs, she approached the table, reaching for the wineglass on it. She knocked it over, and it crashed on the driveway. Tiny shards of glass sparkled in the lights that framed the garage.

Fiona looked up at him and giggled. "Oops," she said.

He scooped her up and headed for the open front door. "Come on, Princess, I think you've had enough."

"Okay," she said with a goofy smile. She wrapped her arms around his neck and snuggled against his chest with a sigh.

For a man who hauled lumber and bags of concrete for a living, carrying Fiona Han was the easiest thing in the world. He breathed her in, separating the scents of paint and polish and wine until he smelled *her*, a heady mix of jasmine and sandalwood. He wanted to sink into the couch, settle her in his arms, and share his heartbeat with hers. Instead, he carried her to her room and placed her on the bed.

Fiona wouldn't let go. She opened eyes that were big and brown, unguarded and trusting, and fixed them on his face. "I love your eyebrows."

Said eyebrows came together in a frown.

"Ooh. I especially love it when you do that. All frowny

and forbidding." She released one hand and drifted her fingers softly across his eyebrows and down the side of his face. "You're like an Aztec god."

He didn't feel like a god. He felt like a man close to a beautiful woman he'd very much like to kiss. Frozen in place by her touch, he held still as she traced his lips with one hand, and drew him down with the other.

She was drunk.

She was distraught.

He shouldn't be there.

Tomas touched her lips lightly with his own, and drew back. Her plump bottom lip held a trace of moisture. Holding her gaze, he leaned in and tasted her, stroking his tongue along the seam of her lips. Her lips parted and invited him in. He cradled her face, the scarred, brown skin of his hands a contrast to her pale, porcelain perfection.

Fiona moaned beneath him, a sound that echoed deep in his throat. She whimpered when he pulled back and sat up.

"Stay," she said.

It was incredibly tempting, but he shook his head. "Another time." He ran a hand through her hair, removing the remaining pins and placing them on the bedside table. Holding her gaze, he said, "I promise."

Fiona sighed and turned to her side, snuggling into the pillow. He found a blanket and covered her. Stroking a finger down her cheek, he tucked a strand of silky, dark hair behind her ear, and reluctantly rose. She looked so peaceful but it would all come back to her tomorrow, and he vowed to be there for whatever she needed.

Every day for the next four days, he called. Each call went to voicemail.

None were returned.

CHAPTER 2

Present Day....

He'd hit his thumb right on the fingernail. It was red and would soon turn black, but it wasn't bleeding, and he hadn't broken the skin. Hopefully he wouldn't lose the nail.

He was a highly trained professional. How had he managed to whack himself with a hammer?

"Sorry, dude. I didn't see you."

Oh. Right. A young man with shaggy hair and a sheepish expression stood beside Tomas. Wearing a hard hat and yellow safety vest, he looked like a carpenter but wasn't quite there yet. Tomas gave the accident-prone student a murderous glare. "Gibson, put the phone in your pocket. This is a job site. Inattention causes accidents."

He ground the words out when he really wanted to push the kid up against the drywall and whack him with a hammer.

Gibson's Adam's apple bobbed in his throat as he nodded. He stuffed his phone in his pocket and scuttled off, nearly knocking Vincent over in his haste to get away.

"And?" Vincent inquired with a raised eyebrow.

Tomas shoved his hammer into his toolbelt and rolled his eyes. "I hit my thumb when the kid bumped into me."

"What's the problem? You have two," Vincent said with a grin.

Tomas flipped him the bird, which only made Vincent laugh.

"Seriously, do you think he's going to make it?"

Tomas leaned against the drywall and crossed his arms over his chest. Vincent mirrored his pose and they both looked around at what would be a tiny house, but was now a skeleton. Four students from Keeney Community College worked nearby, installing drywall that had been cut to conform with the window and door frames. The thump of a nail gun and whine of a power saw provided background music for their industrious dance.

Tomas and Vincent taught construction and contracting to young adults for whom traditional schooling didn't work. Keeney Builds was a joint project between the college, a local non-profit named Keeney Works, and Keeney Building Supply, the company that employed both men as contractors and handymen. Tomas and Vincent were uniquely suited as instructors because they'd both served time and could advise young people about the reality of living behind bars.

The program mixed classroom instruction, on-the-job training with KBS (both in the store and one-on-one with a contractor) and culminated in the entire class of twelve working together to build a tiny house from the ground up. The houses were then delivered to a community that featured affordable housing.

"I sure as hell hope so. I'd hate to mess with our stats," Tomas muttered.

Three classes of students had successfully completed the twelve-week program over the past year. All were now employed in their field, with one exception, and she was at home with a newborn.

"What's the problem? I worked with him on a cabinet install, and the kid was good."

Tomas shook his head and examined his still-throbbing thumb. "Lack of attention. Over the last two days, he's been glued to his phone. I hate social media. People need to focus on the real world."

"Sure, Grandpa." Vincent shoved him with an elbow. He turned toward Tomas and said, "Maybe there's something going on. It could be more than the newest posting on a gaming site."

Tomas narrowed his eyes as he considered the comment. The students gravitated toward Vincent, who smiled often and was generous with his praise. He might know more about Gibson's background. Tomas and Vincent looked alike to the casual observer, both with copper skin, dark hair, and hard muscles. Tomas's stockier build, military-style haircut, and tattoos set him apart, as well as his perpetual scowl. His demeanor did not invite casual conversation.

"Yes!"

They turned as one in the direction of the shout. Gibson careened around the corner with a face-splitting grin. "She got the job." The smile dropped when he saw Tomas's frown. "Um. My mom. She, um, has been out of work for a while. And had a job interview yesterday."

Vincent smiled. "That's good. Glad to hear it." He thumped Gibson on the shoulder as he passed him. He turned and mouthed "See" to Tomas behind Gibson's back.

Tomas glared in response, then tried to turn it into a more pleasant expression before speaking to Gibson. "Good stuff. You gonna be able to concentrate now?"

Gibson smiled broadly. "Absolutely," he said, bouncing off to resume work.

. . .

A few days later, Tomas approached the conference table in the offices of Keeney Building Supply. Less than two years ago, he would have been lining up for mealtime in the minimum-security prison where he served time for auto theft. Now, he was about to eat a catered lunch with respected community leaders.

He picked his usual spot. Ali, the KBS operations director, to his left; Hilary, the CEO and Vincent's wife, to his right at the head of the table; Vincent, directly across from him; his mother Marcia, the marketing director, to his right. Iris, the owner of KBS, was absent. Meetings weren't Tomas's idea of a good time. He'd rather be building something. Fortunately, the others at the table were like-minded, Hilary ran a meeting well, with no messing around, and there was food. The downside to the Monday meetings was that Tomas felt like the odd man out.

Literally.

Newlyweds Vincent and Hilary constantly exchanged lingering looks in a nauseating display of affection. Ali and Marcia were also a couple, although they maintained separate houses. Tomas was sure that would change soon. It was impossible to miss Ali's eyes lighting up when Marcia was around. Tomas was happy for his friends, but still, the giggles and glances left him disgruntled.

He was reaching for a sandwich when Marcia grabbed his hand and stared at the bruise blooming under his thumbnail. "Ouch. How'd that happen?"

Tomas scowled, Vincent snorted, and Hilary made a sympathetic face.

"I thought you were a highly trained professional." Ali elbowed him in the ribs. Tomas's scowl deepened.

"You can razz him later. We've got a full agenda," Hilary said, eyeballing her laptop. "First item: Iris is out of town, so someone needs to—"

There was a flurry of movement in his peripheral vision. Tomas looked up from his meal to see Ali, Marcia, and Vincent touching their noses and wearing shit-eating grins. "What?"

"Not it!" they said in unison.

"What am I missing?"

Hilary rolled her eyes and gave Tomas a wry smile. "That means you get the honor of representing KBS at the next Keeney Works board meeting."

Tomas's eyes went wide before he glared at his coworkers. "Oh, hell no," he muttered.

Iris McLeod owned KBS and, in the complicated relationship that combined the community college, Keeney Works, and Keeney Builds, sat on the board for all three. In her absence, a senior KBS employee took her place.

"I have to be somewhere else," Tomas said.

"You don't even know the date yet," Marcia replied.

Ali and Vincent both had their mouths full and merely smiled.

"I'll put the date, time, and location on your calendar," Hilary said, then moved on to the next order of business.

Tomas pushed his plate away. He was no longer hungry.

CHAPTER 3

The smartwatch on Fiona Han's wrist vibrated. She turned off the alarm, typed a few more words, saved the document, and closed the lid of her laptop. She stood and went to the closet in the corner of her office. Opening the door, she reached up to the top shelf and pulled down a lipstick from the basket that sat there. She checked her appearance in the full-length mirror on the inside of the door while reapplying the light pink lipstick. Her long black hair was up in its customary French twist, not a strand out of place. The pearls at her throat matched the pearls in her ears. She tucked her pale pink blouse into the waistband of her beige pencil skirt and reached for the matching jacket. She kicked off the ballerina flats she habitually wore in the office and slipped her feet into nude patent leather pumps with four-inch heels. At five feet one, Fiona needed every extra inch she could get.

She picked up a small pouch holding her phone, pens, pencils, and extra lipstick, then grabbed her laptop and a stack of papers from her desk. Squaring her shoulders and taking a deep breath, she strode out of her office, down the hallway into the boardroom of Keeney Works, spotted the scowling face of the very handsome and irritated Tomas Alvarado, and promptly stumbled over an invisible impediment.

Strong hands grabbed her arms. She looked down at the scarred brown hands that gripped her. Then up at Tomas. How had he moved so quickly? He let go, bent to pick up the papers now strewn over the floor, set them on the conference table, and returned to his seat. All without saying a word.

In an automatic response, she ran a hand over her hair and smoothed her skirt.

"You look perfect," Tomas said without looking up from the papers in front of him.

"Thank you," Fiona replied, sitting down and busying herself with her laptop. Where was a black hole when you needed one?

No one else was present in the boardroom. She was highly aware of Tomas's presence, though he didn't make a sound. Dressed neatly in a clean, white button-down shirt, his woodsy, lime scent hung in the air. She fought against the memories his scent aroused. Not all of them were pleasant. In fact, most were humiliating.

When she saw him for the first time and mistook him for a waiter.

When her now ex-husband shouted at her, calling her a frigid fuck—in front of him.

When he insisted on driving her home, put her to bed, and turned down her drunken invitation to stay.

He'd kissed her, though.

A kiss the likes she'd never had before. It was hard to believe such an intimidating man could be so gentle. But she hadn't wanted gentle, and pulled him down, wrapping her arms around his neck. The kiss turned ravenous, with tangling tongues and deep-throated sighs. He'd pulled back, kissed her on the forehead, and said, "I'll call you." Which he did.

Fiona never answered, and never returned his calls.

Now, he was in the boardroom. All broad shoulders, bronze biceps, hard jaw, kissable lips, and a tattoo peeking out from beneath the sleeve of his rolled-up shirt.

How the hell was she going to run this meeting?

But run the meeting she did. For ninety minutes. Ninety minutes of explaining the budget, defending decisions, praising partners, and sharing a vision. Because Fiona Han *did* have a vision. A vision where mistakes of the past didn't prevent people from finding and maintaining jobs that would provide a living wage.

That was the mission of Keeney Works. Its community partnership that resulted in Keeney Builds encouraged the staff and board to look further. Ideas were brewing as to what other schools and businesses they could partner with.

Tomas did not participate in the discussion, although he paid attention to each speaker, occasionally taking down notes in a battered spiral notebook.

Once, she saw him smile at Betty Ann, the tiny woman sitting next to him. And—*ohmygod*—he had dimples. But then, he caught Fiona's eye and immediately closed down.

The meeting ended, Tomas stood, and helped Betty Ann out of her seat. The septuagenarian owned a popular boutique and faithfully hired employees from Keeney Works. She favored huge black, rhinestone-studded glasses and leopard print kitten heels. She leaned on Tomas's arm as she made her way around the table. Fiona could have sworn she'd walked into the meeting under her own power. Perhaps this was an opportunity to fondle his biceps.

"Good job, dear," Betty Ann said to her with a pat on the arm. "Tomas is going to help me to my car." She smiled blandly at Tomas but gave Fiona a subtle wink.

"Thank you both for being here," Fiona said, casting a swift glance at him.

He lifted his chin in acknowledgement then spoke to Betty Ann. "Hermosa dama, do you want to give me the keys and I'll bring your car around?"

Betty Ann giggled and said, "Oh Tomas, if you let me hold your arm, I'm sure I can make it." She raised an eyebrow at Fiona in passing, and the two slowly made their way out the door.

The room emptied, and Fiona breathed in deeply. Dammit. She could still smell him. Why had she not returned his calls?

Because she never thought she'd see him again.

Because dealing with the end of her marriage had overwhelmed her.

Because—

All the reasons that seemed so valid at the time sounded like lame excuses. Humiliation hit her as she realized she'd never thanked him for painting her garage door in the middle of the night.

An hour later, she saved a document and closed her laptop as her cellphone rang. The display said "Linh Han." Great, her mother was calling. Could the day get any better?

"Hello, Mother." Fiona leaned an elbow on her desk and rubbed her forehead, grateful that her mother preferred voice-only calls as opposed to FaceTime.

"Hello, Fiona. You are well?"

It wasn't exactly a question. Her mother was merely being polite. "Yes, Mother."

"Good. What is Joseph up to?"

Fiona sat up straight. Her brother Joseph was thirty-six and the apple of their mother's eye. He was the properties manager for Han Family Holdings, in charge of purchasing and maintaining HFH's many commercial properties: strip malls containing restaurants, dry cleaners, hair and nail salons, and other small businesses. While he had an office, he was rarely in it.

"I have no idea. Is something wrong?"

"He's hiding something."

That was bad. Joseph and Fiona were expected to answer questions immediately and truthfully when their mother asked a question.

"I want you to find out what is going on and report back to me."

"Yes, Mother." There was no point in arguing. Fiona resumed her slumped position and idly drew on the legal pad next to her laptop. Her mother moved on to the next item on her agenda.

"The divorce is final, yes?"

"Yes, Mother."

"A realtor will be out to the house tomorrow to see if it needs staging."

"What?" Fiona stiffened in surprise.

"You are no longer a married woman. You will return home and live with your family."

"No. I can't move back home. And I don't want to sell my house."

Her mother's emotionless voice continued, "Your father and I bought the house for you as a wedding gift. Without a husband, you cannot afford the mortgage payments."

Thoughts raced through Fiona's head as she tried to regroup. Her mother was right. On her salary alone, Fiona was unable to make the mortgage payments. "I'll refinance. I'm sure I can—"

Switching to Vietnamese, her mother clipped out, "No. It is decided. Unmarried women do not live alone. It is improper. You will move back home. The house will be sold, and the money reinvested in the business."

Tears swam in Fiona's eyes. She was thirty-three. Too old

to be moving in with her parents, but they held all the power. With resignation, she said, "Yes, Mother."

When the conversation ended, she put the phone down, folded her hands in her lap, and contemplated a dismal future.

CHAPTER 4

omas sat in the truck across the street from the entrance of Keeney Works. He knew she was still there; hers was the only car in the parking lot. He knew, because he'd done this before. Not often. He wasn't a stalker; he didn't follow her home. He just made sure she got into her car safely.

He shifted in his seat, not proud of his behavior. He'd treated her badly today, but injured pride would do that to a man.

Like he had every day for more than a year, he wondered what he'd done wrong.

He relived the kiss again because it was the brightest moment of his life. He'd known kissing her was a bad idea, but he couldn't stop himself. Her marriage was falling apart at the time, and she's been strong and stoic and determined not to break.

He wanted her to know she didn't need to maintain that cool, perfect exterior with him. That she could let go, be vulnerable. He wanted to remove the pins from her hair. He wanted to…he just wanted her.

He told himself she hadn't called because the timing was wrong. That she had too much to deal with. He didn't want to think that she didn't want him.

A door slammed and he sat up. Fiona exited the building, walking rapidly to her car, a bulging tote bag over her shoulder. Halfway to the car, the strap on the bag snapped, scattering the contents over the parking lot. Tomas tensed, grabbing the door handle. When she dropped to her knees, hands over her face, he leaped out of the truck.

She covered her face with her hands and gave in. Tears coursed down her cheeks, black with mascara. She didn't care. She'd had enough. She'd had *more* than enough.

A shadow loomed over her, and she gasped, realizing she was a woman alone in the parking lot of an empty building. The bulky body was backlit by the sun, and she couldn't make out any features. But she knew that scent.

"Why are you here? Are you documenting my most humiliating moments? Because you seem to be there each and every time! Here's some more ammunition for you to use against me. Today, my divorce became final, and I have to move back home with my parents. I'm thirty three." Her voice rose shrilly, but she couldn't stop herself. It had been bottled up for too long. "I will sleep in my old bedroom and sit at the dining table, where my mother will recount my failures night after night." She took a breath.

"So there you go. Broadcast that all over Keeney." Fiona subsided and listlessly picked up her belongings.

"Take this." Tomas thrust a handkerchief at her. When she didn't take it, he picked up her hand and closed her fingers around it.

She stared at it. The scary ex-con carried a handkerchief. A neatly folded, clean, blue paisley handkerchief that—she sniffed it—smelled like lavender. Huh.

She mopped her face and blew her nose, not even attempting to be delicate.

While she had her moment, Tomas gathered everything together and stuffed it neatly into the tote bag. Holding it in one hand, he reached the other toward her.

Fiona stared at it. Tentatively, she took his hand, and he wrapped his fingers around her own. The broad, calloused palm felt rough against hers, and the clean, blunt nails were in stark contrast to her perfectly polished pink manicure. With little effort, he pulled her to her feet. She stared at the top button of his shirt, not wanting to look into his eyes.

When he released her hand and stepped back, dismay engulfed her. White knight moments happened in fairytales, and she didn't need rescuing. She needed—she had no idea what she needed. Shoulders slumped, she watched him beep her car unlocked, open the door, and then toss her tote bag onto the passenger seat. He handed her the keys and held the door open for her.

Fiona sidled around him, feeling the heat of his big body as she passed. He turned and strode across the parking lot.

"I should have called."

Tomas halted, his head turned to the side.

"I…I was overwhelmed and wasn't ready to…I wasn't ready." She twisted the handkerchief in her hand and finished lamely, "I'm sorry."

He nodded and continued walking.

It was probably the sun in her eyes, but it looked like his shoulders were less stiff. She took a chance and asked, "Why are you here?" Her heart pounded. Who was this guy, and why was he present whenever she fell apart?

Turning to face her, he replied simply, "To pick you up."

They stared at each other a moment before he nodded again and went to his truck.

Collapsing in the car seat, she watched him drive off, then banged her head softly against the steering wheel. Sounds of the summer evening floated toward her. A ballgame was in progress somewhere, a lawnmower droned, and close by, an insect buzzed. Fiona opened her eyes to see a fat bumblebee hovering by the open car door as if it were checking her out. Perhaps attracted by the scent of the crumpled-up handkerchief she still held in her hand. It wandered off, and Fiona closed the car door.

She pulled into her driveway, turned off the car, and stared at the stark white garage door, imagining she could see Eddie's accusatory word and her artistic response that had been painted over long ago. Not for the first time, she wondered what her life would be like if she had not married Eddie McLeod.

They'd attended the same high school. Fiona, the mousy little brainiac everyone wanted for a science partner but no one invited to parties, and Eddie, the big man on campus, looking like the star of a teen movie, always suspected of causing trouble but never caught. Their one and only interaction had been sharing a microscope in biology. An interaction Eddie forgot, but Fiona remembered right down to the color of his polo shirt.

They were at the same charity luncheon four years ago, each representing their family's business. Fiona arrived early, found out where she was seated, then moved the place cards around to seat herself next to Eddie when she realized he was there, too. At twenty-nine, with an MBA in her back pocket and wearing four-inch Manolos, she was ready to make an impression.

Eddie arrived smelling of vodka. He didn't appear drunk, but he was far from sober. He ignored the others seated at their table, slung his arm over Fiona's chair, and made loud, smart-ass comments about the speakers during the meal. She was mortified, far from impressed, and left as soon as she was able.

If capturing Eddie's attention was her goal, she'd achieved it. For the next week, he attempted to contact her. When she refused to take his calls, he sent notes of apology. When she ignored them, he sent flowers. When that didn't work, he showed up at Han Family Holdings and waited in the reception area until she consented to see him.

Fiona shook her head at her naivete and climbed out of the car. Eddie was the first man to pay any attention to her. She fell hook, line, and sinker. And now she was adrift in the ocean. What she hadn't known was that he wasn't interested in her, but her family's business. When marrying her didn't earn him a seat at the table, his interest went elsewhere.

And now…Tomas. Big, rough, and slightly scary. Rarely spoke and smiled even more rarely. He confused her. She'd treated him like crap, yet he'd literally picked her up today. Twice. She unlocked the door to the house, kicked off her shoes, and padded barefoot into the kitchen. The kitchen she would soon be packing up and leaving. The thought exhausted her. She dumped her tote bag on the island and mechanically emptied it, putting her lunch bag near the sink and plugging in her cellphone, all while imagining living under her mother's roof again. Under her mother's rules. Her fingers closed around the soft fabric of Tomas's handkerchief.

She pulled it out of her bag and smelled it again. Washing it would lose the scent, but she'd used it to blow her nose. It definitely needed washing. She might just keep it. Or, perhaps, use it as an excuse to see him again…. Who was she kidding? Other than crossing paths with him for work, she had no business seeing Tomas. He was a good man. She sensed he was a man who didn't *date* a woman but a man who *committed* to a woman. And that woman wasn't her. She'd done that once and wouldn't do it again. She shook her head, dropped the handkerchief into the kitchen garbage, and strode from the room.

Minutes later, she approached the garbage, retrieved the handkerchief, and took it to the laundry room.

CHAPTER 5

"*E*ducation Needed to Become an Architect."

Heart thumping, Tomas closed the lid of his laptop and peered over his shoulder. "What are you? Training to be a ninja? You scared the shit out of me?"

Vincent smirked before taking a drink from his water bottle. The asshole loved sneaking up on him. He tipped his chin at Tomas's computer. "Seriously, which student is that for? I'm thinking Marissa. She's focused, intent, and certainly has the determination to complete a four-to-five-year program."

Four to five years? Shit. Tomas was thirty-six. Could he afford to spend the next five years in school? He'd barely finished high school. Too macho to disclose how difficult reading was for him, he instead opted to be the class clown and resident troublemaker. To compensate, he'd convince someone to read instructions aloud and would commit important stuff to memory.

Entry into the prison's general contracting course required taking an aptitude test. Vincent saw his struggle and helped him through the exam. Determined not to be a regular in the state's penal system, Tomas worked his ass off to make it through the contracting program. Now, reading was not easy, but he worked at it, employing technology for text to audio as much as possible.

Vincent was his closest friend, but Tomas wasn't ready to share his dream with anyone yet. Instead, he said, "Yeah, Marissa's a good choice."

"Good choice for what?" Hilary entered the KBS break room, gave Vincent a quick kiss, and poured herself a cup of coffee.

Vincent pointed at the computer. "Tomas is researching architect programs for the students."

"Really? Huh." Leaning back against the counter, Hilary crossed her arms, looking deep in thought.

The two men grinned at each other. They recognized the look. The look that preceded an idea that would mean work for them.

She squinted at them, then walked slowly back to her office, muttering to herself. "Hmmm. Funding…where to get the funding."

Vincent slapped Tomas on the shoulder and followed his wife. Tomas stared at the computer; he hadn't even thought about the cost of tuition.

Moments later, Hilary popped her head around the door. "I'm going to set up a meeting with Fiona Han. Any particular day work better for you?"

Tomas gawked at her. "What? Me?"

"It's your idea. You should be there."

Drumming his fingers on the closed laptop, he stared at his boss. Should he tell her it was supposed to be for him? No. If he couldn't tell Vincent, he definitely couldn't tell Hilary. But maybe, this way, he could get some answers. *And you could see Fiona.* He chased the thought away. This was about work. To Hilary, he replied, "Just let me know. I'll make it work."

She gave him a thumb's up and was gone. Leaving him

wondering how he was going to talk to Fiona about something he knew nothing about but deeply wanted for himself.

❄

Fiona snapped her head up at the ring of the doorbell. She put down the packing tape and headed for the entryway, skirting around neatly labeled boxes and stacked luggage. In front of a wall mirror, she stopped and smoothed her hair back. She peered through the peephole on the door, half hoping it would be Tomas. It was not. It was Iris. Fiona sighed, pasted a welcoming smile on her face, and opened the door.

The whole time Fiona had been married to Eddie, she'd thought her mother-in-law disliked her. Not only disliked her but looked down on her for her Vietnamese heritage. Conversation was stilted the few times they were together, and Fiona was always happy to leave. Not until her marriage was falling apart did she realize Eddie had blocked the relationship from developing. He'd led his parents to believe that Fiona thought they were beneath her. Since Eddie landed in jail for embezzling from his mother, Fiona and Iris were finally becoming friends.

"Hi." She pulled the door wide and stepped back, allowing Iris to enter.

Iris leaned forward as if to hug Fiona, who flinched. Iris drew back, a frown on her face. Fiona shook her head and stepped toward the older woman and grasped her outstretched hand in both of hers. "Sorry," she said. "I need to work on that." Her mother was not a hugger. In fact, signs of affection were few and far between. Perhaps that was why Eddie thought her so cold and unresponsive that he'd had affairs.

Iris gave her a small smile, her eyes soft with understanding. "We've got time for that." She stepped into the living room and turned around slowly, taking in the organized chaos. A box was open on the coffee table, piles of packing paper and framed photographs next to it. A box on the floor was filled with throw pillows. The walls were bare. Artwork that was too large to be boxed up leaned against the walls. She raised eyebrows at Fiona in silent inquiry.

"The house is going up for sale. Not sure how long it will be on the market, so I figured I'd be prepared."

Iris nodded slowly. "You've gotten a lot done." She cocked her head to the side like an inquisitive bird. "Did you forget we're going out for lunch today?"

Fiona whipped out her phone. "That's tomorrow!"

Iris placed her purse on a taped-up box and removed her pale blue cardigan. "No, sweetheart, it's today."

Fiona scowled at her calendar and groaned. "I'm so sorry. I got caught up and—"

"Not a problem." Iris eyed a framed photograph before wrapping it in paper and placing it in the box. "We can make this a working lunch. I'll call the deli and get some sandwiches delivered."

Fiona hurried forward and placed a staying hand on Iris's arm. "That's not necessary. I can—"

Iris placed her hand over Fiona's. "I know you can. But you don't have to do this by yourself." She met Fiona's gaze straight on. "You're not getting enough sleep," she said gently.

Fiona stepped back, lifting her hands to her face. "Does it show?" Since the conversation with her mother and the confrontation with Tomas, sleep had eluded her. She tossed and turned most nights, waking up wrapped in sheets so tight she felt like a burrito.

Laugh lines crinkled around Iris's faded blue eyes. "Only to someone who cares enough to look for it. Now, is there something specific I can order for you? I know the Saturday special is a Reuben sandwich."

Fiona shrugged. Her appetite had disappeared with her

ability to sleep. She looked down at the worn jeans and baggy t-shirt. And apparently her ability to dress as well. "Sure. That would be great."

Iris nodded sharply. "Good. I'll order, then finish up in here. Where are you moving to? One of the new apartments downtown?"

Downtown Keeney used to be comprised of three square blocks. But the outward expansion of Seattle had transformed the sleepy little town at the top of Lake Washington. Now, there were many shops, cafes, and even a hotel. Five residential multi-story buildings had recently gone up with retail space on the bottom floors.

Fiona shook her head and twisted her jade bracelet. "I'm moving back home." Iris had been rummaging through her purse but gave Fiona her full attention. Fiona squared her shoulders and continued, "My family requires it. It's um… complicated."

Her lips thinned, Iris said, "I see. And your belongings? Do your parents have room for them?"

"No. I'll put everything in storage for now. I'll go through them when I have time and sell off what I don't need." Fiona glanced around the room. Eddie had picked out most of the furniture, so getting rid of it wouldn't be a hardship. She just didn't have the energy to deal with it right now.

Iris must have been a mind reader. "I have a friend who is adept at buying and selling things online. Would you like her to take care of this for you?"

Fiona shook her head. "Oh, I couldn't—"

"Please. Let me. I want to help you."

Fiona closed her eyes and sighed. The one good thing that had come from being screwed over by Eddie McLeod was her friendship with his mother. The tightness in her shoulders relaxed, and she opened eyes filled with thankful tears. "Thank you. That would be great." She headed back to the kitchen, not wanting to give in to emotion yet again.

Half an hour later, loud voices heralded the arrival of Marcia Ortiz, Iris's best friend and a business associate of Fiona's, who probably knew everything about Fiona's current situation.

From her spot in the kitchen, Fiona watched the two women approach. Where Iris was pale, thin, and bird-like, Marcia was best described as robust. Rounded in face and body, her dark eyes were sharp, and her dark hair glittering with gray. Both were in their sixties, and they each had important roles in Keeney non-profits, in addition to full-time jobs. Iris worked with Fiona at Keeney Works as the client coordinator, matching up clients with internships. Marcia worked for Keeney Builds. She wrangled the students, ensuring their attendance, assignments, and presentations were up to snuff. Together, she and Iris were contacting other trades to link in with Keeney College and Keeney Works to provide classes and internships beyond carpentry and contracting. In order to work at Keeney Works, Iris had hired Hilary Ortiz, Marcia's daughter-in-law, to oversee her business, Keeney Building Supply.

At the moment, the two no-nonsense businesswomen looked more like giggling schoolgirls. The pleasure they took in each other's company drove a pang of jealousy through Fiona. She had never once had a friendship as deep and strong as theirs.

Marcia clocked Fiona's presence and barreled toward her, pushing past the extended hand and engulfing her in a warm embrace. Fiona stiffened, then relaxed into Marcia's arms like a small child being comforted. Tears filled her eyes, and of their own accord, her arms rose to return the hug. Through watery eyes, she met Iris's questioning gaze. Fiona nodded. Iris rushed forward and wrapped her arms around both Fiona and Marcia. The three women rocked back and forth as a solid unit until Marcia spoke, "Right. I've got calzones and stuffed pepper soup. Whatever we don't eat now, Fiona, you can have for supper. Now, what is it you need me to do?"

Fiona fished a soggy tissue out of a pocket of her jeans and wiped her eyes. "Pretty much all of the furniture can go. I'm not going to need it and it's not really my taste." She grimaced apologetically at Iris, who waved a hand in dismissal.

Marcia was writing in a notebook. "How much do you want for each item?"

Fiona blew out a gust of air and frowned. "I hadn't thought about it. What do you suggest?"

Marcia hoisted herself up on a stool at the kitchen island and looked at the dining room table. "It's in great shape and wasn't cheap. We should be able to get you enough to give you first and last month's rent on an apartment."

Fiona tilted her head and looked at Marcia in confusion. Then her face cleared. "Oh! No. I'm not moving in with my parents because I can't afford a place of my own. It's just… my mother…."

Marcia said, "Now I'm confused. Is your mother ill?"

Fiona shook her head and inhaled deeply before speaking. "My mother is very traditional. It is unseemly for an unmarried woman to live by herself. Now that the divorce is final, and she is selling the house, I have no excuse not to move back."

Iris and Marcia exchanged glances. Not for the first time, Fiona thought they could read each other's thoughts. Marcia nodded, and Iris cleared her throat before turning to face Fiona. "You could move in with me," she said softly.

"What?"

"Hilary and Vincent bought a house and moved out."

"Oh!" Fiona said. "I didn't know." Seeing Iris's tentative smile, she guessed that the women didn't want to subject her to someone else's happiness in the midst of her own pain. Iris's house was the reason Hilary and Vincent met. Hilary had rented the floor above Iris, while Vincent lived in the tiny house on the property.

Marcia leaned forward, clasping her hands. "Technically, you wouldn't be living *with* Iris, but does your mother need to know that?"

Fiona shook her head slowly, not looking at the eager faces in front of her. "She doesn't know that Iris had the house renovated. And, you *are* family." She looked back in time to see the smile bloom on Iris's face.

"You'll do it?" Marcia pressed.

Fiona opened her mouth to reply, but the ring of her cellphone stopped her. She pulled it out of her back pocket and dropped it on the island. "It's my mother." She stared at Iris and Marcia in horror. The phone continued to ring while the women gaped at each other before going silent.

Fiona exhaled sharply.

Iris grasped her elbows.

Marcia said, "Oh, for God's sake. Rip the bandage off and tell her."

Fiona stared at her dumbly.

Iris sighed.

Marcia climbed down off the stool, rounded the counter, picked up the phone, and slapped it into Fiona's hand. "Do it and get it over with. Iris and I will go take pictures of the furniture." She grabbed Iris by the arm and hustled her out of the kitchen, leaving Fiona alone with her racing thoughts and ringing phone.

Minutes later, Marcia asked, "How did it go?" She and Iris peeked around the wall at Fiona sitting slumped on a stool.

Fiona waved them in. "Well, it took a while, but she caved."

Iris and Marcia fist-bumped and entered the kitchen, smiling broadly.

"I may have fabricated a bit. I said that you were feeling poorly and weren't comfortable living alone." Lying didn't come easy, but it was more of an embellishment than a fabrication. Part of the reason Fiona had asked Iris to come and work for her was because of Eddie's betrayal. Iris still hadn't quite recovered. Still, Fiona was glad it was a phone conversation with her mother and not a face-to-face meeting.

"Well, you did have that cold last week," Marcia pointed out. "And you said you'd be lonely without Hilary and Vincent around."

"True," Iris agreed, nodding vigorously.

Fiona twirled her bracelet and rolled her lips between her teeth before saying, "I think she liked it that I referred to you as honored mother-in-law."

Clutching her cardigan, Iris said softly, "I'm the one who is honored to be your mother-in-law."

Fiona smiled through watery eyes and sighed. At Marcia's cough, she straightened her shoulders. "Shall we eat?"

The older women busied themselves laying out the food. Over lunch, plans were made for Fiona's next chapter. A chapter she was writing with help from new friends.

While perfect for a boardroom, her heels, skirt, and pearls were not what others wore in a building supply store. Fiona stepped aside for a burly man in work boots carrying a lighting fixture to exit. From the entryway, she scanned the store and spotted the windows of the second-floor offices. Her gaze tracked down and located the doorway on the back wall. She nodded at an employee by the cash register and made her way through the aisles of hammers, screwdrivers, and other handheld tools. The faint smell of burnt popcorn tickled her nose, and a power saw droned in the distance.

She headed up the stairs and stood on the landing, taking in the four doorways; the bathroom, the break room, a small filing room, and an open doorway through which she could hear Hilary's voice. She followed the sound and stood in the entrance to a conference room. Hilary waved at her and held up a finger, indicating she would be done with her phone call shortly. She hadn't given Fiona much detail about why they were meeting at KBS, only saying they had another avenue to explore for people in the trades who wanted to further their education. Finding a date and time that worked was the hard part, as both women were up their eyeballs in commitments.

Fiona smiled and walked toward the large table, and placed her bag on the seat of one of the six chairs. The table butted up against a wall of windows. On the creamy yellow walls hung the photographic history of KBS.

She stepped toward the first photo and followed the progress of the company. Iris and her husband Darryl in front of the original storefront, then a photo of Iris, Darryl, and a young Eddie near a stack of lumber. It was a photograph she'd never seen before.

She hadn't known her father-in-law well. Partially because he died not long after she and Eddie were married and partially because Eddie didn't want her to interact with his parents. Eddie, as a gap-toothed boy, looked so innocent and harmless. Not for the first time, Fiona wondered what prevented him from being happy, triggering his need to hurt others.

Dismissing the dismal thought, she moved on to the next picture. A photo of Vincent, Tomas, Carl, and the first graduating class of Keeney Builds in front of a tiny house. Fiona stepped closer to the wall to inspect the photo. She told herself she was looking at the students, but her eyes focused on Tomas.

He was turned slightly away from the camera, toward Vincent, and was…smiling? Laughing? Fiona shook her head, not believing that the intimidating Aztec god of a man was capable of laughing. She turned her head at a sound behind her. As if studying his image had brought him to her, Tomas stood in the doorway. His gaze fixed on hers, he tipped his chin at her, gave a small wave to Hilary, and went to the table to pull out a chair and sit.

Fiona was in a quandary. Hilary was still on the phone. If she sat at the table—which was the polite thing to do—she'd have to talk to Tomas and make conversation. She'd known he'd be here. Hilary had said so on the phone, but Fiona hadn't prepared for his presence.

That was a lie.

She'd spent the night worrying about what to wear. In her mind, she'd tried on and discarded numerous combinations of skirts, blouses, and jackets. Had even considered slacks. In the end, she went to her standby: nude pumps, beige skirt, peach silk blouse, pearl earrings, pearl necklace, and her hair in a twist. It was effortless, slightly colorless, all business. Did it give her confidence? Perhaps. She knew if she were to stop by her mother's office, Linh Han would be wearing a variation of the same thing.

Self-consciously smoothing a hand over her immaculate hair, she settled into a seat, fixed a smile in place, and said, "Good morning."

Tomas looked up from the notebook in front of him, mirrored her tight smile, and then glanced back down.

She looked to her left, ostensibly out the windows to the floor, but the windows reflected beautifully the glory of all that was Tomas. Smiling to herself, she studied his dark head, the closely shorn hair, thick dark eyebrows, blade of a nose, and full lips. Lips that were clamped firmly into a tight line. As if drawn, he turned and caught her eyes in the glass. One eyebrow raised, he smirked.

Fiona quickly looked away, busying herself with the contents of her briefcase. Her cheeks flamed. She longed to hide her face in her hands but settled for pulling out her laptop and setting it up. Thankfully, Hilary ended her phone call before the floor opened up and sucked Fiona down into its depths.

"Sorry about that. There was a mix up with a delivery, and the contractor had to mansplain the workings of the loading dock to me." Rising from her desk, Hilary shot a grin at Fiona and snorted at the confused look on Tomas's face. "Check the Urban dictionary for that one."

Fiona bit back a smile as Tomas's heavy dark brows cater-pillared together. She took in and admired Hilary's bold appearance. She wore heels, a pencil skirt, and a silk blouse as well, but there, the similarity in their clothing ended. Hilary's skirt and shoes were electric blue, and her blouse was a geometric print of white and black. She walked with a long, confident stride. Not for the first time, Fiona envied her.

Two years previously, Hilary moved to Keeney. She was a breast cancer survivor who went through a double mastectomy. When her body rejected implants, her husband rejected her. Her new, much younger husband, Vincent, coaxed her out of her colorless cocoon, convincing her that a sexy woman was more than a pair of breasts.

Glancing down at her bland outfit, then swiftly up at Tomas, Fiona wondered if, by not returning his calls, she'd lost her chance at happiness. She banished the thought as Hilary spoke.

"Tomas had an excellent idea, and I asked you here so he can share it, and we can brainstorm ways to support it." She sat at the head of the table, shifting her glance between the two, the large silver cuff on her wrist clinking against the wooden surface.

Fiona switched her attention to the man seated across from her. He swallowed, and her gaze followed the up and down movement of his Adam's apple, then farther down to the open collar of his white button-down shirt and the coppery skin exposed there. *Stop it!*

His lips crooked up in the barest hint of a smile, Tomas nodded. "Keeney Builds is coming along nicely. We have a full slate of students signed up for the next quarter, and there's a large demand for their skills."

Fiona bobbed her head in agreement. Her agency, Keeney Works, had no problem finding jobs for the graduates.

Skilled labor was in high demand in Puget Sound's booming construction industry.

Tomas continued, "We have our limits, though. We have… students who want more than construction management. Some have shown interest in becoming architects. That's a five-year degree program that Keeney College doesn't offer. Only WSU and UW offer it. To get in, you have to first have college level math, English, and read at a high level. Few of our students are there yet."

At some point, while Tomas spoke, Fiona stopped focusing on the man and started focusing on his passion. He leaned forward, big hands clasped together on the table, looking directly at her as he itemized the costs and obstacles facing a high-school dropout wanting to be an architect. It seemed very personal to him.

Not for the first time, Fiona thanked her parents. Neither went past high school, yet they pushed their children to succeed in school, knowing that doors opened wider for those with college degrees.

"Scholarships," she said, turning toward a nodding Hilary. "And full-ride ones at that. These aren't the kind of classes you can take while working full-time." Out of the corner of her eye, she saw a grimace flicker across Tomas's face.

She opened up a search screen on her laptop and began looking into architecture programs. She didn't doubt Tomas's findings, but sourcing funding for programs was her business. Above the screen, she looked directly at him. "How many students do you think would be interested?"

"Two."

"Really?" Hilary asked, eyebrows raised. "I thought it was just that one girl."

Tomas looked down at his notes, flags of color high on his cheekbones. "No. There's a guy…I think would want to do it." His gaze flicked up at Fiona and then back down.

Could he look less interested in her?

Concentrate! This is work.

"Okay." She tapped away on her keyboard for a few minutes, immersing herself in the question of where to find funding. Hilary went back to her desk and her own laptop. It was hard to concentrate with Tomas across from her, but she steadfastly kept her eyes down.

He rose from the table, pocketing his notebook and cell-phone. "Need anything else?"

His dark eyes were focused on her, and her lips parted as she thought about what she really needed from him. "Umm… I'd like to interview the students, get their backgrounds, school records. Can you text me their contact info? I'll give you my number. It's—"

"I've got it." Tomas scowled. Pushing in his chair, he flicked a hand at Hilary and stomped toward the door.

Of course he did. The enthusiasm that buoyed her moments ago followed him out the door. She listened to his heavy footfalls retreating down the stairs, the slam of the door at the bottom. Turning to the window, she craned her neck, hoping to see him down on the floor. He must have gone a different direction. He was out of sight, but not out of her thoughts.

CHAPTER 7

The three contractors sat at the table in the break room at KBS, comparing notes about their day. Small, tattered notebooks lay before Tomas and Vincent. Carl used his cellphone. The older, experienced contractors tried to convince him that an old school, wire-bound notebook and a pencil, had a longer lifespan on a construction site, but Carl was determined to prove them wrong. Vincent and Tomas recorded their job notes on paper first and then typed them into a computer file at a later time, but Carl wrote his notes in an email, which he then stored in the cloud. Their age difference was not that great—a matter of a dozen years, but Tomas and Vincent had learned their trade in prison without access to smartphones and weren't convinced that technology was always the best way to go. Hilary, their boss, didn't care which method was employed as long as detailed notes were kept on every job they did for KBS.

"Hey, you ready to go?" Vincent picked up his notebook and pencil when he spotted his wife at the door of the break room.

The slim, attractive woman shook her gray curls and held

up a file folder. "Not quite. Iris forgot to sign a document. I'm stopping by Keeney Works to get her signature before heading home."

"Can't it wait until tomorrow?" It was close to six o'clock, and Vincent looked annoyed. He'd been telling Tomas and Carl about the time-sensitive meal he'd planned for dinner.

Tomas watched the interplay between the couple, happy for his best friend, knowing that was what he wanted. A relationship. A wife. Someone to go home to. Sensing Vincent's frustration with the delay in his evening's plans, Tomas said, "I'll take care of that." He ignored the three sets of eyes staring at him. He didn't have to explain himself. "If I leave the file on your desk first thing in the morning, will that work?"

Hilary nodded and stepped forward to give Tomas the folder. "That would be great. I've flagged where she needs to sign."

Vincent rose and clapped Tomas on the back. "Dude, I owe you." He followed his wife out the door. They'd barely gone five steps before Hilary giggled.

Tomas narrowed his eyes at Carl, who smothered a grin and stared down at his phone.

He sat in his truck, rubbing his hands up and down his thighs. He pulled down the visor and checked himself in the mirror. No food in his teeth, he'd need to shave sometime soon, but he looked okay. He made a face. *Why is this so damn hard?* She'd apologized for not calling. Before yesterday's meeting, he'd caught her staring at him. She *was* interested. Right?

The meeting itself made him hopeful that there was a way for him to get to school, to be able to study architecture. He wasn't stupid. If he were to expose his learning disability, accommodations would be made. But that felt like…cheating. He had to do this like everyone else. But a scholarship…

that would mean he could go to school exclusively, not struggle through work and school at the same time.

College wasn't something he'd ever aspired to. After squeaking through high school, he'd gotten one job after another until discovering he liked building things, so construction it was. He had a boss he liked and who liked him, and had made him a crew boss shortly before Tomas went to jail. As shitty as that was, jail had led him to where he was now. Sitting in a KBS truck, trying to get up the courage to go into Fiona's office.

He knew that she knew some of his history, but all of it? If she did, what would she think of him? She was brilliant. An MBA, head of a non-profit. He'd never met a person so smart and so…sexy.

Wrong word. Fiona didn't ooze sex like his former girlfriend, Gloriana, who made old men drool when she walked past. No, Fiona's small, feminine form encased in prim clothing was a package he wanted to unwrap. He remembered the night of the kiss. Fiona, drunk, barefoot, hair wild about her shoulders. He wanted to be the man who got to see that woman again. Would she let him? Not if she found out he was lying to her.

Was he lying to her, though? Not exactly. Just…withholding information. He'd have to tell her eventually that he was the other student. But not right now. Now was a chance to get to know each other. This was the perfect opportunity to start fresh. He'd knock on her door, casually ask her to go for coffee sometime, get the signature from Iris, and get out of there. Piece of cake.

He climbed out of the truck, grabbed the file, and strode across the parking lot. Pulling open the door to Keeney Works, he smiled at the receptionist, pleased that she was the same one he'd met before. "Hi. I need to get a signature from Iris."

The woman reached for the telephone. "I'll have her come out for you."

"No need. I helped her move into her office. I know the way."

Before the receptionist could protest, he smiled again and walked quickly to the hallway leading to the back offices. Rounding the corner, he stuttered to a halt. Fiona's office door was closed.

An hour later, Tomas sat in his truck, the signed document in its folder beside him. The job was done, but it wasn't exactly mission accomplished. Sitting in Iris's office while she chattered away at him, Tomas had angled his chair to watch the closed door across the hallway. When it finally opened, two people left, and he had a view of Fiona at her desk. Scowling intently at her laptop, she hadn't seen him. He waited impatiently while Iris searched for her glasses, located a working pen, and signed the paper. Folder in hand, he turned to the door to see the back of Fiona's head. She'd turned her chair around, deeply engrossed in a phone conversation. Unwilling to interrupt, he left, and now, he was sitting in his truck, mentally kicking himself for being a coward.

The ball was in his court, and he hadn't dropped it, he'd run away from it. But dammit, he was gonna go after it. When Fiona emerged from the building, he pulled the keys from the ignition and opened the door of the truck. Motion from the other side of the parking lot halted him. A man climbed out of a late-model sports car and approached Fiona. Glued to the seat of the truck, Tomas watched the man pick Fiona up and spin her around. When she wrapped her arms around his neck, threw her head back and laughed, Tomas took that as his cue to leave.

"Put me down! Joseph, I mean it."

Grinning, Joseph Han lowered his sister to the ground. "Is hugging your brother in public too undignified for the executive director of Keeney Works?"

Fiona narrowed her eyes and smacked him on the arm, thrilled to see him but annoyed at the mess he'd made of her outfit. She dropped her bag to the ground, tucked in her blouse, and smoothed her hair back into place. "You are such a pain."

"Yes, but you love me." His grin was unrepentant as he picked up her tote bag. "Where do you want to go to dinner?"

"How about following me back to my place? If you don't like what I have in the fridge, we can order in." Joseph would be the first guest in her new home, and she was eager to show it off. The first place that she had ever decorated solely for herself.

"Sounds good. Do you want me to pick up drinks?" He opened the passenger door of her car, placing the bag on the floor.

"I've got white wine. If you want something else you'll have to get it yourself." She climbed into the driver's seat and buckled the seat belt.

"I'll get some beer. I have your address so I'll meet you there." Joseph closed the car door and turned toward his own vehicle.

With a wave and a smile Fiona exited the parking lot and headed home. Home was the upper level of a two-story house that had been converted into two apartments. Iris lived in the lower apartment. The house was at the end of a long driveway on a quiet street. The large yard, surrounded by a mix of conifers and deciduous trees, was quiet and private, but enough sunlight came through so that if Fiona wanted to sunbathe in the nude—not that she wanted to— she could do so. Fiona parked her car on the left side of the driveway, leaving the center open for Iris to get in and out of the detached garage. The right side of the driveway was available for additional parking, reserved for another tenant. At the back of the property stood a tiny house. Originally a garden shed, Vincent Ortiz had renovated it after completing the renovations to the main house. The pretty, little, tiny house now stood vacant while Iris took her time finding the perfect tenant.

Fiona climbed the stairs leading to the upper deck and the apartment's French doors. She smiled in appreciation of the freshly mowed lawn and the abundance of flowering shrubs edging the property. The upper deck contained a wooden outdoor table and seating that had been built by Darryl, Iris's dead husband. The table had become Fiona's favorite place to have her morning coffee as well as a glass of wine in the evening. At times, Iris would join her.

Both women had been wounded by Eddie, a self-centered, entitled man-child presently serving time for embezzling from his mother and attempting to lay the blame on Fiona. Eddie's path of destruction was wide. Considering what he'd done to Vincent, it was a testament to the strength of the bond between Iris and Marcia that their friendship hadn't disintegrated.

Fiona unlocked and pushed open her door, kicking off her shoes and dumping her tote bag on the counter to the right side of the door. The kitchen was U-shaped. A large window above the sink faced the backyard. The fridge took up most of the back wall, while the stove was against the wall separating the kitchen from the living area. There was an abundance of cabinets and countertops, which ended in a peninsula that further divided the kitchen from the dining area. Directly in front of the door was a square bar-height table with four tall chairs, all in dark wood. A traditional dining room table with lower chairs would have been easier, but the petite woman had been drawn to the less formal table, bare except for a glass bowl filled with apples. Ignoring her shoes for the moment, Fiona looked over the living room for anything out of place.

Just past the dining table stood a brick fireplace with an exposed wooden mantel holding three colorful vases. Above it, a large mirror reflected the light coming in from the front window. Below the window stood a denim-covered couch with bright yellow throw pillows. Kitty corner to the couch sat a comfortable armchair. A large rectangular ottoman stood before the couch. Upholstered in the same cheery yellow check as the chair, it stored afghans and extra pillows. Currently, the flooring was bare wood. Fiona was contemplating area rugs but for now, was happy with the cool wood against her bare feet.

Looking at her watch, she dismissed her decorating concerns and hustled to the bedroom to change. She stepped out of her navy pencil skirt and tossed it over the back of an armchair. Originally intended for a comfortable reading space, it was now the temporary repository for her wardrobe until she got around to hanging things up. The light blue silk blouse followed suit, and she pulled a sleeveless, bright pink polka-dot sundress out of the closet. Turning to the en suite bathroom, she loosened the clips holding her hair in place. She shook out the heavy, dark mass, running her fingers over her scalp and sighing. Deciding it was too hot to leave it down, she found a hair tie and piled her hair on top of her head in a messy bun. She nodded at her reflection in the mirror.

Joseph was her brother and wouldn't care what her hair and makeup looked like. Turning back to the bedroom, she smoothed down the soft blue paisley bedspread and hung up her clothes. A knock sounded, and she made her way back to the front door.

Joseph's smiling face was framed in the glass of the French doors. In one hand, he held a six-pack of a local microbrew, in the other a bouquet of flowers, grocery store flowers for sure, but flowers nevertheless. Returning his smile as she opened the door, she hadn't realized how much she was looking forward to connecting with her big brother.

"Thanks." She took the flowers and beer, placing them on the counter. "I made pho and banh mi yesterday. How does that sound?"

"Works for me. Do I get a tour before we eat?" Joseph, dressed in slacks and a pale pink button-down shirt with thin blue stripes, rolled up his sleeves and glanced around the apartment.

"Sure." Fiona twisted her fingers as she led him past the table and into the living room. The small space was a huge contrast to the house she'd lived in with Eddie. He had decided on everything from the wall paint to the furniture to the artwork to the area rugs. It had been heavy, ostentatious, and impersonal. Fiona hated it. She'd tried to provide input, but he overrode her. While her parents bought the house for them, his parents gave them the money for the furniture. Eddie reasoned that the money came from his parents, so the furnishing choices would be his as well. It wasn't the first argument she lost to Eddie, nor was it the last.

"This is so you!" Joseph's words dragged Fiona back to the present. "It's bright, cheerful, and comfortable." He sat on the couch, running his hands over the fabric, then leaned forward, opened the ottoman, and pulled out a crocheted afghan. "You still have this?"

Fiona snatched back the old afghan, made with misshapen granny squares in clashing colors. "Yes. Ba Ngoai helped me make it. I was ten. What do you expect from a first attempt?" She folded it carefully and placed it back into the ottoman, then glared at her brother.

"It's ugly as sin. Good thing you keep it in there." He stood and bumped her shoulder with his own, his smile taking the sting out of his words. "Let's see the rest of the place."

She led him down the hall, past a bathroom, showed off her home office, then stood in the doorway while he looked over the bedroom.

"Really nice. It looks like you've settled in." Following her back to the kitchen, he snagged a beer and leaned against the peninsula. "Are you happy?"

Fiona shot him a quick glance before opening the fridge to retrieve the Okanagan Porch Banger wine. His usual smile was replaced by a look of concern. She nodded. "Yeah. I feel like…like I can finally relax. My life is my own. Does that make sense?" She put the wine on the counter and opened a cupboard to get a glass.

"Yeah. I'm sorry I wasn't there for you. I should have—"

"Don't go there. I look at it as a learning experience—crappy as it was—but now I know what I do and don't want in a relationship."

Sipping his beer, Joseph's eyebrows rose. "Relationship? Are you starting to date?"

She snorted. "The ink is barely dry on my divorce papers. And I am not interested in dating." Tomas's image leaped into her mind. He wouldn't date. He would court with a single-minded intensity, seeking something more permanent than seduction. While *permanent* didn't interest her, being the focus of his attention intrigued her.

Immediately, she busied herself in the cool fridge, chasing away thoughts that wouldn't lead anywhere. Not wanting further scrutiny, she deflected. "How's work going?"

Joseph managed the extensive properties of Han Family Holdings. He had four employees working under him, handling rentals, fielding property concerns, and working with the city. He was a dutiful son, working without complaint, but Fiona knew he would rather use his law degree for something else. She wasn't sure what because he'd never said anything, but she sensed his dissatisfaction with the company business.

Shrugging, he looked out the kitchen window. "It's fine. Although, have you heard Mom's newest idea for her legacy?" At Fiona's head shake, he continued. "A memorial garden and an outdoor chapel beside the church."

"What? This is Washington. Who wants to attend a service in the rain?" The Han family were good Methodists. Both Joseph and Fiona attended church regularly while living at home. Now, Fiona attended once a month or so to appease their mother. She had no problem with her mother leaving money to the church, assuming it would be used for a worthy cause.

A look of displeasure crossed Joseph's face. "I don't understand it, either. There are far better things the church could do."

"Keeney United Methodist has a new pastor. Do you think he's sweet-talking Mother?"

"Possibly. I'll talk to her and see if I can convince her to do something more worthwhile."

Fiona pulled bowls and plates out of the cupboard. "Oh, Mother thinks you're up to something."

Joseph bobbled his beer. "What?"

"What is it? You look guilty."

"It's nothing I want the family to know about."

"Are you doing something illegal?"

"God, no!" He propped his hands on his hips and blew out a sigh. "I just want to keep this to myself for a while."

"Okay…." She busied herself serving up the soup. Was he dating someone? Joseph kept his private life very private. She wasn't even sure if he preferred men or women. She glanced up at her handsome brother and smiled. "Are you hungry?"

Joseph nodded at the pot of soup. "Absolutely."

Hurrying into the busy restaurant, Fiona slung her purse over the back of one chair and sank into another opposite Hilary. "I am so sorry I'm late. City council members came for a tour, and then the mayor wanted a photo op. I couldn't get rid of them." She scowled her frustration. Punctuality was a virtue, and she was mortified not to be on time.

Hilary waved away her concerns, setting her e-reader down on the table. "Politicians are a necessary evil. Besides, I got in some reading."

Smiling her thanks, Fiona picked up her glass of water and drank deeply. When Keeney Builds was in its infancy, she and Hilary met regularly, fine-tuning the intricacies of the program. Now, with three rotations of students completed, the weekly meetings weren't necessary, but a friendship had developed, and the women continued to meet weekly for drinks instead of lunch.

Seeing Fiona's arrival, an attentive waiter approached, reached into an ice bucket for a chilling bottle of chardonnay, poured wine into each of the women's glasses, then left them alone. The women raised their glasses in silent salute, then drank.

Fiona sat back and sighed. "Is it me, or was this the longest week in history?"

"Pretty sure it's among the top three, and it's only Tuesday," Hilary agreed. "But forget about work. How are you settling in?" She'd been the previous and original tenant in Fiona's apartment.

"Good. Really good. You were right about that outlet in the guest bedroom. Sometimes it works, and sometimes it doesn't. Should I tell Iris or hire an electrician? I've never had a landlady before, and I don't know the protocol."

"Crap! I totally forgot about that." Hilary put her glass down and dug around in her purse for her cellphone. "I'll put it on the schedule and get one of the guys to take care of it."

"You don't need to do that," Fiona protested.

Rolling her eyes, Hilary said, "When you tell Iris, she'll call me, and I'll wind up doing the same thing. Let's see… Tomas can take care of it on Friday at four o'clock. Will that work for you?"

"No!"

Hilary raised an eyebrow at her outburst.

"I mean…I'm sure Tomas has more important things to do. Can't you send an intern? Don't they need the experience?" Fiona struggled to come up with an excuse.

"Interns are always accompanied by a contractor," Hilary said as if explaining to a child. It was a condition she and Fiona had ironed out when the program was put in place.

Nodding weakly, Fiona buried her nose in her wineglass. Maybe she could leave the key under the door mat….

"Well, crap, that's not going to work," Hilary looked up from her phone. "Tomas isn't free. I can send Carl, though. How's that?"

"Perfect!" Fiona sent up a prayer of thanks. Although he

was a sweet, good-looking guy, Carl didn't make her fumble and stumble in his presence.

"Done." Hilary put her phone on the table. "Has your mom been by to see the place yet?"

"No. I'm not sure I want her to. I'm not ready for her to look down her nose at my decorating choices."

Raising an eyebrow, Hilary gave her a sympathetic smile. "You don't know that she will do that."

Fiona rolled her eyes. "Umm hmm. Oh, but get this. I went to give Iris the rent, and she told me it had already been paid. By my mother."

"That's nice. Isn't it?"

"No!" Fiona glared at her friend. "It's a control thing. She'll hold this over my head in the future." Her mother was an expert at manipulation.

Reaching across the table, Hilary removed the knife Fiona clutched tightly, and put it next to her own.

Chagrined, Fiona relaxed her hands, picked up her wine-glass, and sat back. "But I have a plan. I'll set up a separate account specifically for the rent money and deposit it there. When my mother decides to play the I've-been-paying-your-rent card, I'll write her a check for the amount and throw that back at her. Yes, I know it's petty, but that is my mother's love language, and apparently, it's mine as well." Fiona drank deeply, rather pleased with herself.

Hilary shook her head. "You are not a petty person. You always give the other person the benefit of the doubt. Are you sure you want to do that?"

Before Fiona could reply, a text came in on Hilary's phone. "Oh! Vincent just finished up an estimation at a shop on Main Street. Do you mind if he joins us?"

Although disappointed that their alone time was being cut short, Fiona acquiesced upon seeing the look of pleasure on her friend's face. In her years with Eddie, she didn't think she'd ever worn that joyous an expression on her face. "Not at all!" She reached for the bottle of wine and refilled her glass.

The conversation then became less personal and more general, Fiona reaching for her wine frequently as she considered Hilary's words. Did she really give people the benefit of the doubt? Maybe before Eddie. But since his betrayal and deception, she had developed a hard shell. One that she was not willing to allow anyone to penetrate.

Thoughts of penetration turned to thoughts of Tomas and thoughts of—

"Hey!"

Hilary's greeting roused Fiona from her thoughts. Blinking rapidly, she pressed her thighs together, shifting in her chair. Taking a deep, centering breath, she pasted a smile on her face, looked up, and saw Vincent approaching their table, followed closely by Tomas.

❄

*K*nowing she was seeing someone, knowing she was unavailable, should have made Tomas resigned and accepting of his fate. Knowing full well Fiona would be there, he should have declined Vincent's suggestion of going out for a beer. Instead, he'd gone, and was a dick.

He greeted Hilary and ignored Fiona.

He talked to Vincent and Hilary and ignored Fiona.

When Vincent glared at him, trying to bring Fiona into the conversation, Tomas ignored Fiona.

When Fiona asked him directly about the progress of the latest class, he answered with one word, "Fine."

When a visibly wilted Fiona got up to go to the restroom, Hilary rounded on him, letting loose with both barrels. "What the hell is wrong with you? She's a friend of mine and a work associate. You'd better have a good explanation for treating her like shit."

Before Tomas could respond, Vincent punched him in the arm. "What she said. What's going on?"

Tomas scowled but remained silent.

Locking her gaze on her husband, Hilary's voice turned saccharine sweet. "Honey, isn't the fashion show at the Senior Center coming up soon?"

"Yeah. And?"

"KBS gets a lot of goodwill when our employees volunteer as escorts for the models. You and Carl looked so handsome in tuxedos."

Crossing his arms, Vincent said flatly, "I'm not doing it again."

"You don't have to. Another of our contractors will be doing so." Hilary looked directly at Tomas, eyes narrowed, and lips thinned.

"Oh, hell no." Tomas went pale, the thought of being on stage in front of a crowd making him sweat.

Hilary leaned across the table. "Then tell us why you're being mean to Fiona."

Shit. Glancing between his boss and his friend, Tomas realized there was no way out. He raked his fingers through his hair and blew out a breath. "She kissed me." His back stiffened when exclamations of shock followed his announcement. Then Hilary's surprised expression softened into a smile.

"Spill, before Fiona gets back here," she ordered.

He told them about driving her home, her getting drunk and painting the garage with nail polish, him carrying her to bed, her kissing him then ghosting him, seeing her at the board meeting, her apology in the parking lot, and ended with his last visit to Keeney Works. "Now, she's seeing someone." While it felt good to share, exposing his wound did not feel like a healing process.

Hilary's mouth opened as if to speak, when Vincent grabbed her arm. "Shh, she's coming back."

The three turned to watch her approach. From across the crowded restaurant, Tomas was free to observe her. The woman could not hold her alcohol and wove slightly. A strand of hair had broken free from her tight bun and hung in front of her ear. Absentmindedly, she raised a hand to push it back, the movement causing her to sway even more. God, she was cute. More than cute, she was perfect. She stood out from the Keeney happy hour crowd in her form-fitting pale pink skirt and matching short-sleeved blouse. The ivory heels gave her another four inches, but even with that, Tomas knew, that holding her, she would barely reach his shoulder. A tiny piece of perfection, if only she were his.

Reaching the table, she picked up her purse, her gaze passing over Tomas as she smiled at Vincent then spoke to Hilary. "I'm gonna get going. I'll talk to you soon."

"Got a ride?" Vincent asked.

"Yeah." Fiona shifted her gaze to him. "I Ubered over, and my brother Joseph is picking me up."

"Is that who you had dinner with the other night? Iris said a handsome man was at your place." Hilary's foot connected with Tomas's shin as she shot him a side-eye.

Fiona nodded. "He came to see my new place." Her phone chimed in her purse. "That's him. I'll see you later."

"You moron!" Vincent smacked Tomas, who ignored him, feeling like the dick he was, as he watched the tiny, perfect woman walk away.

CHAPTER 9

Tomas reached blindly for his ringing phone as early morning sun peeked around the blinds of his bedroom window. Locating the phone among the detritus from his pockets on the nightstand, he pressed it to his ear. "Mom, you have a husband and two other children, why do you always call me?" He rolled to his back, pressing fingers against his forehead, trying to push away the headache making its presence known.

"Because I've loved you the longest," Louisa Santiago chirped in his ear.

He never got tired of hearing that response. For years it had been Tomas and his mother, after his father left. Then she'd met and married Carlos and had two daughters, Sylvie, twenty-five, and Cara, twenty-eight.

Clearly with an agenda, she carried on, "Carlos left for the market and my car won't start. I need you to drive me to church. After that, I'll take you out for breakfast."

Groaning inwardly, Tomas threw back the covers and climbed out of bed. "It's Wednesday. Who goes to church on Wednesday mornings?"

"We have a new pastor. He started the weekday worship a few months ago."

"Fine. What time does it start?" He shuffled out of the bedroom, wincing at the sight of the empty tequila bottle on the coffee table. Ignoring it, he proceeded to the bathroom in search of ibuprofen.

"In forty-five minutes."

He pressed his forehead against the cool mirror of the medicine cabinet. "K. While you're there, I'll take a look at your car."

"Thank you, sweetheart."

Grunting, he turned off the phone and turned on the shower.

Forty minutes later, he pulled up in front of Keeney United Methodist, idled at the curb, and looked at his mother over the top of his sunglasses. "Why are you bringing tamales?" She had chattered the whole time she'd been in his truck, and this was his first opportunity to get a word in edgewise.

"For Pastor Tran. He's thin, doesn't eat enough." Louisa pulled the visor down to check her makeup in the mirror.

He searched his memory for the pastor's name when he'd attended Sunday School, pretty sure it was something different.

"Pastor Tran? You have a Vietnamese pastor?"

Louisa thinned her lips. "Yes, you have a problem with that?"

"Not at all." Tomas raised his hands, palms up. "I didn't know there were Methodists in Vietnam."

"Seven percent of the population is Christian. You would know that if you attended church once in a while."

Church was a big part of his mother's life. She rarely missed a Sunday and served on multiple committees. It didn't surprise Tomas that she'd taken on feeding the pastor.

Leaning over, he kissed his mother's cheek. About to

speak, his attention was caught by two women meeting on the sidewalk in front of the church. Both impeccably dressed, with dark hair arranged in tight hairstyles at the back of the head, the younger woman greeted the older woman by bowing her head. "Who's that?"

Louisa sniffed. "Linh Han."

"You don't like her?"

"She's just…" Lousia waved a hand toward the well-groomed woman.

"What, Mom?" In addition to being opinionated, his mother was a good judge of character. His heart sank at the thought of her not thinking well of Fiona.

"I told the Bible study group that Sylvie was starting a new job, and Linh Han gave me that simpering smile of hers and asked how many jobs Sylvie had had since finishing college. Then she said how sad it was that she couldn't hold on to one. Sylvie's never been fired. It's just that she's a dabbler. Likes to try new things." Louisa stuck her jaw out pugnaciously. "So I asked how Eddie was doing in jail and if we should put him on the prayer chain."

Tomas whipped his head around to gape at her. "You didn't."

"I did."

"That's not exactly," he searched for the word, "Christian." If the woman was as proud and condescending as his mother implied, being reminded of her connection to Keeney's most notorious criminal mustn't have gone over well.

"I know," she huffed out. "She just—irritates me. Like her family is perfect. Like her shit doesn't stink."

A snort of laughter slipped out, and Tomas grinned. "Then what happened?"

"Pastor Tran—and he did this so well I wasn't aware of it at the time—led us in prayer, reminding us to treat each other the way we'd like to be treated and that we are all equals. And I said five Hail Marys on the way home."

"Is that something Methodists are doing these days?"

"No," she said with a smile. "But the Catholics have some great rituals. It's a shame not to use them."

"Anyway," she went on, pointing out the windshield. "Unlike her mother, Fiona is lovely. She's just started coming to the Wednesday service in the last few weeks so I don't know her well. I thought you worked with her?"

He kept his face neutral, not wanting Louisa to know that he had a Fiona-induced hangover. "I've been in meetings with her a couple times." *And dream about her every night.*

"Well, from what I understand, she's very hardworking and a dutiful daughter." She turned and smiled slyly at her son. "She would make a wonderful daughter-in-law. I could teach her to make tamales."

Glaring at his mother, he exited his truck, went round the hood, and opened the door for Louisa. "I'll be back in an hour."

"Thank you, sweetheart." She gathered up her purse and the tamales and walked toward the church.

Tomas's gaze followed her, noting the morning sun highlighting the blue-black glossiness of Fiona's hair as she stood outside the church door, talking to an older woman. As Louisa approached, Fiona turned and smiled her way, leaning forward for her kiss. He relaxed. The two women he cared about the most…liked each other.

"*T*hat's awfully kind, Mrs. Santiago, I'm sure Pastor Tran will enjoy the tamales." Fiona smiled politely while inwardly rolling her eyes. What was it with the older women of the church bringing food to the new pastor? So far, she'd seen him receive three Tupperware containers.

"Do you like to cook, dear?" While much darker and rounder than her mother, Mrs. Santiago had the same shrewd focus carefully hidden behind good manners. Her children probably got away with nothing, either that or had learned subterfuge at an early age.

"I do." Fiona nodded, then inclined her head toward her mother. "But not nearly as well as my mother. Her banh bao are to die for."

For some reason, Mrs. Santiago's lips thinned. Then, looking over Fiona's shoulder, she smiled broadly and waved her hand in a come here motion. "My car wouldn't start this morning, and my husband wasn't around to fix it, so my son is here to pick me up."

"Is your husband a mechanic?" Fiona asked politely while wondering when she'd be able to escape. Joining her mother for church in the middle of the week put her behind at work. She'd be working late again this evening to make up for it.

Pride oozed out of Mrs. Santiago. "Carlos rebuilds and customizes old cars and is looking to buy the Woodbine automotive shop. That's got to be cheaper than all the supplies he buys. Now, let me introduce you to my son."

Ignoring her mother's quiet, disapproving sniff, Fiona twisted around to meet the new arrival, and froze.

Her reaction didn't go unnoticed. Striding toward her on long legs encased in tight jeans, Tomas removed his sunglasses as he approached. Reaching his mother, he bent down to kiss her cheek before turning to Fiona with the sweetest smile she'd ever seen. In his deep, rough voice, he said, "Good morning."

Unable to move, she stared up at his warm, dark eyes. Eyes that had glared at her less than twenty-four hours ago. They crinkled at the corners as his smile turned into a grin. "I see you've met my mother."

Unaware that a crowd of curious parishioners were watching, Fiona stepped toward him as if hypnotized, and shifted her gaze from Tomas's face to Louisa's. "You have the same eyes," she spoke as if to herself.

Louisa wrapped an arm around Tomas's waist. "He's my oldest. Tomas is a contractor at KBS and an instructor at the college," she said loudly to Fiona and the women gathered around. "We're going out for breakfast. Would you like to join us?" This was aimed specifically at Fiona.

Seeing Tomas's surprise and remembering their last interaction, she demurred, "Perhaps another time. I'm expected at work shortly." She stepped back to join her mother, ready to accompany her to the parking lot.

"Are you free for coffee this afternoon?"

Feeling a jolt, Fiona looked down to see a big hand resting on her forearm. Her gaze moved across scarred knuckles, up a thick forearm to the tattoo peeking from beneath the white T-shirt stretched across a bulging bicep.

"Please," he added. His grin had altered into a soft smile, and his eyes reflected the entreaty.

Looking the other way, she caught her mother's narrow-eyed glare, curled lip, and flaring nostrils. Her silent "no" all but dripped with disdain.

Stiffening her spine, Fiona turned to Tomas and said, "I can make that happen."

CHAPTER 10

After Tomas and Louisa walked off, Fiona's mother grabbed her arm and hustled her to the parking lot.

"What are you thinking?"

"I'm thinking that I will meet Tomas this afternoon to have coffee."

"Don't be disrespectful. You will cancel."

They squared off over the hood of her mother's BMW. She dug through her purse for the keys to her own car. "That would be rude. We collaborate on projects, blowing him off would make things very uncomfortable at board meetings and events."

Why she chose now to stand up to her mother, Fiona didn't know. All she did know was the look of relief in Tomas's eyes when she'd agreed, and the pitter-pat of her quickly beating heart.

"Thank you," he'd said. *"I'll call later."* With that, he'd squeezed her arm, nodded at her mother, and escorted his mother to his truck.

"That man is on the board of Keeney Works?"

Technically, no, but her mother didn't need to know the details, so Fiona nodded.

Her mother tapped a manicured nail against the glossy paint of her car. "He looks hard."

Fiona bent her head and beeped open the door to her own car, hiding her reddening face from her mother's scrutiny. Tomas was definitely hard, but her mother didn't need to know that, either. "He is a colleague. We are working on a project." Again, not exactly true, but not exactly false, either.

"Just coffee, and just business." With a pointed look, her mother climbed into her car, dismissing Fiona in the process.

Later that afternoon, Fiona closed her eyes and willed her heart rate to settle down.

"You look lovely."

She turned away from the mirror to see Iris standing in her office doorway, hands clasped in front of her. With a guilty start, she put the lipstick away and closed the closet door. "I was just, um...."

"It's okay. Tomas is a very nice man, and it's good for you to go out."

"Really?" Was her former mother-in-law encouraging her to start dating? Smoothing her damp palms along her thighs, she inquired, "How did you find out? Not that I was keeping it secret."

Waving away her protests, Iris took a seat in one of the two chairs facing the desk. "Louisa told Marcia, and Marcia told me."

"Of course," Fiona muttered, eyes narrowing at the grin on Iris's face. This was so not what she had planned for the day. She reached for her phone. "I should cancel."

"No!" Leaning across the desk, Iris grabbed the phone and pulled it out of Fiona's reach. "You will be fine."

"But what will we talk about?" Fiona had been unable to concentrate all day. She'd start something and then get distracted, remembering the feel of his rough hands on her arm.

Her mother's disapproval didn't help, either. She'd texted

multiple times to remind Fiona to keep things on a professional level. Her last text was a demand for Fiona to attend dinner that night. Fortunately, Fiona answered honestly that work prevented her from doing so.

"Keeney Works, Keeney Builds, KBS. You have a lot in common," Iris replied.

Slumping in her chair, Fiona fingered the cool jade of her bracelet, trying to calm her racing heart.

"You share the same passion for working with people who haven't had a break, and you know his story. You know where his heart is at. Loosen up; you'll be fine." Iris placed the phone back on the desk and moved it closer to Fiona.

"Loosen up," Fiona repeated softly. She caught her reflection in the black screen of her laptop, then yanked the pins holding her hair firmly in place. The heavy, dark mass fell around her shoulders. She finger-combed it, tucking a strand behind an ear.

Iris shook her head, eyes wide. "I don't think I've ever seen you with your hair down."

An incoming text prevented Fiona from replying. Reading it, she stood from her chair and smoothed her hands down her skirt. "He's here." She walked around the desk and bent down to kiss Iris on the cheek. "Thank you."

The older woman reached up and patted Fiona's cheek, blinking back tears.

On wobbly knees, Fiona entered the reception area. Legs wide, posture straight, Tomas's back was toward her. She looked at the reception desk where Gina, a fiftyish volunteer, sat staring at Tomas's butt. When she noticed Fiona's arrival, she winked. At Fiona's scowl, she grinned and said, "Fiona's here, Tomas."

He glanced over his shoulder, then turned completely around, gaze roaming over her face and hair as she approached. "Hi," she said.

In the intervening hours, he'd shaved and exchanged his

T-shirt for a short-sleeved, button-down shirt and his faded jeans for dark wash jeans that clung to thick thighs. Lips turning up at the corners, he reached out and took a strand of her hair, rubbing it between his fingers. He wrapped the strand around his finger and gave it a gentle tug. "You ready?"

Wordlessly, Fiona nodded, then turned big eyes toward Gina, who waved a hand as if fanning herself. Turning back, she took Tomas's extended hand and followed him out of the building.

He led her to a KBS truck, opened the passenger door, and stepped back. She eyed the distance between the ground and the seat, then was lifted up and deposited in the truck. "Hey!" she protested. He grinned, closed the door, walked around the truck, and climbed behind the wheel.

"I could have done that myself," she grumbled.

"Yeah," his gaze flicked over her, "but it's more fun my way." With that, he started the truck and pulled out of the parking lot.

She wasn't going to say anything, but secretly, she agreed. Being held by him, even for that brief moment, sent her pulse racing. Her gaze roamed the interior of the truck, noting how clean it was, in contrast to what she'd thought a contractor's vehicle would be like. But it smelled like Tomas, woodsy with a hint of lime. With a quick side-eye, she took in his profile, the firm chin, hawk-like nose, dark eyes with ridiculously long eyelashes topped by thick, straight brows. Like every time she had seen him before, he was clean-shaven. Unusual, given the current trend for men was a carefully sculpted stubble. To prevent herself from swooning, she fixed her gaze on the rosary hanging from the rearview mirror. It swung and swayed with the movement of the vehicle, the silver cross flashing in the sunlight. When the truck stopped, she glanced out the window. They'd pulled into the parking lot of the Keeney River Park.

"I thought we were going for coffee?" She turned bemused eyes on Tomas.

"Here." He handed her a cold take-out cup from the drink holder. "Iced, non-fat, vanilla latte, right?"

Fiona nodded, accepting the drink.

"I asked Iris what you liked. I'm not one for sitting still, so I'm hoping you won't mind if we walk a little."

They both looked at Fiona's sling-backed wedged heels, then she met his questioning gaze. "I'll be fine. Maybe a little help on the gravel, though."

Tomas was out of the pickup and rounding the hood before she'd managed to get the seat belt off. He opened the door, spanned her waist with his big hands, and lifted her down. He reached in, grabbed the drinks, and handed one to Fiona. Then he closed the door, took her other hand, and guided her to the path, not letting go, even when they reached stable ground.

She was holding hands with a man.

She was holding hands with a man who looked like an Aztec god, had bothered to find out what her favorite drink was, and drove his mother to church.

He squeezed her hand then released it.

"I owe you an apology." His deep, rumbly voice drew her gaze up to his. Stopping them in the middle of the path, his eyes were soft and filled with remorse. "I was a dick last night. I was rude, and you deserve to be treated so much better."

"Okay…." She bobbed her head, accepting the apology. "But why were you like that? Did I do something?"

His eyebrows drew together in a fierce frown as he looked over her head, heaving a deep sigh. "A few days ago, I saw a man holding you, and I thought you were seeing someone."

"Wait…*what?*" Fiona cocked a hip and propped a fist on it.

When was the last time a man held her? Besides Tomas helping her in and out of the truck. "Where was this?"

Shoving a hand through his hair, red flags of color appeared on Tomas's cheeks. "The Keeney Works parking lot." His face looked pained. "It was a couple days ago. I stopped by to get a signature from Iris, saw you leave and jump into a guy's arms."

Leaning forward, Fiona enunciated clearly, "That was my brother."

"I know that now!" Tomas put a fist on his own cocked hip. "I didn't last night."

The scowl didn't work with his blush.

A lock of hair fell into her face, and she flipped it back over her shoulder, trying to figure out what to say.

"Like I said, I was a dick. I'm sorry." There were no smiles, just contrition on the hard, flushed planes of his face.

She wasn't used to men who apologized. Eddie never had. But he was less than half the man standing before her. She nodded again. "Okay."

"Yeah?"

"Yeah. But for the record, if you want to know something, ask me."

He grinned, and there it was again, warm, crinkly eyes making her insides melt. To hide her reaction, she sipped on her straw, turning back to the path.

For the next little while, they meandered the path bordering the slough, stepping aside for cyclists and speed-walking geriatrics while getting to know each other. They each had a casual relationship with the Church but deeply respected their mothers' faith and commitment to community. They weren't strangers; Tomas knew about her divorce, and Fiona knew about his time in jail. He shared the surface story: how stealing his stepfather's car landed him there, and how that's where he'd learned construction.

He did not share about the years when he and his mother were alone after his father left, his struggles in school, or his learning disorder. She was part of one of Keeney's leading families, held an MBA, and was the executive director of a non-profit agency. As much as he wanted to, he had no idea if he would get further than coffee with her.

Tomas slowed his pace, taking shorter steps to match Fiona's. It was hard to keep his hands to himself. The breeze would blow her hair into her face, and she would flip it back, the scent of jasmine filling the air. Knowing the weight and softness of her hair, he wanted to touch it, brush it back from her face, hold his hand against the soft curve of her neck. Instead, he shoved his free hand in his pocket.

Her watch beeped, and she crinkled her nose as she checked the time. "I have to get back. I have a Zoom meeting in half an hour."

Turning, they returned to the truck, Tomas taking her hand to guide her across the gravel, and once more lifting her to place her on the seat. He shrugged at her scowl. "Wouldn't want you landing on your dignity."

She snorted. "As if being lifted into a truck is dignified."

When he started the truck, she rolled her window down. Soon, her hair was blowing, and jasmine filled the cab. They got to Keeney Works, and he parked by the curb, lifting her down once again, and walked her to the door. Through the window, he saw the grinning receptionist watching them.

"Thank you, I enjoyed that." Smiling up at him, Fiona attempted to tame her windblown hair.

Unable to resist, he smoothed it back for her. "When I call, you'll answer?"

Biting her lip, she glanced down, then up at him. "Why me? I didn't exactly treat you well, and I'm a hot mess. I did very little dating before marrying Eddie, and you know how well that turned out. I'm not sure what you expect from me."

The vulnerability in her words ate at him. He wished he'd met her long before Eddie, but he didn't have the power to turn back time, and who he was at that time was not a man worthy of Fiona. He wasn't sure if he was now, but he sure wanted to be. With one hand still holding her hair back, Tomas linked the other with one of hers. "I'm not expecting anything. But I admire you and want the chance to get to know you. That's all. We can see where this goes." Reluctantly, he released her to step back, repeating his question, "Will you answer the phone when I call?" His heart beat rapidly while he waited for her answer.

"Yes," she said in a firm, steady voice.

"Good." Nodding at the receptionist, he opened the door and held it for Fiona to enter. She passed the reception desk and, before entering the hallway leading to the offices, turned, waved, and smiled brightly.

Tomas smiled as well. It was a good start. They hadn't opened up about everything, but that would come. While he wanted to know everything about her: favorite food, favorite movie, morning person or night owl, he wasn't ready to share about wanting to be an architect.

Would she laugh? Would she scoff at his lack of education? Not for the first time, he mentally kicked himself for not accepting help in high school.

He'd been such a jackass. Hanging out with idiots and not listening to his mother and stepfather. Finding work wasn't hard. He'd been strong and good with his hands, but not being able to read had limited his future. Going to jail even more so.

The pay was good, and the work at KBS and Keeney Builds was satisfying, but could he have more? And what would more look like? Fiona's face came to mind, and he smiled.

CHAPTER 11

$\mathcal{H}$umming softly, Fiona sat in her car reading her text conversation with Tomas. He used emojis more than words and preferred talking on the phone. Which she didn't mind. Their schedules wouldn't line up, so for the past few days, they had talked on the phone late into the evening. Now, reading the message she'd composed, she bit her lip before hitting send.

Fiona: If you're willing to take a chance on my cooking, would you like to come to dinner tomorrow night?

The response was immediate.

Tomas: Yes. What can I bring?

"Gah!" she shrieked, a knock at the window interrupting her car seat happy dance. She scowled at her brother Joseph, bent double in laughter. "Not funny! Now go away. I'll be out in a minute." She finished her text with Tomas and climbed out of the car. Opening the gate leading into her parents' backyard, she found Joseph waiting for her by the back door, merriment dancing in his dark eyes.

"Car dancing, huh? What was that all about?"

Fiona shoved her phone into her purse and narrowed her eyes at him. "None of your business."

Joseph waggled his eyebrows. "I'll find out. I'm patient."

She shouldered past him, knowing full well that he would because she'd never had the ability to hold out on him. For now, she wanted to keep these feelings, these tap-dancing, squishy feelings, to herself.

As adults, Fiona and Joseph were expected to join their parents for dinner on the first Sunday of the month. Sunday night dinner at the Han household was a tense gird-your-loins-and-prepare-for-the-worst event. Her mother held court from the end of the table, alternately reprimanding her children for sloppy table manners and demanding details of their schooling, jobs, and personal lives. Her father sat silent at the other end, occasionally nodding or grunting when he felt it was necessary.

While they were married, Fiona had suggested to Eddie that they alternate the monthly Sunday night dinners between her parents and his. He'd demurred, telling her that Iris and Darryl were part of a Sunday night supper club. For the first two years they were together, Eddie was a regular at her parents' table, complimenting her mother's cooking and attempting to draw her father out in conversation while largely ignoring Joseph.

When he realized he would not be made a part of Han Family Holdings, their appearance at the dinner table began to wane, and Eddie's controlling behavior over Fiona increased. Contempt for her family and for her culture dripped from his words. Anything in their home with a Vietnamese influence disappeared. The porcelain tea set from her aunts, the decorative wall hanging in the entrance way, even the exquisite throw pillows Fiona's grandmother had sewn from the rich red silk fabric of her wedding dress. All vanished one day while she was at work. She'd confronted Eddie. He flew into a tantrum, snarling in her face about gooks reneging on deals and needing to learn their place. He didn't touch her, but his words flayed her skin.

She'd taken her car and raced from the house, calling her mother. Expecting shelter, her mother's words stopped her short.

"A marriage is a merger between two parties. It works best when the parties have like-minded goals and there is mutual respect. I'm afraid that Eddie did not live up to his end of the deal. The promises he made to HFH did not come through, and I had to let him go."

Fiona pulled to the curb. Her husband had verbally abused her, yet her mother was talking about dismissing an employee. "I don't understand."

Her mother clicked her tongue as if exasperated with a dense child. "When Eddie approached me about marrying you, he promised to open doors for the business and secure property to develop. That never happened. His promises weren't worth the paper they were written on."

"I didn't know," Fiona whispered.

"You didn't need to know," her mother carried on as if the fracturing of her daughter's world were a minor interruption to be dealt with. "The marriage can continue, however the merger of KBS and HFH will not happen. Eddie will not end the marriage, that would look bad for both of us."

Her mother continued, but Fiona didn't hear anything else. *Both of us.* Fiona's safety and well-being were not factors. Everything was business to her mother.

She ended the call and sat in her car. Through the windshield, she saw a strip mall. A strip mall owned by her family. Right. Marriage as a business. Squaring her shoulders, she turned her car around and drove home. That night, she moved out of the master bedroom.

It was her father who convinced Fiona to return to Sunday dinner. Shortly after Eddie's arrest, unannounced, David Han showed up at Keeney Works carrying an African violet. Fiona rose from her desk to greet him; he nodded, then turned left and entered Iris's office. A surprised Iris motioned him to a chair. He sat and spoke quietly to her for a few minutes. Rooted to the carpet, Fiona stood in her own office, unable to hear, watching the changing expressions move across Iris's face. Whatever he said caused tears to well in her eyes. Finally, he stood, patted Iris on the hand, and approached Fiona.

A quiet man, her father was always in the shadow of his wife, seeming content for her to make the decisions, running both the business and the family. Away from work, he could be found in his greenhouse, listening to baseball games and tending to his plants. He took both of Fiona's hands in his, wrinkles fanning out from his dark eyes, a gentle smile tugging up the corners of his mouth. "The people we love the most have the power to hurt us the most. We are not responsible for their actions, nor should we be ashamed of loving them."

Blinking back tears, Fiona lowered her eyes and stared at her father's hands holding hers, unable to speak.

"When you are up to it, please come to dinner. I miss you."

Fiona looked up to see a lone tear slide down her father's cheek. At her nod, he squeezed her hand, then left as silently as he'd arrived. Her gaze shifted when she heard Iris sniff. She exchanged a watery smile with her mother-in-law, then returned to her desk.

Now, entering the kitchen of her parents' house, she hung her purse on a hook by the back door before going to the sink to wash her hands. From his position at the island worktop, her father looked up from the vegetables he was chopping and winked. "How can I help?" she asked.

Her mother turned from the stove, her gaze traveling over Fiona from head to toe, then nodded toward the dining room. "You can finish setting the table. Joseph, I need you to get down the serving platters."

"Yes, mother," they said in unison and went to do their jobs.

Listening to the chatter of her mother and brother with one ear, Fiona set the table and then stood in the doorway to the kitchen. "Who's the extra place setting for? Is Grandfather joining us?" Linh Han's father had lived with her parents for five years since the death of his wife. Sunday afternoons and evenings usually found him at the Vietnamese social club where he played mah jong and smoked the disgusting cigarettes Linh Han would not permit in her house.

"No. Pastor Tran will be joining us."

Fiona exchanged puzzled glances with Joseph, finished setting the table, and joined her father at the island. From her place at the stove, her mother began the interrogation. She started with Joseph, grilling him about various properties and tenants. "And dating, are you seeing anyone?"

Joseph flicked an irritated glance at Fiona before answering, "No, Mother. I've been concentrating on work."

"Perhaps you should try a dating app. I heard there is one called Meet Cute that is very useful. Mrs. Smith says her daughter has had great success with it."

From her place beside her father, Fiona snorted. Joseph bit his lip.

He muttered, "I'll look into it."

The doorbell rang.

Thank God! Fiona avoided the dissection of her love life. "I'll get it."

"No. Joseph will get it. You will help serve the food." Linh Han removed her apron and smoothed down her hair. She gestured at her husband, who patted Fiona on the arm and followed Joseph out of the kitchen.

"Of course," Fiona mumbled, slipping into the role of dutiful daughter. It was better to go along with it, and she'd be able to leave in a couple of hours.

Voices heralded the return of the men, and the women stepped into the dining room.

Having only seen Pastor Tran in his clergy robes, Fiona wasn't sure what to expect. The slim, smiling man in a pale blue Polo shirt and rumpled khakis wasn't it. He looked to be in his late thirties, with slightly messy hair and a relaxed manner.

"Mrs. Han, thank you so much for inviting me for dinner." He stepped forward with one hand extended and a bottle of wine in the other.

Linh Han accepted it with a regal nod. "You are welcome. I apologize for not having invited you sooner. You've met my daughter Fiona."

"Yes." He switched his gaze to Fiona, extending his hand as well.

"Pastor Tran." Fiona smiled and shook hands.

"Please, call me Andy." His smile was big and contagious. "Your home is lovely, Mrs. Han."

Fiona refrained from snorting aloud. It wasn't until they'd been in college that their mother allowed her and Joseph into the dining room and living room unsupervised. To say that she was meticulous about order and cleanliness was an understatement.

"Thank you. Please, take a seat. Joseph, open the wine. This meal is best eaten when hot." She gestured at Fiona to start serving while the men seated themselves at the table. Father at the head, Joseph on one side next to Fiona's empty chair, Linh Han at the foot, and Pastor Tran opposite the Han children. On a large tray, Fiona brought in a variety of dishes and set them near her mother. She took the tray back to the kitchen and then sat beside Joseph.

"Pastor Tran, please say the blessing."

"It's Andy, Mrs. Han. I don't see the need to stand on formality."

Fiona watched her mother's lips all but disappear. Linh Han was a very formal person.

"Of course, Andy."

Hands were joined, heads bowed, and the food was blessed before dishes were passed around.

"Mr. Han, I noticed your garden, your plants look healthy and well cared for."

David nodded but continued to eat his meal. His wife led the conversation.

"Pas—Andy, I understand you are from California."

"Yes," he swallowed before continuing, "I was born in San Francisco. Except for a brother in LA, my family is still there."

"And you went to Stanford?"

Under the table, Joseph nudged Fiona's foot with his own. She nudged back. Andy's presence was saving them from being grilled.

"Yes. I have a degree in social work. I worked for the city of Sacramento for a few years before I answered the call."

"The call?" Fiona tilted her head in question.

Before Andy could respond, Joseph answered, "He means he heard God calling him to go into the ministry."

Joseph's cheeks reddened as the entire table focused on him.

Andy bobbed his head. "Exactly! The work for the city was unfulfilling, and I felt that my gifts could better be used elsewhere."

Face pointed down at his plate, Joseph murmured, "I know what you mean."

Fiona wondered if she was the only one who heard.

"You are a lawyer?" Andy looked at Joseph, one eyebrow raised.

"Joseph manages all of our properties. He is skilled at development and handling the tenants," Linh Han answered from the foot of the table.

Andy nodded and directed his attention back at Joseph. "You must meet some interesting people. Do you enjoy your work?"

"Work is not to be enjoyed, it is simply work," Linh Han interrupted again to redirect the conversation. "Fiona is the executive director of a non-profit. I'm sure you know of Keeney Works." It was a statement, not a question.

If the pastor was fazed by her mother's interference, he didn't let on. "I have heard about it. I would love to talk to you further about it."

Fiona opened her mouth to speak, but again, her mother was there first.

"My daughter is very good at everything she does. Her cooking is exceptional."

A flush of color rose on Fiona's face. Then, it dawned on her that her mother was trying to set her up with the pastor. She managed not to groan out loud.

"I'm sure it is," Andy murmured to Fiona, meeting her gaze, appearing fully aware of her mother's manipulations. "And Joseph, are you an exceptional cook as well?" He grinned at her brother.

Fiona felt her brother tense beside her. Twisting her head slightly, she saw the knuckles whiten on the hand holding his fork. "I get by," he said between stiff lips.

Fiona darted a glance at her father. He, too, was watching Joseph, a frown wrinkling his brow. He caught Fiona's look and raised an eyebrow before returning to his dinner.

Oblivious to the silent conversations going on around her, Linh Han continued, "You are not married. Do you have a fiancée?"

Andy leaned back in his chair, glanced around the table before settling his gaze on Joseph. "No. I haven't found the right man yet."

An awkward silence descended on the table before David

picked up a dish and turned to Andy. "May I serve you more rice?"

Andy held out his plate, then the two men settled into an easy conversation about baseball.

Fiona swiveled her head between her parents. At one end of the table, her dad, who rarely said more than two words, talked with Andy. Meanwhile, her mother sat stiff and speechless. This was a situation she had obviously not anticipated.

If it weren't for the tension radiating from Joseph, Fiona would have enjoyed herself. It wasn't often her mother was caught flat-footed. And she was off the hook from a fix-up. Cutting her eyes to the right, she studied Joseph. He was normally sociable. Why so silent now? She puzzled it over in her head while eating her meal.

Joseph dated. She knew that. He'd mentioned dinners and events, but when questioned, he'd say, "Someone I met online," or "You wouldn't know them." He hiked and kayaked. The photos he posted on Instagram were of the outdoors and the guys accompanying him.

The penny dropped, and Fiona wanted to smack her fore-head. Then she wanted to apologize to Joseph. She'd been caught up in her own drama the past few years and had paid him little attention. From beneath lowered lashes, she cast furtive glances at him while listening to the flow of conversation around her. Somehow, Father dominated, drawing both Andy and Mother into a conversation about replacing the church's roof. He sent questions Joseph's way to draw him in, and gradually, her brother relaxed. Participating slightly, Fiona watched her parents. Father was clearly relaxed and in the know. Her mother…? It was hard to read her mother. She didn't look surprised, though. Now Fiona was hurt. Was she truly the last to know?

After dinner was finished, and Andy departed, Fiona and Joseph washed the dishes and walked to their cars.

"Why didn't you tell me?" She couldn't help the whine in her voice.

"What?"

She gusted out a sigh. "That you're gay?"

Joseph frowned down at her. "Why? Do I need your permission?"

"No. Of course not. It's just that…I guess I'm just embarrassed that I don't know that about you. You're my brother and I love you, and I haven't been paying attention." The last words came out with a few tears. She dashed them away with the back of her hand. "Shit. Now I've made this about me."

Long arms circled her. "You've always been a bit of a drama queen." She heard the smile in his voice.

She stepped back and grinned up at him. "When did you come out to Mom and Dad?'

A wry smile tugged at his lips. "I didn't need to. Dad saw me on the kiss cam at a Mariners' game."

At Fiona's frown, he explained. "Between innings, a camera pans around the crowd, and zooms in on couples. They caught Hugo and me. It was during Pride month a couple years ago."

Fiona did the math in her head. Where was she two years ago? Trying to stay afloat between Eddie and work. Totally checked out from anything except her own drama, obviously.

"Hugo?" She crinkled her nose at him.

Joseph snorted. "Yeah. Unfortunate name. Great kisser, though."

"Are you still seeing him?"

Leaning up against the hood of her car, Joseph crossed his arms. "No. He moved to LA shortly afterward. I've dated a few guys since then, but no one steady."

Fiona turned and settled against the hood of the car as well, staring out at her father's greenhouse, sorting things in her mind. "You used to date girls, though?"

"Yeah." He shrugged. "I've been with both women and men, and I like guys better. Does that bother you?"

Shaking her head, she looked up at him. "I've only had sex with Eddie, so I have very little expertise to comment on."

"Maybe you should switch teams."

She smacked him on the shoulder. "Yeah, I don't think so."

"If you change your mind, let me know. I could introduce you…."

With a grin, Fiona straightened and dug through her purse for her keys. "Sure. I'll do that. So, what do you think of Andy?"

In the light from the kitchen window, she saw Joseph's blush. "He's cute. He gave me his number, but I don't know."

"Mom would love it."

"Yeah," he murmured, "but if it went sideways, that would be all kinds of awkward."

"True. Well, you know what you're doing." She reached up and wrapped her arms around him in a hug. "Talk to you soon?"

"Yeah."

Fiona climbed into her car, waved at Joseph, and headed home. That was an interesting dinner.

CHAPTER 12

"Shit!" Tomas looked at his watch before going to his locker. If he went home to shower, he'd be late for dinner. He pulled the clean shirt and shaving kit that he kept on hand for meetings with clients out of his locker and slammed it shut. Striding to the restroom, he tugged off his KBS t-shirt along the way and used it to wash away the sweat and sawdust at the sink. He scooped up water, scrubbed his face, and ran his wet hands through his hair.

"You have a date!"

He looked up to see Carl, the third contractor at KBS, leaning against the door jamb, a large smile white against his dark brown skin. "Yeah. And I'm running late."

Carl strolled into the room like he had all the time in the world. Fifteen years younger than Tomas, he'd started being Vincent's assistant while going through the contracting program at the college. Ali had then hired him. Talkative and outgoing, he tended to annoy Tomas, but he was good at his work, so Tomas put up with him.

"Who is it? Do I know her?"

Tomas glared at him through the mirror, not about to discuss his personal life.

Leaning against the counter, Carl crossed his arms, tapping a forefinger against his chin. "I *do* know her. Hmm… is it the barista over near City Hall? She's all kinds of cute."

"None of your damn business," Tomas growled. He tossed the wet shirt into the sink and pulled on the long-sleeved, blue button-down.

Immune to Tomas' taciturn ways, Carl asked, "Where are you taking her?"

With a grimace, Tomas grabbed his shaving kit and wet shirt, and shouldered past him.

Carl called to his retreating back, "Make sure you have protection."

Tomas righted himself before stumbling down the stairs. He hadn't thought about condoms. There was no time to go to the store. He walked back to Carl. "You got any?"

Waggling his eyebrows, Carl reached into his back pocket for his wallet and produced two packets.

"Thanks." Tomas narrowed his eyes at the younger man. "Not a goddam word to anyone." Snatching the condoms, he turned and stomped down the stairs, Carl's laughter trailing behind him.

*P*ulling the pins out of her hair, Fiona stared wildly into the mirror. Up or down? Tomas would be here any moment, and she needed to decide. Her workday chignon was far too formal, but wearing it down felt too…expectant. She growled in frustration, finally grabbing a hair tie and putting it up in a messy bun. With a grunt of satisfaction, she surveyed her outfit. The navy blue, high-necked tank top was a good choice. It would hide stains, and Fiona was a messy cook. The white denim capri pants were a little snug. She twisted to see her butt in the mirror. No panty line, and if she refrained from wiping her hands on them, she'd make it through the evening without looking like a slob. She slicked on nude lip gloss, turned off the bathroom light, and surveyed the bedroom. She fluffed the pillows and straightened the pile of books on her nightstand. "Give your head a shake," she murmured aloud. There would be no bedroom action tonight. But she'd shaved her legs and put on her sexiest bra and panties, just in case.

A knock at the door sent her flying down the hall, through the living room, past the table, and to the French doors. Outlined against the evening sun, Tomas stood, his head twisted to the side, looking over the deck and yard. In one big hand he held a bottle of wine, and in the other a bag with the KBS logo on it.

"Hey," she said on a breathless sigh, holding the door open for him to enter.

He twisted back and surveyed her from top to bottom and back up, dark eyes settling on her face, moving back and forth as if memorizing her features.

While they had talked and texted, they hadn't seen each other in five days. She swore he'd gotten better looking. Straight dark eyebrows over bold black eyes, framed with inky lashes, a blade of a nose, and hard but kissable-looking lips. She sighed, and those lips quirked up in the smallest of smiles.

"Hey, yourself." He leaned forward and brushed her cheek with those lips, then his gaze met hers, eyes crinkling at the corners in the sweetest of smiles. He sniffed, brows drawing together in a fierce frown. "What's that smell?"

"Oh crap!" Fiona darted away and went to the oven. Grabbing up potholders, she yanked the oven door open and dove in with both hands to pull a pan of burnt crostinis out of the smoking oven. Settling the pan on the top of the stove, she dropped the potholders on the counter. "So, no appetizers tonight." She directed her mortified gaze to the pot of chili simmering away. A sound had her turning back to Tomas.

He was biting a lip, staring at her with an amused expression. "That's fine." He placed the wine on the peninsula countertop. "I remembered you like chardonnay. If you show me where the glasses are, I'll pour one for you."

Wordlessly, Fiona pointed at a cupboard, then stood back and watched the big man move about her kitchen, totally relaxed, making himself at home. Her hostess skills resurfaced, and she said, "I bought you beer." She opened the fridge with a Vanna White flourish. "There are three different kinds. I hope they're okay."

Tomas handed her a glass of wine, then bent to look in the fridge. Reaching in to snag an IPA, his distinctive woodsy lime scent trailed off him. Standing, he pulled the door of the fridge closed and stepped closer to her, effectively pinning her in the corner where the two countertops met. Her stomach fluttered as a big hand moved toward her face. She held her breath. A long finger brushed across her lips, freeing a strand of hair stuck to her lip gloss, then tucking the hair behind her ear.

"Thanks." He stepped back, and a sigh escaped her. *Oh my God, how would she make it through the night?*

"The chili looks good."

"Yes! That's something I can make." Fiona scooted around him and motioned with her wineglass. "Do you want to take our drinks outside for a bit, or do you want to eat now?" Screwing up the crostini messed up her plans, and she was all kinds of awkward.

He glanced out the window and then down at her. "Let's go outside." Taking the beer and the KBS bag, he opened the door for her. She moved past him with a murmured thank you, and led him to the outdoor chairs on the deck.

The furniture was new, two armchairs, a small couch, and a table. She'd arranged and rearranged them until finally placing the couch against the wall of the house, the two chairs angled on either side of them so that each seat had a view of the backyard. They came with beige cushions, and she'd bought bright red pillows that drew hummingbirds to her deck.

She took a chair, and Tomas sat on the couch near her and handed her the bag. "This is for you. A housewarming gift."

"Oh." She placed her wineglass on the table and took the crumpled paper bag.

He looked sheepish. "I suck at wrapping gifts."

The admission melted her insides. The Aztec god had a flaw. "I'll try not to hold that against you."

Opening the bag, she pulled out a pink zippered case. She dropped the bag, examined the case for a clue, then unzipped it to reveal a power drill. Eyebrows drawing together in puzzlement, she said, "Thank you. This is so…."

"Practical. I know." He shrugged and sat back, angling one long leg over his knee. "This brand makes tools specifically for people with small hands. They were originally all in pink for women, then someone clued in to the trans world, and now they come in a lot of colors."

Fiona held the drill up. She'd never been comfortable with tools, precisely because they were too heavy and awkward to handle. But this one, she pressed the power button, and it whined. "Oh!"

"I charged the battery."

"Thank you." She turned the power tool in her hand, holding it like a weapon. "Do I need to get a license to drill?" He rolled his eyes, and she widened her own. "It was there. I had to use it."

She pressed the power button a few more times, oddly pleased to have received the drill. "Thanks again, but, umm, why?"

"My dad left when I was small, and my mom was useless

at fixing things," he said, staring out at the yard. "Anything that was broken had to wait until one of my uncles could fix it, and they showed me how to do things. When Mom married Carlos and had my sisters, she decided they would learn how to use tools, make their own repairs, change tires. That kind of shit."

One hand holding the drill, Fiona picked up her wineglass and sipped, not interrupting.

"Last year for Christmas, I bought Sylvie, Cara, and my mom each one of these." He shifted his gaze to Fiona. "Women should have the tools to take care of fixing things themselves."

"You mean like that wonky outlet?" Tomas was unavailable, so Carl came to fix it and was in and out in less than an hour.

"Yesss," Tomas drew out the word. "But that's electrical and should be approached carefully. Maybe start with something less—"

"Shocking?"

He smiled, revealing that dimple she was enamored with. "I was going to say less life-threatening."

"Did you give your mom and sisters lessons on how to use the drill?"

His head bobbed. "Sort of. Sylvie was putting together a television console and was having trouble. I couldn't help her in person, so I made a video and sent it to her."

"Great idea. I've found all kinds of instructional videos on YouTube. Is yours up there?"

"I sent it directly to Sylvie, so I doubt it."

Fiona sat back and sipped her wine speculatively.

"What? You're thinking of something." He nudged her knee with his own, a relaxed smile on his face.

He was easy on the eyes and easy to talk to. Unlike Eddie, Tomas seemed genuinely interested in hearing her thoughts and ideas. "I'm thinking about making instructional videos.

Maybe get tool companies to sponsor them. We could film you teaching one of the female students in the program—"

Raising his beer bottle, he interrupted her, "Not to burst your bubble, but that's already been done. To pass one of the classes, students have to demonstrate competence with different tools—explain safety stuff, different uses. One kid came down with Covid and couldn't do it in person, so she sent in a video recording."

"The videos could be of students explaining to *you* how to operate a tool effectively!"

"Me?"

She was getting excited now. She reached over and squeezed his knee. "Yes! This would be excellent exposure for Keeney Builds. Prospective *employers* could see the students demonstrate their knowledge, and prospective *students* would see what's expected of them in the program."

"I get that. But why do I need to be in the video?"

Fiona snorted and waved her hand up and down. "Because you are all that. And there will be multiple views." *Did I just say that? The wine is going to my head.*

Tomas blinked. "I'm all that, huh?"

She squirmed. "Yes," she squeaked.

He leaned toward her, tracing her cheekbone with a finger. "I think you're all that as well."

Staring at his full lips, Fiona forgot all about power tools and instructional videos. A thrill shot through her as his gaze darkened, and his hand slid around her jaw to cup the back of her neck. She parted her lips in an invitation, moving closer.

"Hello!" A voice came from the bottom of the stairs. "Can I come up or am I intruding?"

The moment broken, Tomas removed his hand, sat back, and drank from his beer.

"Hey, Iris," Grimacing at him in apology, Fiona called to her landlady and mother-in-law, "Come on up."

Tomas rose as Iris came into view. Turning slightly so his back was toward the stairs, he adjusted himself, drawing Fiona's eyes to his crotch. *Oh my.* Her gaze swept up to his, catching the slight narrowing of his eyes. Then he winked. And she blinked, wondering just how red her face had gotten.

"Hi Tomas," Iris said, "Please, sit down."

"Would you like to join us?" Fiona asked. "I can get a glass of wine for you?" *Please say no, please say no.*

The older woman shook her head and walked toward a chair. "I'll sit for a minute, but no wine for me. I'm headed to Scrabble."

"We were talking about a new idea for KBS and Keeney Builds."

Iris's gaze bounced between Fiona and Tomas, eyebrows raised in silent question.

Aware that he was now sitting closer to her, Fiona ignored him to focus on Iris. "He brought me this power drill, and we started talking about instructional videos for women."

"Videos? Like on YouTube?"

"Yeah. The intended audience is women who want to make small repairs around the house."

"I can see that." Iris nodded. "I've been selling power tools for years, but I barely know how to use them."

"Exactly!" Fiona shifted to pick up the drill. "Tomas says this company makes tools in smaller sizes, so they aren't as bulky and unwieldy. Perhaps they would want to sponsor."

Crossing her arms, Iris tipped her head to the side. "Have you thought about classes as well?"

"I already teach classes," Tomas said.

Iris shook her head. "Not like the classes for your contracting students. I'm thinking of the Senior Center. There's a big multi-purpose room with counters. It's been used for flower arranging classes and cooking demos. This would be the same kind of thing."

"That's an excellent idea." Fiona beamed at Tomas. "What do you think? Or is that stretching you too thin. You've got the contracting jobs for KBS and the classes for the program…."

Tomas rubbed a long finger back and forth across his bottom lip. "Let me talk to Hilary and Vincent. There's a student or two we may recommend that Ali hire for KBS."

Iris asked, "Do you want to teach classes to women?"

Fiona hadn't even thought of that. She studied Tomas for his response. Attuned to his presence, she noticed a slight stiffening before he shrugged, saying. "I don't know. I like building houses, and I like teaching students about building houses because there's a specific plan, and they're kids wanting to learn a profession. Not…."

"Old women looking for something to occupy their time," Iris deadpanned.

That drew a snort from both Fiona and Tomas.

Moving to the edge of her seat, Iris's grin switched to an earnest expression. "Keeney Builds has really come along. It's no longer a way to get people jobs in the trades. I know that you're trying to get students into architecture, and you need funding for that. For funding, you need attention. Classes for the community—some for seniors and some for kids—draw that attention. Some of your students may want to go into teaching themselves, and this would be a good training ground."

She rose from her chair and reached over to pat Tomas on the arm. "I've heard graduates talk about how good you are. Yes, you're cranky, but you hold them to high standards and are patient." She walked to the stairs. "Think about it. We could make this work, as well as those videos you talked about." With a final wave, she descended the stairs.

Fiona and Tomas were silent as they listened to her car start and move down the driveway.

"Sorry, I didn't mean to railroad you." Fiona knew so little about him and they weren't at a place where she should be pushing him. This was their second date after all.

Smiling absently, he took her hand, tugging her toward him. Without resistance, she rose from her chair, moved around his long legs, and settled beside him on the small couch. He stroked his thumb over the back of her hand and leaned in to place a kiss on her cheek, close to, but not on the lips. "You didn't railroad me." He tilted his head at the drill Fiona still held in her other hand. "I thought I was bringing you a gift, not a springboard for a new training program."

She crinkled her nose at him. "Ideas fly at me all the time, and I can get carried away." Holding up the drill she added, "I really like this. Will you teach me how to use it?"

"Do you want private lessons with power tools?"

Glancing down at his crotch, then up at his dark eyes, she replied, "Is that an innuendo?"

"Yeah."

"Then yeah." She set the drill down on the table. Twisting around, she reached up to stroke his cheek, opening her lips in invitation.

Tomas accepted the offering with a growl. Twisting around, he brought his hand to the back of her neck, then into her hair, drawing her head closer and sealing his lips over hers. He tasted and teased and sucked gently on her bottom lip, leaving Fiona breathless. She climbed into his lap and wrapped her arms around his neck, and went back for more. The man could teach a master class on kissing, and she wanted to be the only student.

CHAPTER 13

The condoms didn't get used after all. Despite Fiona's willingness, *he* wasn't ready. She was more than a quick lay, and he wouldn't treat her that way. However, as great as kissing and holding her was, he fully intended to do more, and would be prepared for that time. So Tomas bought two boxes of condoms on his way to work the next morning. One stayed in his truck, the other he left in a paper bag on the table in the break room, Carl's name scrawled on it. He doubted they'd go to waste.

Through each interaction during the workday, he thought about what he enjoyed. He didn't voice that out loud, knowing people would look at him strangely. But he paid attention.

Supported by the college and Keeney Works, Keeney Builds had been up and running for twelve months. After completing the general contracting program at the college, students rotated through three sessions in groups of four. One group worked in the KBS store under Ali's supervision. The gruff old man patiently taught them the flip side of contracting: processing orders, handling materials, and dealing with customers. Students initially rolled their eyes, impatient to strap on a tool belt and build stuff, but by the end of their three weeks, they nodded their appreciation. Another group worked with two of the contractors, going out on calls to repair and build whatever the customer wanted, installing plumbing, replacing flooring, and building decks. In addition to practical application, they learned to be punctual, courteous, tidy, and efficient. This part of KBS's business relied on customer satisfaction, and students learned that the ability to wield a hammer or Skil saw wasn't the only requirement for the job. Lastly, under the supervision of one contractor, they worked on a tiny house. The city contracted Keeney Builds to provide homes for a tiny house community. Not only did the students build the houses, they delivered them to the location and oversaw the installation.

Tomas was in his element building the tiny houses. At first, supervising the students was like herding cats, but he figured out a system. Each day started out with a detailed to-do list, from inspecting work completed the day before to checking supplies were correct to the building itself. He believed in measuring twice and cutting once. He'd learned that from his stepfather Carlos, and it was ingrained during his program in prison; supplies were not plentiful, so there was little room for error.

Each new group of students soon learned he was exacting, yet he explained steps carefully and patiently, leaving time for students to ask questions and parrot back instructions. After a confab with all interested parties, Hilary, Vincent, Ali, and Marcia, it was decided that Tomas would work exclusively with the tiny houses; he didn't have the patience or customer skills for house calls.

Today would be a little different. A delay in the delivery of electrical equipment meant that his students had the day off while Tomas would do a KBS contracting job solo. He eyed the tidy little bungalow from the truck, then glanced down at the clipboard. Ernest Gardiner needed banisters installed on either side of his staircase. He exited the truck and approached the house, pasting on his politest smile.

A curtain twitched in the window, and the front door opened before Tomas knocked. Hunched over a battered walker, a tiny man with gnarled hands peered up with open hostility. "You're not Vincent."

"Nope, he's on another call." Tomas pulled a business card out of his shirt pocket, blessing Ali for reminding him to carry them. He handed the card to the old man, noting the swollen knuckles as the man awkwardly accepted it.

"Tomas Alvarado," he sniffed. "Got ID?"

Gritting his teeth to hold back an expletive, Tomas fished out his wallet and displayed his driver's license to the old guy.

Through rheumy eyes, the man stared at the license, then up at Tomas, before grudgingly moving back. "Come on in."

Silently stepping into the foyer, Tomas eyed the small space. A hall led back to the kitchen from the front door, the living room on the right. Along the left side of the foyer, a staircase gave access to the second floor. "I understand you need two banisters installed, Mr. Gardiner." There was no point in small talk, he figured he should just get to work and get it over with.

Ernest Gardiner grumbled, waving a hand at the staircase. "I don't *need* them. My kids paid to have them installed. Too busy to do it themselves." He glowered at Tomas. "I could do it myself, but they insisted and, what the hell, it's their money."

Tomas put his tool chest down, carefully wiped his feet, and walked over to the stairs. A banister was recently installed on one wall. He suspected it had been put in around the same time the old man started using a walker. He grabbed it and shook. Definitely loose. On the other wall was a banister that was obviously installed when the house was built. He gave it a shake as well. A little firmer than the other, but he saw the wisdom of replacing both.

"What they really want is to put me in a home. Sell this house and split the profits."

Tomas listened with one ear as he climbed the stairs, knocking against the wall to locate and mark the studs.

"Don't you have one of them stud finders?"

"I do," Tomas looked over his shoulder at the old man. "But this is just as effective in older homes."

Ernest grunted, whether in approval or disapproval, Tomas didn't know, or particularly care. He descended the stairs and moved to the door. "I'll get the materials and get started."

"About time. I'm not paying for you to stand around."

Tomas brushed past him with a tight smile and stalked to his truck. This was why he preferred working with students. He opened the tailgate and sorted through the materials, wondering why he just hadn't taken a day off. His cellphone rang. "What?" he growled into it, not caring who was on the other end.

"You must be at old man Gardiner's house." Ali boomed out with a laugh.

Leaning against the side of the truck, Tomas glanced at the house to see the old guy staring at him from the open door. He waved, then twisted away to speak into the phone. "What did I do to piss you off?"

Ali laughed again, ignoring the question. "You're gonna really impress him when you tell him you have to come back to KBS."

"Why?" Cradling the phone between his ear and his shoulder, Tomas picked up the two banisters in a show for the old man.

"You haven't got the right hardware. Whoever packed the truck—and I will find out and chew their ass accordingly—gave you the wrong stuff."

"Great. The old guy barely trusts me and now is gonna think I'm incompetent."

"Give him the phone and I'll sweet talk him."

"Fine." Carrying the materials, Tomas walked back to the house. "Mr. Gardiner, I have to go back to the store. My supervisor will explain it to you. Here." He put the phone on speaker and held it closer to where the old guy sat on his walker.

"Hello?" he yelled into it.

Tomas stood holding the phone while Ali patiently explained the mix-up, emphasizing that Tomas was not responsible, and that KBS would reduce the installation cost to compensate for the inconvenience. When the conversation was over, Tomas tucked his phone in his back pocket. "I'll be back shortly," he said.

"Take your time," the old man said. "My lunch will be delivered soon, and I don't want you banging around while I'm eating. But I expect you back in an hour 'cause I won't pay for overtime."

With a tight nod and managing not to slam the front door, Tomas stalked to his truck, climbed in, and took off. Stopping for lunch himself would go a long way toward improving his own mood.

He opened the door to *Hola!* smelling the familiar onions, garlic, and peppers. The restaurant was located in a small strip mall filled with Asian-owned businesses, and it was originally a Korean barbecue restaurant. Patrons were confused at first but soon adapted to the new owners and food. Many years later, the restaurant had expanded, taking over the shop beside it. Now *Hola!* consisted of the original restaurant, an adjacent banquet room, and a food truck. Tomas had been out of the house when his mother and stepfather started the business and, unlike Sylvie and Cara, spent little of his teenage years in the kitchen. But he knew his way around it, had helped out when necessary, and admired the work ethic of Carlos and Louisa. When he'd gotten out of prison, and before working for KBS, he'd put in a few shifts, preferring the kitchen to serving customers.

It was the pre-lunch setup, the servers and cooks bantering back and forth in the empty restaurant. Tipping his chin at the young hostess, Tomas made his way to a back booth where his mother sat wrapping cutlery, and flung himself down.

Louisa smiled up at him, not bothering to comment on the frown on her son's face. "Hello, sweetheart, this is a nice surprise." She angled her cheek in expectation of a kiss.

Tomas dutifully kissed her, then poured himself a glass of water from the pitcher sitting in the center of the large table. He grunted before downing the entire glass.

"Want some lunch? Stevie's experimenting with a new soup."

At his nod, Louisa made to get up.

Placing a staying hand on his mother's arm, Tomas rose. His mother spent most of her day on her feet. She didn't need to wait on him as well. "I'll get it. Want some, too?"

Louisa nodded and settled back down.

The kitchen went quiet as he entered. Looking around, Tomas saw smiles disappear and spines straighten at his presence.

"Relax, it's nobody important," the head cook called out from her position by the big stove. The tiny woman grinned as Tomas wound his way toward her, stopping next to the stool from which she could see the entire kitchen as well as parts of the dining room through the pass-through.

"Hey, Stevie." He nudged her shoulder before peering into the large stockpot on the stove. "Mom says you're making a new soup."

"Hey yourself, hot stuff. Try this." She ladled a serving into a bowl and presented it to him. At his appreciative smile, she crossed her arms and smirked. "Right? Not bad for vegan. We're catering some dinner where they want all vegetarian and vegan. What the hell is wrong with people?"

It was a rhetorical question. Stevie Swan had been reigning over the kitchen for ten years. A distant cousin of Carlos, she and Louisa were thick as thieves, brainstorming new recipes in their downtime, unafraid to stray from the traditional path. Tomas often wondered what role his stepfather played in the business other than as a peacemaker. It was loud when Stevie and Louisa disagreed, but it generally didn't last long.

Pulling a bandanna from an apron pocket, Stevie swiped it across her forehead. Another bandanna held back spiked gray hair. Unlike Louisa, who was always stylish, Stevie never wore makeup, cut her own hair, and lived in baggy jeans and Converse high-top sneakers.

Tomas finished the bowl of soup during Stevie's diatribe, then held it out for more. "I'll take another for me and a bowl for Mom."

Filling the two bowls and handing them to him, Stevie said, "Go. Eat. Your mother doesn't see you enough."

Accepting the scolding with grace, Tomas joined Louisa in the dining room. He ate the second bowl more slowly while his mother fired questions at him. He explained about the delay and the job for old man Gardiner, unable to keep the irritation out of his voice.

"You've always hated looking incompetent."

Tomas grunted.

"Ernest Gardiner owned the auto shop over on Woodbine. Remember the place?"

Tomas nodded. Woodbine Automotive was the place to buy parts for cars built before computers were installed. If they didn't have it, they knew where to get it, whether salvaged from a junkyard or ordered from an obscure source across the country. Carlos bought most of his parts there for the custom low-riders that were his passion and lucrative side business.

"Ernest stopped working on cars when his rheumatoid arthritis got too bad. Then he broke a hip last year and can't drive. He's probably unhappy to lose his independence. It must kill him to have others do the work around his home."

Watching his mother deftly wrap cutlery in paper napkins, Tomas listened as she went on, thinking about the gnarled knuckles and how hard it must be to hold a tool.

"His kids aren't interested in taking over the shop and it's up for sale."

"Is Carlos going to buy it?" he asked.

"Hopefully." Lousia wagged her head back and forth. "Stevie has the kitchen under control. I handle the front of the house, and the food truck is doing well. Carlos doesn't have to be so hands-on anymore, he's getting restless."

That wasn't news to Tomas. His stepfather wasn't lazy and was at his best when he had a project to complete.

"Do you want to take some food back to Ernest?"

"Nah. He was expecting a lunch delivery."

Louisa waved away his answer. "Bring him some tamales. If he doesn't eat them today, he can have them tomorrow."

Tomas grinned. His mother thought food was always the answer. "I'll do that." Kissing Louisa on the cheek again, he stopped in the kitchen before heading out to his truck, feeling much better for the food.

He returned to the Gardiner house carrying two bags.

Ernest stood in the doorway. "It's about time," he said, eyeing the bags. "You planning to eat your lunch here? I ain't paying you for that."

Tomas rolled his eyes, placing the bag of food on the walker. He withdrew the hardware from the other, which he placed on the stairs and a small power drill. "Here. The food is from my mother, Louisa Santiago. She says hi."

Ernest sniffed appreciatively. "Good. That lunch was crap." He tipped his chin at the drill. "What's that for?"

"These were sent to KBS by a tool company that wants us to be a test market. To see if people are interested in buying them. The box was broken on this one, and we can't sell it. Thought you could use it." Other than the color, it was an exact replica of the one he gave Fiona.

Ernest closed the front door and leaned against it for support before releasing the walker and picking up the tool. The handle fit snugly in one hand, and he raised the drill to examine the buttons. They were large and bright, and the lettering was easy to read. Ernest pressed the power button, and the drill came to life with a whine. "What the hell am I supposed to do with it?"

Waving at the banisters lying on the floor, Tomas said, "This will go faster with another set of hands. Can you sit on the stairs and install the lower hardware while I do the ones at the top?" He was lying through his teeth. By himself he'd be able to have both banisters installed in less than half an hour.

A gleam entered the old man's eye, but he snuffed it quickly before glaring at Tomas. "Fine. If it gets you out of my house faster. Take the food to the fridge while I get settled."

Picking up the bag of food, Tomas complied. When he returned from the kitchen, the old man was seated on the stairs, powering the drill on and off, a look of glee on his face. Tomas ignored it. Instead, he stepped around the old man to carry the banisters, hardware, and his own drill up the stairs.

Having spent his life around cars, Ernest was no stranger to tools. But he required a little instruction. An hour later, the job was done. Tomas bent over his toolbox, placing the extra hardware and his drill inside.

"Here."

He twisted to look up. Ernest thrust the drill out at him.

Tomas waved it away as he stood. "You keep it. Ali was gonna toss it, anyway."

The old man didn't protest. A small smile quirked up his lips, and he stood a little taller as he shuffled to the front door. Shouldering past him, Tomas started for his truck when Ernest cleared his throat.

"There's a bunch of floorboards on this porch that need nailing down. This drill will come in mighty handy. I think I'll get to it after I have a nap."

The two men exchanged silent nods before Tomas walked off. He stowed his toolbox in the truck bed and climbed into the cab. On the passenger seat lay the open box of the power drill, the receipt tucked inside. Even with his employee discount, it hadn't been cheap.

He considered the differences between working with the students in Keeney Builds and working with the old man. Unlike the younger people, Ernest Gardiner didn't think Tomas was a contracting god, hanging on his every word. But the experience was satisfying. He still didn't want to work with individual customers, but he'd been given a lot to think about.

CHAPTER 14

"Are you there?"

Fiona nodded, then realized he couldn't see her. "Yep."

"So, will tomorrow night work for you?" Tomas asked.

She placed a hand over her chest to keep her heart in place.

"Sure." It came out as a croak. She cleared her throat. "I'm looking forward to it."

They arranged the time and ended the call. Bending over, she banged her head slowly against her desk. She'd just agreed to have dinner with his family. *Holy crap!*

Sitting back, she stared around her office. "Give your head a shake." She was the executive director of a non-profit agency. She lunched with local politicians and spoke at fundraisers. She could do this. She knew Louisa Santiago. She was a wonderful person. But Tomas's stepfather and sisters? Yikes!

Meeting Eddie's parents was the only experience she had. And it had been a disaster.

Walking down the stairs from her bedroom in her parents' house, she'd found Eddie and her mother in a hushed conversation. They drew apart at her approach, Eddie looking smug. He kissed her on the cheek in greeting while her mother gave her appearance the once-over and wished them a good evening.

Outside the house, Fiona hurried to follow Eddie as he strode down the driveway. He beeped the locks on a new bright red Audi and was ensconced in the driver's seat, revving the engine when she got in the car. She'd barely buckled the seat belt before they were off.

"Here," he said, thrusting a folded piece of paper at her.

Bewildered, she scanned it as he drove through the winding streets of her neighborhood. It was a two-column list, one labeled DO and the other labeled DON'T.

"I want my parents to accept you. So I made a list of things you can and can't talk about."

Fiona looked between the list and the man beside her, ice trickling down her spine.

It had been a dull gray day, typical of fall in the Seattle area. She was one month into dating Eddie and three months into her new job.

Supported by local churches and the town council, Keeney Works had been formed to combat joblessness. Their clients were those who struggled to find and maintain steady employment. Some battled addiction, some had multiple brushes with the law, while others dealt with health issues. Fiona was the youngest person to apply for the role of executive director. She worried that she'd only gotten the job because of her mother's influence, so she was determined to excel at her work.

Eddie's attention overwhelmed and flattered her. She'd expected him to be aggressive after his drunken behavior at the fundraising luncheon. Instead, his kisses, while nice, never led to fiery make-out sessions with roaming hands. On the days when they didn't see each other, he texted, making her laugh at silly memes. Exactly what she needed after busy, stress-filled days at work. She'd been looking forward to this evening; Iris and Darryl McLeod were respected in the community, and she wanted to make a good impression. But the words Eddie said made her stomach sink.

She studied the list. "Speak only in English. Why wouldn't I?" Her parents had immigrated from Vietnam as small children and spoke English fluently. She was raised speaking Vietnamese and English, had learned Spanish and French, and was now studying Tagalog. Eddie thinned his lips and raised his eyebrows in response. Was he implying his parents were bigots or racist? She looked back at the list. *Make minimal eye contact and avoid touching.*

"My mother will try to hug you but don't let her. That will annoy my father, and we don't want that."

"Okay," she murmured, subsiding into her seat. Looking at the profile of the handsome man beside her, she wondered what she was getting into. Yet, her mother approved of Eddie and was pleased about the dinner. Fiona was determined to be open and positive despite the churning in her belly.

The evening limped along at the expensive seafood restaurant in Kirkland. Fiona sipped wine sparingly, answered questions politely, and watched the tension escalate around the table. Eddie directed the conversation, at one point cutting off Fiona as she was explaining the funding behind Keeney Works when Iris asked about it. No one wanted dessert, and soon, they were heading back home in Eddie's car.

"Sorry, babe." Eddie squeezed her knee, then placed his hand back on the steering wheel. "You were getting into the weeds there. Mom wouldn't have understood, and Dad would have thought you were boasting."

"How was that boasting? I was explaining—"

"That's just it. Dad doesn't like…" he flicked his gaze over Fiona, then back at the road, "women explaining things to him. He's old-fashioned."

Misogynistic was more like it. She didn't speak during the rest of the drive. She'd sleep on it but was pretty certain she wanted nothing more to do with the McLeod family.

Entering the house, she followed the sound of the TV to the family room, where her parents sat watching a cooking show.

"How did it go?" her mother asked, muting the sound.

"Not," she said, slumping into a chair and rubbing her temples. "They were polite. I don't know if it was because I wasn't white or because I'm Vietnamese, but they don't like me."

Eyes narrowed, her mother leaned toward her. "What did you do?" Even in a bathrobe and slippers, Linh Han was intimidating.

Fiona's eyebrows drew together. She hadn't expected her mother's vehemence. "Nothing. I was polite. Asked questions—"

"Did you talk too much? No one likes a girl who talks all the time. Or giggles. You giggled, didn't you?"

"I did not giggle!" She looked over to her father, not expecting him to participate, but it would be nice if he supported her against her mother for once.

"There must have been something. I hope you haven't messed this up."

"I don't know how I could possibly mess things up. But it doesn't matter. I'm going to break it off with Eddie. I don't want to date a guy whose parents can't accept me." She made to rise from the chair, but her mother's words had her frozen in place.

"You will not. You will send a note to the McLeods thanking them for dinner. You *will* make them accept you. This is a good match."

Dumbfounded, Fiona sank back into the chair. "You can't be serious. Eddie gave me a list of things I shouldn't say or do around his parents. I don't want to be with someone when I have to walk on eggshells."

Her father leaned forward, mouth open to say something, when Linh Han shot him a look and shook her head. He sent a regretful look to Fiona and shifted back into his chair.

"You are a smart girl. You can figure this out. But you will *not* be breaking up with Eddie. Now, goodnight." Her mother raised the remote and turned up the sound on the TV.

Fiona and her father stood at the same time. He patted her on the shoulder and spoke softly, "Your mother has your best interests at heart." Then he headed out the door leading to his greenhouse.

Should she have brought wine? Standing on the front porch of the Santiago home, Fiona had her third freakout of the day. The first was about what to wear: a knee-length yellow sundress with white flowers, wedged sandals, and her hair in a side ponytail hanging over her shoulder. The second was about what to talk about. She wrote out six notecards and stuffed them in her purse. Now she stood with the flower arrangement her father made for her, wondering if it was the right gift.

The Uber driver had already gone, and before she could call for another, the door flew open, and a beautiful woman smiled at her.

"Hi, I'm Cara." She held out her hand. "You must be Fiona."

Fiona took her hand and released it quickly, worried her palms were soaked with sweat.

Slightly taller than Fiona, Cara was curvaceous. Dressed in a bright blue sundress, her makeup was understated, and she wore her black hair cut in an angled bob that curled around her face. She smiled easily. "I love your shoes," she said, stepping back to allow Fiona to enter. "Did you get those at the boutique on Main Street?" At Fiona's nod, she carried on. "They have the most divine stuff. It's like the mother ship calling me home every time I go near."

Cara chatted away while leading Fiona into the sprawling rambler. What had Fiona expected? She knew Tomas's parents were successful businesspeople, like her own parents. However, unlike her home, which was so formal, the living room was off-limits unless there were guests, the Santiago residence was warm and welcoming. Big windows let in the evening sun. The walls were painted a soft yellow and hung with bright artwork that drew the eye. The furniture was a mixed collection of comfortable chairs and couches, perfect for relaxing. This was a room meant to be lived in.

"Fiona!" Arms outstretched, Louisa Santiago rushed toward her. Spotting the flowers, she shifted her hug to a side embrace. "Those are lovely. Cara, put those on the table so I can give this girl a proper hug."

Cara winked at Fiona as she took the flowers. "Sorry," she mouthed.

And then she was wrapped in a hug. Louisa's perfume filled her nose as she rocked Fiona back and forth in her warm embrace.

"You can let her go now, Mom."

Over Louisa's shoulder, Fiona spotted Tomas. Propped against the entry to the dining room, he stood with his arms crossed, grinning at her. "I should have warned you about Mom's hugs. They can be intense."

Releasing Fiona, Louisa glared at her son. "She is the first girl you've ever brought home for dinner. Of course, I'm going to hug her." Turning to Fiona, she patted her on the arm and said, "Put your purse anywhere. Tomas will get you a glass of wine, and we'll go out to the back deck. Carlos and Sylvie are arguing over the barbecue. I need to referee." With that, she hurried off, leaving Fiona and Tomas alone.

He pushed off from the wall and moved toward her.

"Hey." His eyes dancing, he kissed her softly, tugging on a lock of her hair with one hand, while circling her waist with the other. "You look great. Thanks for coming."

Leaning into him, she was finally able to breathe. "Your family is…."

"They are that." His dimple came out with his smile. "But you'll survive."

Taking her hand, he tugged her toward the back of the house. "Come meet the others. They're going to love you."

CHAPTER 15

Sitting back in his chair at the outdoor dining table, Tomas smiled to himself. Fiona looked relaxed, sitting beside him, but twisted to talk to Sylvie and Cara. Something about dry shampoo. He barely paid attention, mesmerized by her smile and the way her eyes sparkled when she laughed. He rose from the table and started collecting plates.

"Oh! Let me help you." Fiona pushed her chair back, beginning to rise.

He motioned her back down. "Stay. I've got this."

Cara waved at her brother dismissively. "Let him. He needs the practice."

"Brat," he said, taking the plates into the house.

From the kitchen, he heard his mother talking to Carlos excitedly in Spanish. Standing quietly, he listened for a moment. When it was obvious they had only nice things to say about Fiona, he walked in and put the pile of plates next to the sink.

Louisa turned from making the coffee, clasping her hands in front of her and smiling broadly. "She's lovely. So polite and sweet."

"I know, Mom." Tomas scraped the plates off, rinsed them under the faucet, and handed them to Carlos, who put them in the dishwasher. They worked silently while Louisa chattered away.

"She's a good influence for Sylvie."

Beside him, Carlos stiffened and grunted.

Tomas twisted to see Louisa. "What's wrong with Sylvie?"

Her smile lost its brightness. But it was Carlos who answered, surprising the hell out of Tomas. His stepfather rarely spoke to him.

"She's quit another job."

"Another?"

"She's had six different jobs since graduating."

Tomas let out a silent whistle. Sylvie changed her major twice before graduating with an art degree from WSU. Unlike Cara, who'd known she was going into medical research since the age of twelve, Sylvie's interests shifted frequently.

"Is she like me?" His learning disorder had gone undiagnosed until he was in prison. It wasn't their fault, but he knew that Louisa and Carlos felt responsible, and beat themselves up for being bad parents.

His mother shook her head. "She doesn't have a learning disorder, but she lacks focus. She's just—"

"Drifting." Carlos turned to take Louisa's hand, his face mirroring her unhappiness.

"Has she been to a counselor?"

"You mean a mental health counselor?" Louisa shook her head. "Not that I know of."

Cara had her own place in Kirkland, but Sylvie still lived at home. She wasn't a pampered princess. She paid rent and did her share around the house, often hostessing at *Hola!* to earn a bit more money.

"Maybe a career counselor? Find out what excites her or that she's qualified for?" Tomas was just throwing shit out there. He loved Sylvie and didn't want to see her make the same kind of mistakes he had, letting pride and stubbornness take away years she'd never get back.

"Is that what Fiona does?"

Glaring at Carlos, Tomas replied, "Is that why you asked me to invite her? A free counseling session?"

Louisa inserted herself between the two men. "Of course not! Iris told Marcia, who told me you were seeing each other, and I wanted to get to know her better. I know she runs Keeney Works, but not exactly what she does." She patted Tomas's arm soothingly. "When she and Cara were discussing internships, Sylvie was paying attention, and I thought…."

The worry on his mother's face convinced Tomas that she hadn't an ulterior motive for the invitation. Carlos kissed Louisa on the temple and murmured something in her ear. Her face relaxed.

Carlos said, "That's a good idea. We will suggest Sylvie see a career counselor."

And that would go over like a lead balloon. Sylvie was stubborn, a trait she shared with her half-brother. She would have to be approached carefully.

The dishwasher loaded, Tomas dried his hands on a towel and tossed it onto the counter. "I'll ask Fiona about bringing it up. If she doesn't want to, she might have some suggestions for Sylvie."

"Thank you, sweetheart," Louisa said.

Carlos met Tomas's gaze, tipping his lips up in a smile. Tomas dipped his head in acknowledgement and went back outside.

Sylvie and Cara were scrolling through their phones, but Fiona was nowhere to be found. Cara looked up. "She got a call from her mother. She went out to the driveway to take it."

Tomas looked that way, wondering if he should check on

her just as Fiona turned the corner. She caught his eye and grimaced, still speaking into the phone. As if they had minds of their own, his feet took over, and he walked her way. In rapid Vietnamese, she finished the conversation, eyes firmly locked on his.

"Did you understand any of that?" Her face was pale, but bright dots of color appeared high on her cheekbones.

"No, is it bad?"

Biting her lip, she ducked her head and stuffed her phone in the pocket of her dress. "My mother knows I'm here and is wondering why you invited me to meet your family."

He stepped closer, fingering a lock of hair, loving the silky feel of it. "I think you know why. Do I need to put this into words?" At her head bob, he sighed and muttered, "I wasn't expecting to do this in my parents' backyard."

Her head came up, a small smile on her face. She looked past him and said, "The coast is clear. No one's on the deck."

"Yeah, but they're probably standing in the doorway watching us."

"So speak softly."

Her teasing smile made him growl softly. "I want to be able to kiss you whenever I want. I want to have sex with you. And I want to see where this goes beyond sex." He ran his hand down her arm, taking hold of her hand. "Remember Mom saying I've never brought a girl home to dinner?"

"Yeah."

"There's never been one I liked enough." He brought her hand up to kiss her knuckles. "I'm not good with words. I want you in my life, and I want to be part of *your* life."

She was back to biting her lip again, but her eyes were wide, and she nodded slowly. "I want that, too."

"Is that what you told your mother?"

She shook her head vehemently. "God, no. I told her you and I had started dating, and I was meeting your family. Then I hung up."

"You hung up on your mother? How's that gonna work out?"

Scrunching up her face, she replied, "Not well. But I keep telling myself I'm a grown-ass woman and it's my life."

"Do you want me to meet your parents?" He had little experience with meeting parents, but for Fiona, he would do his best to be charming.

"Yes. But not yet."

Tomas didn't want to put it off. He liked to meet obstacles head-on and take care of them before moving on to the next. His brows came together, and he started to speak, but she went on.

"My family is not like yours. My mother is cold. My father is silent. Dinner with them will feel like an inquisition. Not like this warm embrace." She threw her arms out, looking around the yard, and he tried to see it through her eyes.

His mother loved color. Her yard was a mix of annuals and perennials in every color of the rainbow. There wasn't a scheme to her gardening. She saw something she liked, and she planted it; if it thrived, she planted more. It was a lot to take in, but it was restful in its own way. In the far corner was the swing set Carlos had built when the girls were small. In anticipation of grandchildren, Louisa had left it up.

"My mother doesn't garden," Fiona continued. "She instructs my father what she wants, and the flowerbeds are ordered, almost regimented. We didn't play in the backyard because we might make a mess." She moved closer to Tomas, lifting her head to meet his gaze. "I'd been with Eddie for two years before I realized the marriage was arranged."

Seeing the unhappiness in her eyes, Tomas took her hand. She had more to say, and standing by the back deck was not the place for it, so he led her to the swing set and motioned for her to sit. She did so, pushing herself back and forth with one foot on the ground. He leaned against the support and studied her. His own mother was fiercely loyal to him, pushing and prodding him to be productive. He'd ignored her and screwed up royally, but she still loved him, and showed that love every time she saw him.

"My divorce is an embarrassment, I'm a personal failure to my mother." She raised a hand as Tomas was about to interrupt. "I know she's wrong and that it's her problem. But a couple weeks ago, we had a surprise guest for Sunday dinner. Mother tried to set me up with Pastor Tran."

"Seriously?" Tomas fisted his hands on his hips, but Fiona giggled before he could explode.

"But Pastor Tran is gay and was far more interested in Joseph than in me."

He barked out a laugh. "How did *that* go?"

"Mother needed to regroup, so Dad stepped in, and he and Andy—Pastor Tran's first name— talked about baseball. It went fairly smoothly after that."

Tomas didn't say anything, imagining what it would be like to have such a manipulative mother. Louisa meddled for sure, but Fiona's mother took it to a different level.

"I learned that night that Joseph was gay. I've been so caught up in my own drama, I wasn't paying attention to anyone else."

"Does it bother you that he's gay?" Tomas shifted, crossing his arms, and watched the play of emotion across Fiona's face. For traditional families, especially those with close ties to the church, being gay was still difficult. To Tomas, love was love.

Shaking her head, she said, "Oh no! I get Joseph being protective of his private life, not wanting Mother to interfere. I'm just mad at myself for being so self-centered."

Moving closer, Tomas squatted to bring his gaze level with Fiona's. He curled his hands around hers. "You had a lot of shit going on. If Joseph loves you, he's probably kicking himself for the same thing."

Fiona blinked back tears. "That's what he said." She sniffed, then grinned up at him. "But I think he and Andy are dating. So it's not all bad. However, I want to wait before you meet my family."

"Your call." Tomas stood, taking her hand and guiding her out of the swing. Her parents didn't sound like people he wanted to meet, anyway. "Let's say goodbye and I'll take you home." He leaned down and spoke softly into her ear. "Is it okay if I stay awhile?"

A blush stole over Fiona's face, and she nodded.

"*W*hat is it with you and your stepfather?" Fiona asked as they left his parents' house and walked toward his truck.

She wasn't sure that he would answer. But ignoring the barely veiled tension between the two men wouldn't work. Not if Tomas and his family were to be part of her life. She had enough issues with her own family.

He lifted her into the truck before she could do so herself, then climbed behind the wheel and checked that her seat belt was secure before doing his own.

"You don't need to do that." She rolled her eyes. "I've been doing up my own seat belt for a couple of decades now."

A muscle ticking in his jaw, Tomas stuck the key in the ignition, checked for traffic, and pulled away from the curb. They drove in silence for a few minutes, Fiona wondering what she could possibly have said to upset him. "Look—"

"Did you see the scar on Cara's eyebrow?"

"Umm…yeah. It's not really noticeable, but I saw it."

"I bought my first car when I was seventeen. Carlos wouldn't let Mom give me any money toward it, not even a loan. He probably thought I wouldn't pay it back. So I busted my ass washing dishes in the restaurant three nights a week, plus weekends, to save up enough money. It was a piece of shit Plymouth Valiant. But it was mine. Mom wanted me to help her out by driving the girls to soccer practice and stuff, so Carlos paid to have the car inspected for safety issues. The front passenger seat belt needed to be replaced because the buckle wouldn't latch properly."

Fiona looked down at the buckle pressed against her hip, her heart rate picking up.

"He bought the replacement kit and told me to take care of it." Tomas focused on the road, his voice a monotone.

"You didn't replace it."

He shook his head, then shot her a look filled with guilt, remorse, and self-loathing. "The words swam on the pages when I tried to read the instructions. The latch worked sometimes, so I didn't figure it was a big deal, and I stuffed the kit under the seat and forgot about it. I made the girls ride in the back seat anyways. One day, I was running late. When I picked Cara up, her arms were full and she couldn't open the door to the back seat, so I leaned over, shoved open the door to the front seat, and told her to get in and buckle up."

Heart pounding, Fiona clutched her hands together, eyes focused on his white knuckles clenching the steering wheel.

Tomas flicked a glance at her. "Yeah. I stopped suddenly, the seat belt gave way, and she slammed into the dashboard." He shook his head, muttering so softly she almost missed it, "There was so much blood."

"And he hasn't forgiven you?" she whispered.

"Would you?"

She processed that for a few minutes. "You couldn't read? How did you get your driver's license?"

For the first time in what seemed forever, Tomas smiled. "Cara and Sylvie read the manual out loud to me. I memorized it. I had to take the test three times before I passed."

Fiona returned his smile, happy to see his hands loosen on the steering wheel.

"Carlos wouldn't let the girls ride with me again after the accident. Mom was pissed, but he put his foot down."

"Can't really blame him."

"*I did*. Back then I thought he was a real prick."

"Did you…?"

"Yeah. It took me a week to figure out the instructions, but I fixed the seat belt. Showed it to Mom. But he didn't change his mind."

She shifted in her seat to face him fully. "Things must have been tense for a while."

He shrugged. "We didn't speak to each other. He'd say to Mom, 'Tell your son to cut the grass.' Or I'd say to Cara, 'Tell your dad I went to buy gas for the lawn mower.' Stuff like that. I moved out as soon as I could. We didn't speak again until five years ago."

"What happened then?"

Tomas pulled the truck into the driveway and parked behind Fiona's car. "That's when he called the cops on me."

He got out of the truck, leaving a stunned Fiona staring out the windshield.

She flung the door open. "What did you do? And don't give me that wide-eyed, innocent look. You must have done something." Tomas's big hands spanned her waist as he lifted her out of the truck. She placed her own hands on his chest, pushing him back as he leaned in to nuzzle her neck. "Uh-uh. You have a story to finish, my friend."

Grinning, he set her down, closed the truck door, and followed her up the stairs to her apartment. She unlocked the door, tossed her purse on the counter, and pointed at a chair. "Sit and talk. I'll make tea."

"God, you're bossy." Tomas settled into a chair and plucked an apple out of the bowl on the table. He rolled it between his hands while she moved about the kitchen. "Carlos likes to fix up cars, and he's good at it."

She nodded, thinking about the beautifully maintained car Louisa drove. She smiled at the irony of both their mothers driving BMWs, although her mother traded in her car every three years; the woman wouldn't be caught dead in one as old as Louisa's.

"He'd finished work on this cherry red Chevy Nova SS. The engine had this low throaty rumble, the interior was gorgeous. I'm getting a boner just thinking about it." He laughed at Fiona's glare. "I was pissed at him one night. I'd taken beer from the restaurant. Not the first time, either. This time, he chewed my ass out in front of a bunch of my friends. They laughed. I was humiliated. So I went home, found the keys to the Nova, and took off to Wenatchee for the weekend. On the way back, the cops pulled me over and arrested me for auto theft." He spoke in a matter-of-fact tone.

Standing beside the stove, Fiona watched the anger and frustration play across his face. She could only imagine his fear at the time.

"*I* didn't know Carlos had sold the car and *he* didn't know I'd taken it. The buyer came to get it, Carlos opened the garage, and it was gone. They reported it to the cops."

"And your stepfather got you sent to jail?" She moved over to the table and placed a hand on his shoulder.

He shook his head. "Mom said he tried to talk the buyer down from pressing charges. But the buyer was seriously pissed. I was an angry punk then, which didn't help matters. So, yeah, that's how I wound up doing time."

Fiona pressed into his side, running a hand down his arm to stroke the scarred knuckles of his big hands. Hands that built beautiful homes, designed delicate jewelry, and touched her like she was precious. "Was it…awful?"

Twisting one hand, he interlaced his fingers with hers.

"Yeah. It was a minimum-security prison over in Forks. But I still got beat up a couple of times. There was a nurse who used to live in Keeney. His mom knew my mom, and was able to help me out by getting me a job cleaning up in the infirmary.

"The doc there figured out I had trouble reading. At first, he was a real jerk. Got pissed that I wouldn't follow the instructions he'd written down. Thought I was lazy and trying to piss him off. I think he saw me staring at the paper, trying to figure things out, and he started asking questions about school and stuff. I had to tell him about my learning disorder. The prison had a rehabilitative program with a psychologist on staff. That doctor got me tested, and they figured out how to help me."

He turned wary eyes her way. She didn't know what he was expecting to see in hers, but he seemed to relax and continued speaking.

"I got pulled from the infirmary, which sucked because that nurse, Jaime, made the best cookies." He grinned up at her. "They put me in school. I wasn't thrilled, because school sucks when you can't read. But it was time. If I was gonna have any kind of future, I had to put in the work. There were a dozen guys in the class. Like me, they had learning disorders, although we weren't all the same. It was hard work, but it wasn't like I had anything better to do."

"And you learned to read," she spoke softly, one hand intertwined with his, the other sifting through his hair, gently massaging his scalp.

"Yeah." Now there was pride in his eyes. "I'm still slow. And I do better when I hear instructions instead of reading them. But I read something every day, to work at it, get better."

She cocked her head to the side. "What do you read? The newspaper? Sports stuff?"

"Nope." He shook his head. "I like romance novels."

"Really!"

"Yep." Releasing her hand, he shifted so she stood between his legs, his arms caging her in between his hard body and the edge of the table. "They're kind of like…instruction manuals."

CHAPTER 16

He studied her face closely, watching her eyes widen and lips part as a blush crept up her neck and stained her cheeks. Kissing her on her back deck had been sweet torture, one that he'd happily relive, even though it wasn't enough. Was he moving too quickly? He didn't know how experienced she was, but his gut told him not much. And he seriously doubted that Eddie had done much to make it good for her.

Dipping down, he glided his lips along her cheeks to the corner of her mouth. One hand came up, and he pushed her hair off her shoulder, exposing her graceful neck. She shivered at his touch. Pulling back, he stroked his hand across her collarbone, around her shoulder, and drew her to him.

She tilted her head back and cleared her throat. "Instruction manuals?"

His other hand pulled the hair tie out of her hair, and he sifted his hand through it. "Yeah, I learned how to unlace a corset, and that releasing a woman's garters was hard to do one-handed."

She giggled, then her hands came up and rested against

his chest. He pressed into them, one hand holding her close, the other now massaging her scalp.

"Of course, if you're not wearing a corset or garters, that information isn't going to be useful. Are you?"

She shook her head, a smile playing over her lips as she relaxed into him. He pressed closer, seeing the response in her eyes as his cock pressed against her belly. Her hands stroked over his chest, and a tentative thumb found his nipple. He groaned. She leaned forward, replacing her thumb with her lips, lightly sucking the tight bud through his shirt. He brought her chin up, and found her lips with his. He tried to keep it gentle, but when her mouth opened beneath his, he swept his tongue in and claimed hers. Deep in her throat, she moaned her response, and a shiver went through him.

Since taking her home all those many months ago, he'd dreamed about holding her and hearing those noises, and being free to explore where they might lead. Pulling back, he held her by the shoulders, stroking a thumb over the pulse beating in her neck. Color rode high on her cheekbones as she reached up and took both of his hands in hers, twisting to the side. Releasing one hand, she led him down the hall- way, glancing shyly over her shoulder. Wordlessly, they entered her bedroom, then faced each other. Eyes on her, he didn't take in the details of the room. There would be time for that later.

She stepped closer then reached up to the buttons on his shirt. "May I?"

Swallowing, he nodded.

Her tiny hands made quick work, then she pushed his shirt back, and he shrugged it off and tossed it onto a chair in the corner of the room. He stood tall and straight while her hands and gaze traced over his tattoo. It started above his right pec, went over his shoulder, and halfway down his arm. It was an Aztec sunrise.

"I've been wanting to do this forever," she murmured, her

gaze following the swirls of ink. Then she leaned in and kissed his nipple again.

He sucked in a breath, and she giggled, murmuring, "I read instruction manuals as well."

"Yeah?" Both hands finding the straps of her sundress, he pulled them down off her shoulders and kissed the spot where her neck and shoulder met, then licked his way up to her ear. "Are you good with this?"

In response, she released the zipper of her dress, and her shoulders slumped forward as the loose bodice fell to her waist. Fiona kept her head down as she pushed the dress over her hips to the floor and stepped out of it. She removed her shoes and tossed everything onto the chair. Straightening her shoulders, she turned toward him, exposing herself fully. She wore only panties in a dusky rose color. The same color as the nipples on her small pert breasts.

The bold woman of moments ago was gone. Not looking at him, Fiona stood stiff, hands fisted at her sides as if expecting him to reject her.

The thought never entered his mind. "Hey, look at me," he said, tipping her chin up to meet her gaze. "I don't know what you've been told, but everything about you is perfect. There isn't another woman I want to be with."

The vulnerability revealed when she lifted her eyes made him want to punch the wall. Made him want to hunt Eddie McLeod down and punch him in the face.

Swallowing his anger, he placed a hand behind Fiona's neck and pulled her closer, then kissed her forehead before gliding his nose along hers. Feeling her relax, he guided her hands to the fly of his jeans and waited. It would be damn difficult, but he would wait if this wasn't what she wanted.

Head bowed, she released the button and undid the fly, pushing his jeans and underwear down his hips. His cock sprang free, and her gaze flew up to meet his.

It took all his resolve not to throw her on the bed and rut

into her. "I'm not sure how slow I'm going to be able to take this."

Her gaze locked with his. "We can do slow the next time."

Thank Christ. He toed off his boots and removed his clothes in record time. Then he scooped her up, placed one knee on the bed, and laid her down. Settled beside her and propped up on one hand, he traced a finger over her eyebrows, down her nose, and across her lips. She darted out her tongue to flick the tip of his finger, then drew his finger in and sucked on it. He felt it all the way to his balls, and pressed his hard cock against the smooth skin of her thigh.

She shifted on the bed until they were both lying on their sides facing each other. Continuing to suck on his finger, she reached between them, sliding a hand up the back of his leg, over his ass, drifting it over his hip bone to hover above the tight curls at the base of his cock. Releasing his finger, she said, "I want you. I won't break," and wrapped a small hand around his cock and tugged.

Groaning, he trailed his finger down, circling the tight bud of one nipple before moving downward and stroking it across her panties. She pushed against it, and he felt her wetness. He teased her through the thin fabric while she squirmed, squeezing his cock until he thought he would blow.

"Baby," he growled, pulling her hand away and climbing off the bed.

"Did I do something wrong?" Fiona pushed herself up on her elbows, unconsciously thrusting her tits in the air.

"Not at all." He lifted up his jeans and dug a condom out of a pocket. "Just getting this."

"Oh," she sighed, and made to remove her panties.

He threw the jeans at the chair and prowled back to the bed. "No. I do that."

Her hands fell to the side, and she watched as he approached the foot of the bed and crawled toward her.

"You, princess, are going to lie back and let me worship you."

A shiver ran the length of her body as she watched him through half-lidded eyes. Removing her panties, he parted her legs and kissed his way up the inside of one thigh to press his nose against the silky hair of her mound. His head came up, and he caught her gaze. "Will you taste as good as you smell?" Then he proceeded to find out, the flat of his tongue lapping her from her opening to her clit, then fastening on the tight bud, and sucking.

Fiona's hands came up, grabbing his head and pressing it into her, her head whipping back and forth on the pillow. Mewling, she tensed as her orgasm coursed through her, and he licked her clean. Rising to his knees, Tomas rolled the condom over his hard cock, eyes fixed on the sated look on her face. With a slow smile, she reached for him, and he settled between her thighs, rubbing the tip of his cock through the wetness of her pussy. The tight walls of her sheath relaxed to make room for him as he entered her slowly. He held back until he could take it no longer, and pushed all the way in. Fiona's eyes widened, and he held himself still, watching the play of emotions move across her face.

She sighed, and smiled, and grasped his shoulders to hook her legs around his hips, offering herself completely. Tomas accepted the invitation, and drove himself in over and over until he arched his back in release. Coming down, he unwrapped her legs, and bent to capture her lips and her sounds of contentment. His arms went around her, and he twisted and fell to his back, taking her with him until she was snuggled against his side. When his heart rate normalized, he untangled himself from her, kissed her forehead, and went to the bathroom to deal with the condom.

She was under the covers when he returned, holding one

side back in invitation. He didn't hesitate, climbing in, settling on his back, and pulling her to him.

Rising on her elbow, she ran her free hand up his chest to cup his jaw. "Thank you," she said, her gaze soft and warm.

It felt like a gift, and a smile bloomed on his face while warmth flooded his chest. He kissed her palm before closing his eyes and drawing her tight against him.

Fiona didn't know what to do. Eddie had been her only lover, and their couplings had been just that—couplings. Prior to tonight, the only orgasms she'd ever had were self-induced. Curled up against Tomas's side, her mind raced, while at the same time, under the hand she'd placed on his chest, she felt his heart rate slowing. Tomas shifted, turning to face her, his eyes crinkled, and he kissed her nose. Anticipating his leaving, she smiled faintly. At that, his brow furrowed.

"Did I hurt you?"

"No!" she blurted. "That was…." She felt a blush from the roots of her hair to the tips of her toes. "I mean…."

He kissed her lips lightly. "Good. Do you want me to leave?"

"No!" She closed her eyes in an attempt to corral her thoughts. She didn't want to mention Eddie, but she didn't know how to explain without doing so. "I was married, so I'm not inexperienced. It's just…I never had…." She opened her eyes to find him studying her, one of his big hands stroking lightly over her shoulder. "This."

For a person who spoke before audiences small and large, she wasn't articulating herself very well. Blunt honesty seemed to be her best course of action. "I have a drawer full of toys, so I know what an orgasm is like. What I don't know, is what it's like for a man to want to—" she searched for the appropriate word "—linger." That wasn't right, either. She snuggled against him and kissed his chest. "This."

His gaze softened as his hand moved up to her cheek, and he stroked a thumb across her lips. "Then I'm happy to give this to you."

With a sigh, she draped an arm across his belly, and he held her.

It was late when he left. Barefoot and naked beneath her robe, she'd walked him to the door and watched him drive off after giving her yet another toe-curling kiss.

Turning from the French doors, she retrieved her phone from her purse to plug it in. It rang. Startled, she bobbled it, then looked at the screen. Her mother. *Oh my God!*

Fiona had never defied her mother. But tonight, she'd hung up on her, then ignored her calls. She stared at the ringing phone. Answer it? And what, listen to her mother hurl vitriol at her? She'd just had the best night of her life, a dinner with people she liked, followed by sex with Tomas, which was so good she wanted to relive it again and again in her mind, not share it with her mother. She let the call go to voicemail. Then she silenced it, plugged it into the charger, turned off the lights, and went to bed.

CHAPTER 17

Fiona poured herself a cup of tea before checking her phone for messages. There was one from Tomas and four from her mother. Figuring she'd save the best for last, she listened to the ones from her mother.

"We must have been cut off, because a dutiful daughter would not hang up on her mother. Call me back."

"This is a mistake, Fiona. What are you doing there? Call me back."

"You foolish, stupid girl, we will be talking about this, and you will listen."

"Do you know how many women he has been with? Do not give yourself to him. You are a novelty, and when he is finished with you, he will toss you aside."

Each message whittled away at Fiona's self-confidence. The last was a direct hit. *Was* she a novelty? A notch in his bedpost? She'd awakened with the glow of having been well-loved, and now…now she felt used.

For most of her life, she'd been submissive, doing what she was told to do. Studying business in college, working for HFH, and applying for Keeney Works. She thought she would gain some independence by marrying Eddie. Instead, she traded a controlling mother for a controlling husband.

Was her mother right? Was she wrong to sleep with Tomas?

Did she do it because it was exactly what her mother didn't want her to do? Possibly, but Tomas was everything Eddie wasn't. He was interested in what she had to say. He listened to her. He was protective. *Protective or controlling?* She shook away that invasive thought, pressing the button to listen to his voicemail.

"Morning, princess. I'll be on a job site until six. Don't cook. I'll bring dinner."

Frowning, Fiona sipped her tea. Presumptuous? Possibly, but he was also bringing dinner, which was thoughtful. *But he didn't ask. He didn't ask if you were busy. He just assumed he could show up whenever he wanted.*

There was nothing on her calendar for the evening. But that wasn't the point. Entering the bedroom to finish getting dressed, she stared at the rumpled bed, specifically the dented pillow where Tomas had been. After signing her divorce papers, she'd wondered whether she'd ever wake up to another man in her bed. Apparently not. Tomas didn't stay.

"Give your head a shake," she muttered and made the bed with quick, efficient movements.

It was going to be a busy day, and she concentrated on her calendar as she went through her morning routine: doing her makeup and arranging her hair while standing in front of the bathroom mirror. She wiped out the basin and cleaned off a smudge of toothpaste with a tissue before dropping it into the wastebasket. On top of a condom wrapper.

Novelty.

She stared at the foil package as the word circled in her head, taunting her. She wasn't. Was she?

Chewing off her carefully applied lipstick, she retrieved

her phone to tap out a reply. *Not tonight, but I'll talk to you soon.*

The message disappeared into the ether just as the realization that she'd done precisely what her mother wanted hit her.

She stuffed her phone in her purse and finished preparing for what would undoubtedly be a crappy day.

*S*lam!
The locker door bounced back, and Tomas slammed it again.

"What is going on in here?"

He turned to find Hilary and Marcia standing at the door to the break room, concerned looks on their faces.

Shit. He'd thought he was alone. He grimaced and turned to close the locker fully. "Nothing. Sorry to bother you."

Shouldering past the much taller Hilary, Marcia entered the room and went to the coffee machine. "I talked with your mother this morning. She said dinner went well last night and the family loves Fiona." She filled a mug and topped it with cream and sugar. "Can I pour some for either of you?" She peered over her shoulder at the others. Hilary nodded, but Tomas shook his head.

He wanted coffee, but he wanted to escape the nosy woman in front of him. Not for the first time, he wished he lived in a town where his actions would be anonymous. However, not only was Marcia his mother's friend, she was a coworker and Vincent's mother. Being rude was not an option.

"Thank you, but I have to get going." He shoved his phone in his back pocket and headed to the door.

"Not so fast."

Groaning inwardly, he turned. Marcia and Hilary leaned against the counter, eyes focused on him.

"Taking out your frustrations on a classroom of unsuspecting students will not solve your problems," Marcia told him.

"I don't have a problem." He crossed his arms, trying not to glare.

"Well, something happened between you leaving Fiona's place at midnight and now." Marcia looked up at Hilary and explained, "Iris is a light sleeper. She heard him leave. She said the last few days Fiona has been as giddy as a schoolgirl."

"Then how come she doesn't want me to come over tonight?" Unable to stand still, Tomas prowled around the room. "Last night was great. Fabulous. She got on with Mom and my sisters. Enjoyed herself at dinner. We talked and we went back to her place. And—" He looked up to find the women rapt with attention. "And it was good. When I left, we talked about getting together. So this morning I called, and she must have been in the shower, so I left a message telling her what time I was coming over tonight. *She* texted back and said not tonight, she'd call me soon. What the fuck is that?" Running out of steam, he pulled a chair out from the table and threw himself in it.

"You *told* her you were coming over?" Marcia's voice rose.

"Yeah." He looked up to see Hilary shaking her head and Marcia giving him a flat-lipped glare. "And not to cook. That I'd bring dinner."

"You didn't ask, you *told* her?" Marcia blew out a gusty sigh and took a seat across from him. Hilary sat next to her, folding her hands on the table.

Tomas nodded, unsure what he'd done wrong. But seated across from the two angry women, he knew it was something big.

"Has she told you much about her family?" Hilary asked.

"Some."

"Did you know that everything was mapped out for her? That her mother made all the decisions? Then her piece-of-shit husband told her what to do." Marcia exchanged looks with Hilary and continued. "Taking the apartment was the first time Fiona went against her mother's wishes. And then being with you? That's huge. An independent choice that will seriously piss off her mother. And Fiona will hear about it."

Glancing between Marcia and Hilary, Tomas thought about Fiona hanging up on her mother and what the fallout might be.

Hilary leaned in, her eyes sympathetic. "So you *telling* her, not asking…."

"Is not giving her a choice." He rubbed a hand over his face. Choice was taken away from him when he entered prison. Where he went. What he ate. Who he saw. Fiona's prison didn't come with cement walls and razor wire, but her world had been restricted. "Shit. I have to make this right."

The two women nodded.

CHAPTER 18

$\mathcal{A}$ blinding headache accompanied Fiona into the Keeney Works parking lot. She was coming from an on-site meeting with a large, up-scale nursery that hired both long-term and seasonal workers. They'd been reluctant to come on board when she reached out to them more than a year ago, but they requested today's meeting out of the blue.

The presentation went well. Despite being frazzled, Fiona fielded questions from the management team like a champ, and she anticipated securing a new job source for her clients.

"I'm wondering about our client base. Will the workers' looks intimidate them?"

The question came from a pot-bellied middle manager.

"What do you mean?" One eyebrow raised, Fiona replied with a tight smile.

Four middle-aged white men busied themselves with cellphones around the table, leaving the other man gaping like a fish.

Sitting back in her chair, Fiona silently studied him, wondering if he realized how condescending and racist he sounded. Another time, she might have swallowed back the slight and murmured about Keeney Works teaching their clients about workplace etiquette and dressing like professionals. But today, she was tired and overwhelmed and just done.

The moment lengthened and became increasingly more awkward. With a nod, Fiona closed her notebook, stuffed it in her tote bag, and rose from her chair, murmuring her thanks for their time. No one spoke as she walked to the door. She placed a hand on the knob, paused, then turned back. " I take that back. This has been a waste of *my* time. Keeney Works seeks to improve our clients' lives. I don't see how that can happen here. You care more about the delicate sensibilities of your precious customers than improving the community. This was an opportunity for you to show Keeney that you care about giving someone the benefit of the doubt and a chance to prove themselves. But God forbid you should offend an over-privileged suburbanite by hiring someone who's a different color, or lived rough, or speaks broken English. I won't be calling you again."

She yanked the door open and stalked through the store and out into the parking lot. Stopping at her car, she gusted out a sigh and leaned against the tailgate as she pulled her hair out of its customary bun and massaged her tight scalp. *What had she done?* Having the nursery as a job source would have been a feather in her cap, but she'd blown it in a fit of righteous pique. The board of directors would not be thrilled, and she may have jeopardized her job. She stared around the parking lot at the upscale cars and thought about her parents.

Sponsored by the United Methodist Church, they'd emigrated from Vietnam in the mid-1970s. Her mother and father were both young children, and grew up together in the tight Vietnamese community of Anaheim, California. They were expected to marry and did so. They'd learned English quickly and, like many others in their culture, started out in nail salons. But Linh Han was ambitious, and she and her husband relocated to Keeney and opened up their own nail salon in a strip mall, eventually buying the strip mall itself. As business focused as she was, her mother appreciated the church's generosity and made it a point to give back to the community that embraced her. So while HFH expanded their real estate ventures, they built a cosmetology school in Keeney and awarded scholarships specifically for immigrant students to further their education.

Which confused Fiona as well. Her mother believed in raising up others but didn't want Fiona to be with a Hispanic man. Linh Han couldn't see her own prejudices and biases.

Tomas overcame so much, his lack of education and a learning disability a huge part of it. Then came the obstacles and opportunities he faced when he got out of prison. How Eddie had denied him work, how Vincent had gone to bat for him, and how Iris had taken him on. His success was the kind of thing Fiona wanted for her clients. And if this nursery didn't see the opportunity they'd passed up on, too bad for them. On that conclusion, she beeped her car open and climbed in.

She squinted against the late morning sun in the Keeney Works parking lot, and the pain radiating from the base of her skull. Trudging into the building, she passed the receptionist with the barest of waves, intent on getting to the quiet of her office. Three paces from finding refuge, her steps faltered. Her mother's voice was coming from her office. Fiona must have made a noise because Iris popped her head out of her own office and scurried toward her, an unhappy expression on her face.

"I'm sorry, dear," she whispered. "She arrived thirty minutes ago and insisted on waiting for you in your office."

Groaning inwardly, Fiona patted Iris on the arm. "It's okay. Thank you for letting her in." Running a hand over her hair, Fiona straightened her spine and strode into her office.

Linh Han was speaking rapidly in Vietnamese on her

phone. At Fiona's entrance, she raked her eyes up and down her daughter, her gaze lingering on the hair hanging loose down her back, then pointed at her wristwatch. She finished her conversation while Fiona rounded her desk and seated herself.

"It's about time you got here."

It was on the tip of her tongue to apologize, but Fiona bit it back. Instead, she made a show of looking at her calendar. "I wasn't aware we were meeting today. How can I help you?"

"Don't be impudent," her mother spat out. "We need to finish our conversation."

"No, Mother, we don't."

Linh Han gasped.

Heart pounding in time with her head, Fiona pushed through. "Mother, I am thirty-three. I am a divorced woman living on my own and supporting myself. You have no say in who I see, or what I do." Holding her hand up to stop her mother from interrupting, she snapped, "I'm not finished. I've done everything you wanted me to, up to and including marrying a man who gaslighted me because you thought it would be good for the business. I lived under your thumb, then under Eddie's thumb. I will *not* do so again. It is *my* life, and who I choose to spend it with is *my* business."

"You are wrong. What you are doing brings shame to the business. You are with a criminal!" The anger fairly vibrated off of her mother. "His people are—"

"What? Immigrants? So are you and Father. Tomas's parents are naturalized Americans. They are hard-working business owners. They go to the United Methodist Church, just like you."

Her mother's eyes narrowed. "Louisa Santiago is not like me. She is—"

"Warm, inviting, interested in the lives of her children without trying to control them. She is involved in the community and a great mother."

Linh Han waved her hand in dismissal. "If she was a good mother her daughter would not be flighty and unable to hold down a job, and her son would not have gone to jail."

"Tomas made a bad decision. One he paid for. But through that decision he learned skills that allowed him to become an excellent contractor and an excellent teacher. He is a good man, and I care deeply about him."

"He is beneath you."

Leaning forward, Fiona banged her fist against her desk. "Why, Mother? He treats me well. He's interested in what I have to say. How can he be beneath me? I don't understand."

Rising to her feet, Linh Han screamed at her daughter. "He is an uneducated Mexican! He will always be beneath you."

*T*omas pushed through the door to Keeney Works, determined to make it right with Fiona. Hopefully, a heartfelt apology would work, because more than anything, he wanted her to know that he would not take her for granted. That he would not assume what he wanted was what she wanted. Three women gathered around the receptionist's desk looked at him with big eyes. Loud voices came from the hallway, one that belonged to Fiona. Without a word, he headed toward the heated argument in Vietnamese. When it switched to English, he clearly understood the words being spoken.

In the silence that followed, he leaned against the wall, weak-kneed. He'd faced them before, bigots and racists who judged him by the color of his skin, and he knew he would do so again. But from Fiona's mother? She was Vietnamese, she'd felt the same prejudice. What would it be like to have that woman in his life? Because as Fiona's mother, she would be in his life. Thoughts chased through his head, freezing him in place.

"I think you should leave." Fiona's cold voice released him. His heart started to beat again.

"But—"

"I don't want to hear it, Mother. You've truly revealed yourself this time and I can't talk to you. Go."

There was a rustling sound then Linh Han emerged from Fiona's office. She startled when she spotted Tomas. "You!" she spat out, then stalked down the hallway.

Edging closer to Fiona's door, Tomas spotted Iris in her office across the way. The older woman jerked her head toward Fiona and mouthed the word *"Go,"* moving her hands in an encouraging gesture.

"Hey," he said, rounding the door.

An exhausted-looking Fiona sat at her desk, rubbing her temples with her fingertips. "How long have you been here?"

"Long enough." He tried to speak gently, but keeping the bitterness out of his voice was hard.

Blinking back tears, Fiona looked away. "I'm sor—"

"Don't apologize."

"But my mother…what she said about you…."

"Yeah, it hurts. I won't lie about that. But I also heard you. You care deeply about me?"

Fiona's head jerked up, her lips rounded in a silent O.

Moving away from the door, Tomas crossed the room to where she sat. He turned her chair to face him and kneeled before her. "Yeah, I heard that, too."

Sighing softly, Fiona laced her fingers together in her lap and looked up at him with an uneasy gaze.

"I don't know what to do about your mother, but *your* words made me very happy. Especially after your text this morning."

"I—"

Tomas touched a finger to her lips. "Please. Let me finish."

He waited for her nod, then stroked his finger across her cheek. "I assumed that you wanted me to come over tonight. I was wrong, and I'm sorry. Instead of *telling* you I'm coming over tonight, I should have asked if I could. I know you have a life, and it was wrong of me to think that you'd drop everything for me. You are your own person, and I can't, and shouldn't, make decisions for you." He sat back and waited, hoping he'd said enough. Hoping she'd give him another chance.

Leaning forward, Fiona touched his cheek. "Thank you. You have no idea what that means to me."

He gusted out a sigh, took her hand, and kissed the inside of her wrist. "May I see you tonight?"

Her smile was his answer, and he brushed her lips with his. Rising, he pulled her up from her chair. "What time? And would you like me to bring dinner?"

"Six o'clock. And yes, whatever you want to pick up."

"I hope your day gets better," he said, rubbing her shoulders until the tension eased out of them.

She gave him a crooked smile. "It just did."

CHAPTER 19

Tomas called in his order to *Hola!* and stopped to pick it up before going to Fiona's. The restaurant was beginning to pick up with the dinner rush, but it was a smoothly run operation, and he found his mother at her usual spot, the back booth, where she did paperwork and kept her eye on things. He kissed her on the top of the head before sliding in across from her.

"Hello, sweetheart." She beamed up at him, pushing aside her laptop. "Your order will be ready soon."

Tomas nodded absently, toying with a stack of papers on the table. Louisa moved them out of his reach. "I have those in order. Don't mess them up."

He raised his hands in surrender and poured himself a glass of water from the carafe in the middle of the table. Sitting back, he let his mother's cheerful chatter flow over him. She shared news of the restaurant staff, the car Carlos was currently working on, and the health of various relatives. Nothing that required him to participate. But she was a mother whose son had brought a woman home for dinner.

"Fiona is lovely," she said, glancing up at him.

"Yeah."

"Then why do you look unhappy?"

And there it was. Straight to the point, but laced with concern.

He looked off to the side, watching a family being seated at a table, laughing at something the young hostess had said, then back to his mother. "I overheard Fiona's mother say that I'm beneath Fiona because I'm an uneducated Mexican."

Louisa sat back, muttering in Spanish, but didn't look shocked. "And Fiona?"

"She kicked her mother out of her office. Doesn't want to see her again."

Louisa clucked in dismay. "Poor Fiona."

"Yeah." Tomas exhaled, catching his mother's sympathetic glance. "I don't understand and I don't know what to do. I mean, I know Fiona can do better than me." He held up a hand to prevent his mother from interrupting. "And not because I didn't go to college or that I'm Mexican, but because she is caring, dedicated, forgiving, classy, beautiful, and just so…."

"Perfect?"

"Yeah," he breathed out.

"She does have flaws." It was Louisa's turn to hold up her hand. "Everyone does. But she seems to be perfect for you. She pushes you, and I like that. She draws you out and doesn't put you down. You're a better person when she's around. Carlos likes her. Your sisters like her. *I* like her. I hope you can make this work."

"Thanks, Mom. But I don't know how to help her with her mother. I didn't expect her to be a racist. They're immigrants like us."

Louisa shook her head and sighed. Fingering the small cross she wore around her neck, she said, "When I was in school, maybe thirteen, there was a kid who lived down the street from me. His name was Harvey. He had terrible acne, and he was tall and gawky, and walked with these long bouncing steps. My girlfriends and I would walk behind him and pick on him. We'd call him names, mock him. We were thoughtless and cruel."

Crossing his arms, Tomas studied his mother. "That doesn't sound like you."

She smiled wryly. "Never underestimate the capacity of teenage girls to be mean. When I got older, I was ashamed and wanted to apologize, but he moved away."

"Why are you telling me this?"

"Have you ever done something you regretted and wished you could take back?"

Tomas snorted. That pretty much described his twenties.

Raising her eyebrows at his response, Louisa leaned forward, folding her hands together on top of the table. "I bet Linh Han is feeling that way right now."

He shrugged, unwilling to let it go; there were the words themselves, and the fact that she'd said them to Fiona.

"I think that water pitcher has more warmth than Linh Han. But that doesn't mean she doesn't care about her daughter," Louisa said.

The restaurant was filling up and getting louder. Tomas leaned in to hear his mother more clearly.

"She is a proud, determined woman whose daughter is not following the path she wants her to."

"She married Fiona off to Eddie for the business."

Louisa's normally smiling mouth set in a firm line. "Yeah, that's not right. But still—"

"No buts, Mom. Her pride comes before her family. And this time she's gone too far. She's hurt Fiona too many times, and I don't know if Fiona will forgive her."

An unhappy silence descended. A waitress brought over Tomas's order, and he shifted to get out of the booth. Louisa put a hand on his arm to stop him.

"I believe that Linh Han loves her daughter and regrets what she said. If she apologizes, will you forgive her?"

He wanted to confront the old witch. The words themselves were true, but the way she'd used them to put him down in Fiona's eyes, the way she made her daughter feel small, could he forgive her for that? Frowning, he bent down to wrap an arm around his mother. "I don't know, Mom. Maybe." She hugged him back, and he picked up the food and headed to the exit.

Securing the food in his truck, he closed the door and nearly tripped. "What the—" Winding around his feet was a small black cat with a white splotch on its nose. It sat on its haunches, looked at the truck, and looked at Tomas.

"You better get out of the way," he said, and went around to the driver's side. The cat followed him. "Scram!" He made a shooing motion, but the cat just stared.

"I think he likes you." Stevie stood by the restaurant's back door having a smoke.

"Whose cat is it?" Tomas asked.

"It's a stray," Stevie replied. "Showed up a few days ago, and your mom started feeding it."

"Is she going to take it to a shelter?"

Stevie shook her head. "It's still a kitten and won't let anyone near it."

The cat strolled toward Tomas and wove between his legs, looking up at him.

Stevie snorted. "Nobody but you, apparently."

"A stray, huh?" He eyed the cat.

"Yeah. We get them sometimes. They don't stick around for long, though. They get hit by a car or eaten by a coyote." She flicked a hand to indicate the greenbelt behind the restaurant. "Unless someone were to give it a home."

Tomas shot her a narrow-eyed look, then stared at the cat. It blinked slowly and purred. He sighed. "Got a box?"

· · ·

$\mathcal{H}$ands full, he used his foot to tap at the door of Fiona's apartment.

A frown creased Fiona's forehead when she opened it. "How much food did you bring?" she asked, eyeing the box. She'd changed out of what Tomas considered her uniform. He knew from having seen the inside of her closet that she had half a dozen skirts and jackets in muted shades and a dozen coordinating blouses. Now, she wore navy leggings and a long, loose, silky, wine-colored top. She was barefoot, and her hair was in a messy bun on the top of her head.

He put the box on the table and the bag of food on the counter before taking her in his arms. "Do you have allergies?"

"Not to any foods."

"Animals?"

"No."

"Good," he said. Kissing her lightly, he let her go and opened the box.

The cat poked its head out and looked at Tomas indignantly before turning to Fiona. It meowed and leaped out of the box.

"Ohh," Fiona crooned. "Who is this?" She extended a hand, and the cat sniffed it, butting its head against her fingers.

"I don't know. It's a stray that's been hanging around the restaurant and needs a home."

Sitting on the table, the cat arched its neck as if inviting Fiona to scratch its chin. She did, and the cat closed its eyes and purred. Fiona was practically purring herself, cooing, her face lit up with a smile of pure delight. The cat turned its head and licked her hand.

Fiona giggled. "It feels like sandpaper."

For a stray, the cat looked pretty healthy, with bright eyes and a gleaming coat. It lavished affection on Fiona, alternately licking and rubbing its head against her hand.

"Are you keeping it at your place or taking it to your parents' house?"

"I thought, maybe you'd like it."

"Really?" He hadn't thought it possible for her smile to get bigger.

She scooped up the cat and sank to the floor, holding it against her chest. The cat dug its claws into her shirt as it stretched up to nuzzle her jaw. Fiona nuzzled it right back before grinning at Tomas. Tension leaked out of him as he sat beside them. It looked like he'd done something right today.

A while later, he cleared away the remains of the meal while Fiona sat at the table talking quietly to the cat and looking better than she had earlier in the day. He was rinsing plates in the sink when a tap came at the door. He couldn't see who it was and looked over to Fiona, who made a come in gesture. Wiping his hands on a towel, he stepped over to the peninsula and leaned against the countertop. Two men entered, and it took him a moment to recognize Fiona's brother Joseph, but he didn't know the other man, though he looked familiar.

"Hi," Joseph said, hand extended. "Tomas, right?"

Tomas gripped his hand. "Yeah. Nice to meet you." He turned to the other man, who was Vietnamese as well. Not as tall as Joseph, he was casually dressed in jeans and a t-shirt, a contrast to Joseph's slacks and button-down shirt.

"Andy Tran. I'm the pastor at your mother's church." He shook hands with Tomas and turned to Fiona. "I hope we're not interrupting."

Rising from the table, Fiona shook her head. "Not at all."

Seeing her tight expression, Tomas moved around the counter to stand behind her, ready to take her back with whatever happened.

"You got a cat," Joseph said.

"I did," Fiona replied, holding it against her shoulder. "What's up? I wasn't expecting you."

Joseph and Andy exchanged glances. Joseph crossed his arms and looked tense. Andy shoved his hands in his pockets and turned his gaze to Tomas and then to Fiona. "I got a call from Tomas's mother." He smiled in a way that Tomas could only describe as pastorally. "It sounds like you've had quite the day."

He couldn't see her face, but Tomas could feel Fiona's tension. He placed both hands on her shoulders and squeezed gently while meeting Joseph's gaze. The man appeared to relax slightly, lifting his chin as if accepting Tomas and Fiona. Tomas returned the gesture. "You guys want to sit down?" he asked.

"Yes. Please." Fiona gestured toward the living room. "Where are my manners. Please, sit."

Joseph and Andy seated themselves on the couch. Fiona perched on the chair while Tomas sat on the arm of the chair. He could have brought in one from the dining room, but he didn't want to leave her side.

"Tomas's mother called you?" Fiona spoke to Andy but twisted to look up at Tomas. "Did you know?"

Shaking his head, he said, "No. I told her what happened today, though."

"Why would you do that?"

He studied her face, seeing the hurt in her eyes. "I needed an outlet. It was either talk to *my* mother or drive over to your parents' house and yell at *your* mother."

Their eyes locked. He could see the emotions move across her face. The tightness around her eyes and mouth relaxed, and she murmured, "Good call." The cat grew restless, and Fiona put it down. It made a beeline for a dish of water and lapped daintily at it.

Andy leaned forward, lacing his fingers together and propping his elbows on his knees. "Your mother, Tomas, was very concerned about Mrs. Han and the impact of her outburst on Fiona. She hoped that I might be able to intercede. Joseph was with me when I got the call."

"I am so sorry." Joseph reached over to take Fiona's hands, his angry gaze shifting between her and Tomas.

Fiona shrugged. "You didn't do anything."

"That's the point. I didn't do anything. Mother has been controlling you for years, and Father and I have sat back, allowing it to happen. You seemed fine with it, so we didn't interfere. And now, now that you're finding some happiness in opposition to what she wants, she's lost it." Joseph spoke bitterly. "Andy had the phone on speaker, and when I heard what she said about Tomas, *I* lost it. I called Mother and blew up."

Fiona's gasp was the only sound in the room as brother and sister stared at each other.

Clearing his throat, Andy spoke to Tomas, "Any chance you've got some beer? I wanted to pick some up, but Joseph wouldn't let me."

"Sure."

Tomas stroked a hand through Fiona's hair and stood. Andy rose from the couch and followed him into the kitchen. Opening the fridge, Tomas pulled out three beers and a bottle of wine. "Glass?" he asked. When Andy shook his head, he poured a glass of wine for Fiona and dug the bottle opener out of the drawer to uncap the beers. He handed one to Andy and leaned back against the counter.

Andy did the same and held his beer aloft. "Cheers."

Tomas returned the salute.

"Are you mad at your mom?"

Tomas took a drink, giving himself time before answering. Being talked about didn't make him happy, but his mom set in motion something he couldn't do; improve Fiona's relationship with her brother. "No. My mom is big on forgiveness. I made her life hell and scared the shit out of her when I went to jail." He looked at the pastor to gauge his reaction. Andy nodded, but remained silent. "She wants me to be happy and knows that I won't be happy unless Fiona is happy. So, she called you."

Placing his beer on the counter, Andy crossed his arms. "I was in my office and wasn't expecting Joseph, which is why the phone was on speaker. I'm not sure if it's good or bad that he heard the conversation."

Tomas tilted his head toward the living room where Fiona and Joseph were speaking in low voices. "Good for them. Maybe not good for their mother."

"Are you going to reach out to her?"

Hell no! was on his lips. Instead, he replied, "That depends. If they want me to, I will. But maybe not for a while. It's too fresh, and I'll probably blow up." If he did show up on her doorstep, Fiona's mother would, no doubt, call the cops on him.

"Was your family like theirs?" he asked Andy.

Even when he and his stepfather weren't speaking to each other, Tomas knew that he was loved and that he could depend upon his parents. With a mother like Linh Han, growing up must have been tough on Fiona.

Andy shook his head and smiled. "Controlling? No. They weren't happy that I went into social work instead of engineering like they did because there's not a lot of money in it, even less so in ministry, but they're happy that I'm happy. It helps that they married for love." Seeing Tomas's raised eyebrow, he continued. "The Vietnamese immigrant population was, and still is, very close-knit. David and Linh Han grew up together, knowing that they would marry. Which was not uncommon."

"But that's not the same as choosing who you will spend your life with."

"No. However, Linh Han's parents made that choice for her. And she expected and did the same thing for Fiona."

"And look how well that turned out," Tomas muttered. His blood boiled whenever he thought about Eddie McLeod. The self-centered prick destroyed everyone he came into contact with. The fact Fiona had survived Eddie's gaslighting was a testament to her inner strength.

Picking up his beer, Andy pointed it at Tomas. "Right. And now she thinks she has to find another husband for Fiona."

"One that isn't an uneducated Mexican with a prison record." Bitterness clogged Tomas's throat. He understood the message in his mother's story about the boy she bullied, but that didn't make the hurt go away. Didn't make him feel less angry toward Linh Han.

"There is no excuse for the words she said. Whether you heard them or not." Andy moved closer to Tomas and grasped his shoulder. "You don't need me to tell you that. I'm hoping Linh Han realizes she's fucked up her relationship with her kids and works to heal it."

Tomas snorted. "Are pastors allowed to swear?"

"Hell, yes. Just not in front of the congregation."

The two men laughed.

"What's so funny?" Fiona rounded the corner with Joseph right behind her. She looked like she'd been through the wringer. Both her eyes and her nose were red, but she was smiling. Joseph still looked tense, but when his gaze met Andy's, he dipped his chin in some unspoken acknowledgment.

"This guy swears like a trucker. He'd fit right in on a construction site." Tomas handed the wineglass to Fiona and the other beer to Joseph.

"Not a good idea. I'd get distracted if there were hot guys

in tool belts." Andy winked at Tomas before moving over to Joseph. Nudging his shoulder, he said, "How'd it go?"

"We cleared the air a bit. But we're still angry with Mother." Joseph looked up at Tomas. "If you treat my sister well, that's all I care about. Mother should, too."

Tomas spoke to Joseph, but his eyes were on Fiona. "I will. That's a promise."

CHAPTER 20

"So, that's Tomas?" Joseph had asked after she absolved him of any guilt about their mother. As a son, the pressure he received growing up had eased once he reached adulthood and moved away from home.

"That's him," Fiona replied, eying Tomas where he stood in the kitchen with Andy. Tomas turned toward her, eyebrows raised in question. She shook her head and smiled.

"He looks at me like he doesn't quite trust me not to hurt you."

She gave Joseph the side-eye. "That's because he had quite the introduction to our family."

"Again, I'm sorry. I wish I'd done better."

His sincerity was so apparent that tears welled in her eyes. "I know," she replied.

After Joseph and Andy left, Tomas had gone to a pet store and returned with a mountain of paraphernalia. While the cat zoomed around the apartment until it wore itself out and collapsed on the couch, they batted around names for it. Nothing seemed right, so they tabled the discussion and went to bed. Tomas held her all night long and woke her with soft kisses that led to morning sex, which, she decided, was her favorite way to start the day.

Now, sitting down at her desk, Fiona flipped open her planner to see what the day was supposed to look like. No meetings, thank God, although there was a note to reach out to Hilary. They'd interviewed the first student interested in an architectural scholarship but were having problems setting up an interview with the second applicant.

As screwed up as her family life had been, Fiona knew that her education opened the doors to where she was today. Without her parents pushing her to apply for every scholarship she was eligible for, she would be neck deep in student loans. If she could set up this scholarship program, many other people would be able to realize their dreams without going broke.

She opened her laptop to go through her emails when she heard a tentative knock. David Han stood at the door looking very unhappy.

"May I come in?"

Nodding, Fiona rose from her chair and came around to stand in front of her desk. He rarely visited her office, and after yesterday's drama, she braced herself, not knowing what to expect.

Her father stepped forward, hands clasped in front of him.

She waited for him to speak, watching as he gazed around the room. He moved closer to the long wall displaying photos of Keeney Works' success stories. Pictures of smiling people at work, doing jobs they'd found through the program. The photo she'd hung most recently was similar to one that hung in the conference room of KBS. It was of students standing around Tomas while he delivered instruction at a building site for a tiny house.

"Is that him? Tomas?" Her father pointed at the picture. He pronounced the name as Tom-us.

Fiona corrected him, "Yes, that's Toe-mass." She studied the photo, trying to look at it through her father's eyes. Tomas had been caught unaware, frowning in concentration. Standing with his legs spread and arms crossed, he looked fierce and intimidating.

David Han leaned in, peering closely at the image. "The students are paying attention. Some are taking notes."

She blushed. "I've never really looked at the students."

Her father smiled at her confession. "They look relaxed and engaged. A mark of a good teacher." He stepped back and faced her fully. "I would like to meet him."

This was not what she was expecting. Although he was more tolerant than her mother, they'd always been a united front.

"I…Mother…." The smile left his face as she fumbled to express herself.

"Your mother is wrong. More importantly, *I* was wrong. I've stood back for too long, letting your mother make all the decisions, and not seeing the damage we did to you. You are a flower bud that wasn't allowed to bloom. I should have put my foot down before you married Eddie. But I thought you and he would grow together as your mother and I have. We have had a good life, and I wanted that for you. However, parents, although they mean well, don't always make the best decisions. For that, I am sorry."

His lips trembled as he gazed intently at Fiona. Blinking back tears, she opened her mouth to reply, but he held up a hand to stop her.

"Let me finish. Your mother doesn't sleep well, so for years, we've had separate bedrooms. Last night, I heard her crying. I went to her, and she told me what she said. Those ugly words are unforgivable. She knows that and regretted them immediately."

Fiona couldn't hold back. "She doesn't regret *saying* them. She regrets that Tomas and Iris heard her."

"You might be right. Your mother is incredibly proud and hates when there are witnesses to a mistake."

Her head was reeling. She moved over to a chair and sank into it, collecting her thoughts. "So, if they hadn't heard her, she could pretend it didn't happen? It would have been swept under the rug?" That's the way it had always been in her family. Nothing was ever addressed, just ignored.

"Maybe," he admitted. "We'll never know."

David took the seat beside her, clasping his hands in front of him. "I'm not apologizing for her. And it's up to you and Tomas to decide if you can forgive her. I'm hoping she reaches out to you. I take it she hasn't done so already?"

Fiona shook her head. "I'm not surprised. She's never apologized before."

"She was raised to believe admitting to mistakes and apologizing is a sign of weakness."

Fiona digested that for a moment. "Do you believe that as well?"

"No. To understand when you have made a mistake, and apologize for hurting someone, that is a sign of strength."

This, too, was something to think about. And her thoughts led her back to Tomas and his heartfelt apologies. A warmth spread in her chest, and tension leaked out of her body.

Her father rose from his chair. "I've taken enough of your time."

"Thank you for coming, Father."

He wasn't a demonstrative man, merely nodding. "I hope your mother calls soon."

"I do too," she murmured.

He wandered back to the photo of Tomas and pointed at it. "I would like to meet your young man and see the work they are doing."

Pleased at his words, she smiled. "I'll make the arrangements."

rossing his arms, Tomas sat back and grunted in satisfaction. A beer bottle landed beside him with a thunk, jarring him out of his reverie. "Hey," he said, turning around to see Carlos drinking from his own beer. "What's up?"

"I'm drowning my sorrows," Carlos answered, staring moodily at the oil-stained concrete floor.

"Okay." Tomas sipped his beer and watched his stepfather.

The three-car garage smelled like metal and motor oil. His mother's car was parked in one bay, Carlos's SUV was in the second, and the third bay was Carlos's workshop. It was currently empty as his most recent project had just been sold. One wall was lined with cupboards filled with auto supplies and tools, and a workbench was built under the wide window of the back wall. Tomas sat on a stool with graph paper in front of him. He moved aside to allow Carlos to see what he was working on, knowing Carlos would get to whatever was bugging him in his own time.

"New tattoo?" Carlos asked, pointing at the design.

"No, although that would look awesome." Tomas had drawn his name in thick lines, overlaid with Fiona's name in a delicate swirl. "I'm trying to decide if it should be a necklace or a bracelet."

"Nice." Carlos propped a hip against the bench and changed the subject. "Your mom told me you gave Fiona an apology cat."

"I guess so. I hadn't thought of it that way."

"Still," Carlos said, "it was nice. Considering what her mother did."

Tomas shook his head. Of course, Carlos would know. His mother once said that he and his sisters should expect her to share whatever they told her with Carlos because keeping secrets was bad for a marriage.

"That woman is a piece of work."

"You've met her?" Tomas asked.

"Sort of." Carlos shrugged. "Your mother pointed her out to me at church once. She was giving the pastor the notes she'd taken on his sermon. Rumor has it she's the reason that pastor left Keeney."

Linh Han *was* a piece of work. Tomas stared at the intertwined names on the paper, more determined than ever to protect Fiona as much as she would let him.

Carlos tilted his beer at Tomas, saying, "You aren't beneath Fiona. You know that, right?"

"Yeah," Tomas replied. But it was going to take a while to sink in.

"You are a good man, and worthy of her. Believe it."

Carlos wandered over to close a cupboard door that was ajar. Something blocked it, so he pushed harder. It still wouldn't close. Carlos wrenched the door open, shoved the offending item onto a shelf, and closed the door with a resounding thud.

"You sure showed it," Tomas observed.

"Yeah." Carlos's growl turned into a humorless chuckle. "I got word that someone outbid me for Woodbine Automotive."

"That sucks." And he meant it. Ever since he and Louisa decided they could afford to buy the shop, Carlos had worn a permanent smile. The restaurant was Louisa's passion, and the auto parts store would be his.

"Yeah." Carlos sighed and finished his beer. "A California company bought it and plans to open up a fast-food restaurant. So not only do I lose out, but *Hola!* will have more competition."

"Well, shit. How's Mom doing?"

"She's taking out her frustrations on the appliances and

muttering to herself. She's more pissed on my behalf than worried about the restaurant. She's too good of a business-woman to let this stop her."

"Still, that really sucks for you." Tomas rose from his stool to grasp Carlos's shoulder, shaking it lightly. "I wish I could do more to help, but can I get you another beer?"

"Yeah."

$\mathcal{A}$ car pulled into the parking area while he was in the middle of instructing a student on the proper way to hold a hammer. "Now pull it all the way back," Tomas said.

The student looked at him warily. "But I'm gonna miss the nail."

Tomas nodded. "It's gonna happen, but you'll soon get the hang of it."

"Okay," the girl said, then took a big swing. She hit the nail squarely on the head and squealed in delight. "I did it!"

"You sure did. Keep it up." He watched her a little longer, then turned to see who had arrived.

Fiona stood a few yards away with an older man beside her. "Hi," she said with a bright smile. The man nodded, looking wary.

"Oh, hey. I wasn't expecting you. Is everything okay?"

"Yes. This is my dad, and he wanted to see what you're building. I hope it's okay, I probably should have asked first."

"Not at all." Tomas came closer and bent to kiss her cheek. "You are always welcome." He turned to her father, unsure what the protocol was. If the man refused to shake his hand, things would go downhill fast. He settled for introducing himself. "Hello, Mr. Han, I'm Tomas Alvarado."

Not as tall as his son, David Han had rounded shoulders, graying hair, and a barely noticeable paunch under his short-sleeved button-down shirt. His khaki pants were slightly wrinkled, and his shoes were well-worn. He seemed the opposite of his pompous, rigid wife. He held out his hand. "Please, call me David."

They shook hands, then David stood back and surveyed the work site.

Four students were erecting the frames that would eventually form the walls of a house. It was their third day working together, and they were beginning to gel as a team. The girl Tomas had been instructing scooted across the floor, driving nails to secure the frame into the flooring.

"Wouldn't it go faster with a pneumatic hammer?" David asked.

"Yes," Tomas replied. "But they will have to use a hammer on some jobs, so they might as well get good at it now."

Fiona stood ramrod straight, her smile looking a little strained as her gaze flicked back and forth between her father and him.

What did she want? He wasn't good at small talk, and his anger toward her mother extended in part to the father who'd allowed his wife to run roughshod over Fiona for years. However, Fiona had brought her father to meet Tomas and see him at work, which had to mean something.

Fortunately, the cat, wearing a jaunty bow made from bright yellow construction tape, jumped down from the bed of his truck and strolled over to greet the visitor.

"How's Little One like being on the job site?" Fiona asked, bending to pick up the animal. They'd determined she was a girl and made plans for her to soon be spayed.

"Good. She caught a mouse earlier and was very proud of herself," Tomas replied. She'd left the half-eaten carcass near the entrance to the port-a-potty, which hadn't endeared her to the student who stepped on it, though.

"I guess she didn't like being alone yesterday. So when we were leaving for work this morning, she escaped and got into Tomas's truck," Fiona explained, stroking the cat's ears. "I can't take her to the office because two people have allergies, so Tomas brought her here."

David nodded. If he'd caught on that Tomas spent the night at Fiona's place, he didn't react. "And you've named it Little One?" he asked.

Tomas snorted. "Yeah, we couldn't settle on a name. I thought Hell Cat or Demon was appropriate, and Fiona wanted to call her Precious Kitty. So for now, it's Little One."

Little One scrambled out of Fiona's arms, leaped to the ground, wove a figure eight around David, then sat on her haunches and stared up at him.

"I think she wants you to pick her up," Fiona said with a laugh.

David frowned. "I'm not much of a cat person. I'm better with plants."

Little One cocked her head as if listening, then stalked off with a flick of her tail.

"Did I offend her?" David asked.

"Apparently so." Fiona patted his arm. "It's okay, Dad. Bring her treats when you come to the house, and she'll forgive you."

She walked over to Tomas and stood on tiptoes to kiss him on the mouth before saying, "We'll get out of your way." She said, "Thank you," in a quieter voice, and stepped back.

"Any time," Tomas replied, meaning it. He added, "David, if you ever feel like swinging a hammer or playing with power tools, you're welcome to stop by."

"Really?" David smiled.

"Really," Tomas answered truthfully, his gaze fixed on Fiona.

Fiona walked into the cafe where she'd arranged to meet Tomas. She'd suggested *Hola!*, but Tomas had demurred, so they were meeting at one of the restaurants that hired and trained workers from Keeney Works. She arrived early to speak with the owner and was pleased with the glowing report she received. At present, four of the staff had come through the program, and the restaurant owner was considering training one for a management position.

Driving back from the job site yesterday, her father had commented favorably on Keeney Builds and Tomas's patience with the students. She assumed her mother had told him about Tomas's prison record, but her father didn't bring it up, or comment on Tomas spending the nights at her place. Today, her father messaged about accepting the invitation and setting a date to work on the job site. So when Tomas entered, Fiona was in a good mood.

He spotted her wave and strode over with a frown on his face. It didn't look like his afternoon had been nearly as good as hers.

He leaned down to kiss her cheek, but she turned her head and caught his lips with her own, turning the chaste peck into something deeper. His eyes flashed as he pulled back with a low growl.

The blush on her cheeks warred with the grin on her lips. She wanted this man and wasn't afraid to let anyone know.

He sat across from her and spoke in a low voice, "We should have met at your place." He grinned evilly as comprehension dawned, and Fiona's blush deepened.

The server arrived at that moment, and they placed their orders. Tomas drank from his water and placed it back on the table. His frown returned.

Before meeting up with him, she'd exchanged emails with

Hilary, who said Tomas had the details on the second scholarship student. So Fiona texted and asked him for the contact information. He'd come back with the request to meet for lunch, which pleased her greatly. It was no burden at all to meet with all that hotness in the middle of the day. Sitting across from him and sensing his uneasiness, her stomach tightened. If something was wrong, she wanted to know now. Before she allowed herself to dream bigger.

She steeled herself for the blow. "What is it?"

He placed his elbows on the table and interlaced his fingers. "I need to come clean."

Her heart leaped into her throat, and it must have been visible on her face because he reached out to take her hand.

"Not about us, babe. We're all good. It's about the second student who wants to be an architect." He glanced down at the table and back up at her. "It's me."

Fiona blinked. "What?"

He released her hand and sat back, not meeting her gaze while he spoke. "A while ago, Vincent walked in when I was looking up details for becoming an architect. He assumed it was for the students, and I didn't correct him."

"You want to be an architect?" She drew his gaze back to hers, and he nodded.

"Yeah. At least, I think so. I like building things, and I want to learn how to design, too."

She studied his face. It was earnest and animated. "Have you always wanted to do this?"

He shrugged. "Kind of. When I was younger, I didn't want to put the effort into learning more. It was…." He pointed at his head and rolled his eyes. "But I made it through the contractor's program, and with the work I do at KBS and Keeney Builds, I think I can do it. I just have to take my time and focus."

The server arrived with their orders, and they took a few minutes to eat. Her mind reeling with questions, Fiona forced herself to let Tomas take the lead. This was *his* dream.

"Then Hilary got you involved." He looked up and grinned. "You two were so excited. You see possibilities everywhere, and I didn't want to bring you down."

"How would that bring us down?"

"I'm too old. You can find scholarships for the young ones. They're so eager and fresh-faced. While I'm…."

The frown was back as Tomas shook his head and took a bite of his sandwich.

"You're older? Have a record? *You* are the perfect candidate. You have a great story. Someone who screwed up, and is starting over. When schools hear about you—"

Dark eyes flashing, Tomas leaned in and spoke intently. "That's just it. I *don't want* my story out there. It was bad enough to have to talk about it to get support for Keeney Builds."

Chastened, Fiona turned her attention to her meal.

"Babe," he murmured.

She focused on her sandwich, but when Tomas spoke again, his voice soft and gentle, she looked up to see tenderness and apology in his eyes.

"That came out too harsh. I didn't tell you I was interested in being an architect because I realized what a time and financial commitment going to school would be. And yes, I know a scholarship would offset expenses, but still, I have a learning disorder, it will take a long freaking time to do the program."

"People go back to school as adults, even people with learning disorders. They work full-time and go to college if that's what they really want." Mindful of the people around them, Fiona kept her voice down, but she was angry, disbelieving that Tomas was too lazy to study. It sounded like he was using his difficulties with reading as an excuse, too.

"Yeah. I get it. And I'm not afraid of hard work. But you

and Iris and a cranky old man opened my eyes to something else."

"What?"

"A while ago I had to work on this old guy's house." Tomas chuckled. "He annoyed the shit out of me. But I realized he didn't want someone to work on his house. He wanted someone to work *with him* on his house. Go at his pace and help him. It was a pain in the ass at first, but taking the time, helping him use the tools, that was…satisfying. I think I could teach classes at the senior center, like Iris said. Old people can't be any worse than some of the kids I've dealt with, and the classes would have to be small. I don't know about how-to videos, but maybe if they were in Spanish, Carlos suggested that. But working *with* people, that seems more satisfying than drawing stuff for others to build."

"You want to help people." Fiona concentrated fully on Tomas, trying to see his vision. He barely spoke in more than one-word sentences when she first met him, and scowled more than he smiled. Now, he was talking about teaching. "You've really given this some thought, haven't you?"

He shrugged. "Yeah. If it doesn't work out with the senior center, I could maybe reach out through Mom's church. I'm sure there are families who need work done on their homes but can't afford to hire someone. Or families who can only afford to buy older homes that need a lot of work, and they don't have the skills to do it themselves or the money to hire someone who does. I can help them. Maybe Keeney Builds and KBS could get involved."

Listening, Fiona could already see the possibilities. "HFH!" she blurted out, eyes fairly gleaming. At his questioning look, she explained, "Han Family Holdings is my family's company. We own commercial properties, like the strip mall next to your parents' restaurant. The business could help families buy homes that need work. The buyers use sweat equity to reduce their mortgage. Similar to what Habitat for Humanity does.”

Tomas looked doubtful. “Your mother would do that?”

Fiona looked determined. “HFH is not just my mother. Everyone in the family has shares. And yes, I think my mother would do it. Especially now when she needs to find a way to make amends. My dad is a fan of what you do, building tiny homes for the community, and wants to do more himself. And if we get Joseph and Andy, especially if we get *Pastor* Andy and the church behind it, Mother will be happy to support it. The business looks good, the community benefits, and she saves face. She’s also been looking for a legacy, and this would fit the bill nicely.”

Tomas appeared to mull the idea over. “I didn’t know HFH bought residential properties.”

“They don’t. At least not yet. But let me talk to Joseph. I’m pretty sure we can convince him.”

“Are you sure?”

“Absolutely.” With that, Fiona pushed her plate away and sighed. “I feel so much better. When you walked in here, I thought you were going to break up with me.”

His eyebrows winged up. “Why would you think that?”

She didn’t look at him, fiddling with her bracelet instead. “I don’t know. Just….” It was hard to put her level of insecurity into words. Judging by the looks of others in the restaurant, she wasn’t the only person who found him attractive. Tomas was, by far, the most handsome man she’d ever known, and it was difficult to believe that he wanted her for herself, and wasn’t using her to gain access to her family’s money.

“I haven’t looked at another woman since the first time I saw you.” He unclenched her hand, stroking a finger over her palm to rest on the pulse beating wildly in her wrist. “It was at that event, and you told me to bring you a drink.”

Her face flamed, and she groaned. "I was hoping you'd forget that."

"That's what I get for wearing all black. You weren't the only one who thought I was a waiter that night." He grinned. "You had so much poise and grace, despite having dealt with Eddie's shit. You made quite the impression on me."

She stared at him, hypnotized, enjoying his touch as much as his words. "I did?"

"You did. So unless you tell me otherwise, I'm not going anywhere." Ignoring the people around them, he kissed her long and deep, drawing out her soul with him when he pulled back. "You go. I'll take care of the bill and see you tonight."

"Okay," she replied and floated out of the restaurant.

She was still on a high from Tomas's declaration when her brother called later that afternoon.

"We've got a problem."

Fiona put the phone on speaker and propped it beside her laptop. "Well hello to you, too. I'm fine, Joseph, thanks for asking." She chuckled as she signed off on an email.

"I'm serious."

His tone grabbing her full attention, Fiona closed her laptop. "What's up?"

"Mother blocked Carlos Santiago from buying Woodbine Automotive."

"You're serious?"

"As a heart attack."

She stared blindly at the photo of Tomas on her desk. She'd caught him unaware, asleep on the couch, with Little One curled up on his chest. "Why would she do that?"

"Because she can. Because she saw an opportunity to benefit herself."

"You'd think she'd be trying to make amends, not worsen the situation." Her mother still hadn't called, and Fiona wondered if she ever would.

"I don't know that the two are tied together," Joseph said. "Buying commercial real estate doesn't move that quickly."

Fiona shifted to massage the cords tightening at the back of her neck. "How did you find out?" she asked.

"The company who won the bid is a fast-food chain based out of California. They emailed me to thank HFH for letting them know the property was available. And sent a check for ten grand."

She groaned. Her mother was messing with the community as well. Keeney's family-owned restaurants didn't need competition from the big chains. Then the thought hit her. "How am I going to tell Tomas?"

"Don't," Joseph said.

"What? No."

"I'm pretty sure I can fix this, so just—"

"You don't understand. I can't—"

"Listen!" He exhaled forcefully. "I can fix this, and then you can tell him."

Despite the fact he couldn't see her, Fiona shook her head. "And if you can't? No." Keeping secrets wasn't healthy for a relationship. Not telling Tomas wasn't an option.

"Just—just give me a week. Then you can tell him. Regardless of what happens."

She stared at the photograph, mulling it over. "Are you sure you can fix this?"

"Positive."

"Fine." She disconnected, hoping and praying he was correct.

CHAPTER 22

Joseph met Tomas and Fiona in the church parking lot. The day had been a scorcher, and it was still warm as they approached a side entrance. Tomas had never been in this part of the church and assumed this was where the offices were located. A group of people were exiting, and Joseph moved to hold the door open for them. Fiona and Tomas stepped aside, allowing the group to pass, then followed Joseph inside.

"I smell heaven!" Andy's loud voice preceded him as he popped out of a conference room and beckoned them to enter.

Tomas smiled in agreement. The red chile sauce in *Hola!'s* chicken enchiladas *was* heavenly. The combination of onion, garlic, and jalapenos made his mouth water. Obviously, it was a good choice. The aluminum pan he carried was enough to feed a small army. When his mother found out he was bringing dinner to the pastor, she pulled out all the stops, elbowing Stevie out of the way and preparing the food herself. Fiona carried a bag with freshly made tortilla chips and guacamole, as well as paper plates and cutlery.

"Put everything on the table, I'll be right back." Andy

disappeared, and Tomas and Fiona busied themselves setting out the food while Joseph unpacked his laptop. Andy had rearranged his evening, provided they fed him. He reappeared carrying a tray with a pitcher of ice water and four glasses. "Sit, please," he said.

They each found seats, Tomas and Fiona on one side of the long table, Andy and Joseph opposite them. Loading up his plate, Tomas waited for the others to do so. Andy said a quick blessing, and they dug in.

"Thank you for rescuing me," Andy said around bites of his enchilada. "That was the trustees group. They'd have talked forever. And thanks for insisting on feeding me." He twisted around and kissed Joseph's cheek.

Joseph smiled in response, then turned to Tomas. "He forgets to eat, then gets seriously cranky."

Tomas watched the exchange between the two men. They were relaxed and openly affectionate with one another. He looked at Fiona to see her beaming at her brother. As if feeling his eyes on her, she turned toward Tomas, a warm look in her eyes and a soft smile on her lips. With that look, the tension went out of his shoulders, and he finished his meal in silence, listening to the men's good-natured bickering.

Groaning, Andy sat back with a hand on his belly. "That was so good."

Motioning at the leftovers, Tomas said, "My mother said you'd take the extra food."

Andy nodded. "Yeah, we have a couple of families who will love it. I'll drop off the leftovers on my way home."

Fiona looked at her watch. "Shall we get started? Joseph, will you take notes?"

Her brother pulled his laptop toward him, and all three looked expectantly at Tomas.

He'd had doubts about his ability to contribute to a group of highly educated business and community leaders, and considered begging off. Fiona could easily take the lead and would be more eloquent about it. Then he thought about why he'd told her about his idea in the first place. Telling someone else meant he needed to follow through. Rubbing his hands on his thighs, he took a deep breath and began.

"There are people here in Keeney in need of housing. Already we have the tiny house community going up, but that doesn't help families. The cost of homes is crazy, making it hard for the average person to afford to buy one. And what they *can* afford is often crap; in need of more work than they can do themselves, or afford to hire someone to do." He looked over to Fiona.

"HFH is in the position to purchase homes and work with qualifying families who would work on the homes themselves, with reduced mortgage rates," she said.

Joseph's fingers stilled on the keyboard. "Mother will never go for that."

"Hear me out." Fiona raised a hand and spoke directly to her brother. "Mother is looking for a legacy, and you are looking for something different."

"What do you mean?" Joseph jerked back.

"You aren't happy," Fiona spoke softly but earnestly. "I can see you're restless. I think you want to do more than property management. You know about real estate. You are the perfect person to oversee this project. Find and purchase houses, learn from organizations that help people get into housing, then work with banks to offer loans that won't overwhelm working families."

Tomas could see Joseph's interest growing as he listened to Fiona, and he looked at Andy to judge his reaction. The pastor met his gaze and gave him a discreet thumbs-up. But Joseph wasn't quite ready to commit.

"And Mother? She's not a risk-taker. She only gives back to the community when it benefits her as well. Like the cosmetology school." Joseph glanced between Tomas and

Andy and explained, "Everyone thinks that HFH started the school to train immigrants and students who aren't college-bound. What they don't know is that graduating students intern in HFH salons as part of their training. Mother gets low-cost employees."

"Your mother's motives may not be totally altruistic, but that doesn't mean the community hasn't benefited from the school. I know she reduces tuition in favor of the internships, which makes it easier for students to afford the training. Not every school is willing to do that."

Joseph frowned at Andy's interruption, but Fiona went on before he could speak.

"Mother wants a legacy. And what better legacy than helping families find homes. And, I think right now, after what she said about Tomas, she's feeling repentant, and will be willing to buy in. And yes, I know I am capitalizing on her guilt, but I don't have a problem with it." Fiona sat back, glaring around the table as if expecting to be challenged.

"How can I help, and what role do you want the church to play?" Andy asked. At Joseph's narrow-eyed look, he went on, "Fiona's right. I haven't known you long, but even I can see you want more than to be a landlord. And I can get the church firmly behind you. Affordable housing is social justice, and that's something this congregation strongly believes in."

Fiona grabbed Tomas's hand under the table and gave it a squeeze. His heart lightened. This could work. Fiona's determination and Andy's reasoned enthusiasm were swaying Joseph. Rather than scowling, Joseph looked thoughtful.

"Andy, will you be able to identify families? If not from your congregation, then from other churches?" Fiona glanced at him before digging into her tote bag and pulling out a file folder. "I made a list of action items." She distributed papers, keeping one for herself. All three looked at the list. Andy was the first to laugh, then Tomas, and finally Joseph.

"Can I check off the first item?" Fiona asked with an innocent look.

Joseph rolled his eyes. "Yeah, you sweet-talked me into coming on board."

With an exaggerated stroke of her pen, Fiona ticked off the first box.

Andy nudged Joseph's shoulder and spoke while studying the list. "Yes, I can identify the families. The city has a housing taskforce, and I'll reach out to them. They'll be very excited. We might have a problem, though." He put the paper down and looked directly at Tomas. "Your mother is very well-liked and has a lot of influence in the church. Your mother—" Andy switched his gaze to Fiona and then Joseph "—has a lot of influence. People respect her, but don't particularly like her. I think you are going to have to convince them to work together."

Tomas sat back and studied the others' expressions. His mother's heart was huge. He didn't think it would be difficult to convince her to participate. Carlos, however, was a different story. He didn't forgive easily. He'd have a hard time supporting the project if Linh Han treated his wife the way she'd treated Tomas.

Fiona must have been thinking along the same lines. "Louisa Santiago is one of the sweetest women I know. If Mother treats her badly—"

Joseph cut her off with a hard look. "She won't. Mother's ego is big. I think she will want to do this. We make it clear to her that an apology is required and that this is a communal project. If she doesn't agree, then I'm leaving HFH." He shrugged. "You're right. This is the kind of thing I want to do. I've been stuck for a while, and I want something more fulfilling. If HFH doesn't back the project, I'll find work with an organization that does something similar.

Maybe you can hire me." He looked directly at Fiona and grinned.

She snorted. "Mother won't like an ultimatum. But we will make a compelling argument to the HFH board. I'm sure we'll have the votes when they see our presentation."

"Who's on the board? I thought it was just your family?" Tomas asked.

Joseph shook his head. "Mother, Father, Fiona, and I each own fifteen percent of the company. There are eight other shareholders—our cousins, who have five percent each. They're pretty passive, but we do need their agreement. Mother's the one we have to persuade, though."

"Will your dad be able to help?" Andy asked.

Joseph shot a look at Fiona before sitting back and crossing his arms. "Possibly. The thing is, Mother knows that Dad went to meet Tomas and wasn't happy about that. Like he's choosing Fiona over her."

Fiona stiffened beside Tomas, tension rolling off her in waves.

"It's not all bad because it's about time Mother learns that she can't run our lives." Joseph looked at Andy, then at Tomas. "We get to choose who we want to be with.

"I don't want to put this on the back burner while we wait for Mother to get her head on straight and welcome Tomas with open arms. It's a brilliant idea, and we should move on it."

Brilliant? Tomas's lips twitched in a slight smile. If it was brilliant, it was because of Fiona.

He may have had the original idea, but it was unformed. She was the one who had seen the value and magnitude of what they could do.

Her spine straightened. "Then we better make this a very persuasive presentation."

A tiny furball was buzzing with energy when they got back to Fiona's place. Little One scampered after the toy

Fiona tossed down the hallway, bouncing off the walls in her eagerness to get to it. Fiona put a hand against Tomas's chest to push him back into the bedroom. Resisting the push would have been easier than breathing, but the thought never entered his head. She closed the door and leaned against it, eyeing him up and down like he was a prize she'd won at the fair. He straightened his spine and flexed his pectorals, making them dance.

Fiona let out a surprised giggle. With her hands on his chest, she ordered, "Do it again."

And he did, liking the feel of her touching him. Inviting her to touch him wherever she wanted. Her hands moved from his chest up to the back of his neck, and she tugged him down to claim his lips.

Whether she knew it or not, every time she kissed him, every time she smiled at him, she plucked a tiny piece of his heart, and put it in her pocket. She could have it all, and he would wait as long as it took for her to offer her heart to him.

His hands went to the buttons of his shirt, but she stopped him. "No, let me." Eyes glittering, she kissed each inch of exposed skin as she worked the buttons and pushed his shirt off his shoulders. Light hands danced across his chest and under his arms. She dragged her nails down his spine, leaving him trembling. He thunked his head against the wall, unable to stand without support. Grabbing his ass, she squeezed him hard before teasing along his waistband and unbuckling his belt.

"Babe," he groaned.

"Yes?" She looked up at him with an innocent smile from where she knelt before him.

"Are you going to—?"

"Yes," she replied and took him in her mouth.

"Yes," he sighed, stroking his hands through her hair. "Yes."

CHAPTER 23

Sitting at the table in the break room, Tomas studied his notebook, determining what supplies he needed for the next day's build. Normally, he was more organized, but the presentation for HFH had taken up a lot of his time. He did not want to screw up and look bad in front of their board. More importantly, he didn't want to let Fiona down.

"What do you need?"

"Two by fours."

"No dumbass. What do you need for the presentation?"

Ali stood by the coffee maker, mug in hand, amused look on his face. "How do you—never mind. Fiona told Iris who told Marcia who told you?"

"Uh-huh." Ali pulled out a chair and sat opposite Tomas. He sipped his coffee noisily, eyes never leaving Tomas's face. "It's a great idea. KBS wants to be on board. Hell, half of Keeney wants to be part of it."

"Really?" It never failed to amaze him how quickly news traveled through town.

Ali nodded. "Some because helping people find homes is the right thing to do. Others because it's the flavor of the month and they want to be part of it. And a few because they're looking for a way to benefit from it. Like KBS." Seeing Tomas's narrow-eyed look, Ali chuckled. "We're a building supply company. We'd be stupid if we weren't on board. We can provide supplies at reduced cost—that makes us look good to the community and turns those homeowners into valued customers, who will, hopefully, sing our praises in the future."

"Will other businesses think the same way?" Tomas hadn't thought much beyond the presentation, although he expected Fiona had.

"Oh yeah. Everyone from roofers to plumbers to landscaping companies will want to contribute. It's great advertising and a healthy tax break to boot."

Tomas shook his head. The scope of the project was bigger than he imagined.

"So what's your biggest obstacle?" Ali settled back in his chair, looking like he had the entire day to chat.

"Fiona's mother." At Ali's raised eyebrow, he continued. "First off, she hates me and my family. Second, I think she's community-minded *only* when it serves her purpose. Third, she does not like to appear weak in front of others."

"I don't know her personally, but Marcia and Iris know her from church. They say she gets things done."

Tomas fiddled with his pen, thinking about how much to tell Ali. "Fiona is not like her mother."

Ali barked out a laugh, pulling out a wrinkled handkerchief to wipe his face.

"What's so funny?" It was an obvious mistake to talk to the old man.

Shooting Tomas a wry grin, Ali took his time folding up the handkerchief and stuffing it back into his pocket. "They're as different as night and day. Fiona is a force to be reckoned with. That woman has energy for days. Like her mother, she gets things done. But the difference is that

Fiona's motivation comes from the heart. A real desire to make the world a better place. Linh Han is…calculating."

Tomas looked through the window overlooking the floor of KBS, thinking about Ali's words. In his mind, he saw Fiona and her mother outside the church the morning he asked her out for coffee.

They had been almost mirror images. Conservative clothing and hair, calm expressions. The very picture of successful, competent businesswomen. He blinked, realizing that Fiona had stopped wearing her hair in that smooth twist she'd always worn. He didn't know what she did, but she looked more…relaxed. And what he considered her uniform—pale close-fitting skirt, blouse, and jacket was gone. Now, there was more color and variety in what she wore, as if she wasn't trying to fade into the background. When did that happen?

"So?"

Shaking his head, Tomas returned his attention to Ali. "Sorry. What did you say?"

"I asked how you were going to handle her mother."

"Haven't a freaking clue."

Ali pushed his chair back and took his coffee cup over to the sink. He spoke to Tomas over his shoulder as he rinsed the cup under running water. "If you're in it for the long haul, I suggest going to both her parents."

Tomas rose as well, shaking his head. "I think talking to them before the presentation may piss them off and they won't go for the project."

"No dumbass. You and Fiona. If your intentions are honorable, go talk to her parents. They're old school and will appreciate you coming to them."

Feet frozen to the floor, Tomas stared at Ali as comprehension dawned. Waiting for Fiona wasn't the right move. After being used by her mother and asshat ex-husband, she would not set herself up to be hurt again. She'd want Tomas to state his intentions clearly.

"You do want to marry her, don't you?" Ali twisted around, crossing his arms and leaning back against the counter. "Because if you're stringing her along, holy hell is gonna rain down on you." He jerked his head toward the KBS floor.

Tomas turned his head to follow Ali's gaze. Down below, he saw Iris, Hilary, and Marcia standing near the customer service counter. He swallowed. Ali was right. He'd better get his shit together.

The rest of the day was a blur. He didn't know if he was coming or going. Sitting at a stoplight, all he could think about was a life with Fiona. They hadn't been together very long, yet since meeting her more than a year ago, there hadn't been anyone else for him. Her marriage to Eddie was shit. Would she want to commit to Tomas? Would she want to marry again at all? She'd said she was afraid he'd break up with her. She hadn't said she wanted a commitment. Maybe she was happy with their arrangement and didn't want anything more.

A horn sounded behind him. Shit. Tomas shook off his daze and paid attention to driving. Up ahead was a strip mall, and he spotted a familiar figure exiting a convenience store. Not thinking, Tomas signaled, then turned into the parking lot. He'd barely put the truck in park before he was out the door.

"Joseph!"

Fiona's brother looked up. Spotting Tomas, he waved. His welcoming smile turned to a concerned frown as the scowling man bore down on him. "What's wrong?"

Stopping a few feet from the other man, Tomas said with a growl, "I want to marry your sister."

Joseph blinked. "Um…okay?"

Angry brown eyes searching uncomprehending brown eyes, Tomas let out a frustrated groan and started pacing.

"So what's the problem? Did she say no?"

Tomas shook his head.

"So she said yes."

Tomas shook his head.

"What did she say?"

"I haven't asked her yet." Tomas wheeled around, glaring at Joseph, who had the balls to laugh at him. "It's not funny," he ground out.

"Tomas, what's wrong?"

The two men turned to see Louisa and Carlos standing in the doorway of their restaurant. In his fog, Tomas hadn't been aware he'd pulled into the parking lot beside *Hola!*

"He's in love with Fiona," Joseph called out in a voice laced with amusement.

His mother gasped, clutching her hands in front of her and beaming a huge smile. Behind her, Carlos chuckled.

"Great," Tomas muttered.

"But he hasn't got the balls to ask her to marry him," Joseph explained.

"Just shut up already."

Joseph grinned. "They're your parents; they deserve to know why you're having a meltdown in the middle of the street."

Shop owners and a few customers stood near the storefront, watching the back and forth as if at a tennis match. Sensing his mortification, Carlos walked over and grabbed his arm.

"Let's take this inside."

His mother rushed forward to wrap Tomas in a big hug. Wiping her eyes, she stepped back, allowing them to enter.

Joseph followed behind, stopping to talk to Louisa. "My day just got more interesting. How about yours?"

She beamed at him and nodded.

Carlos led a silent Tomas to the back table, then peeled off. Seating himself, Tomas looked up to see Joseph settling in across from him, wearing a shit-eating grin. "Fuck off," he said.

"*You* came to *me*." Joseph shrugged.

Carlos returned with a bottle of tequila and three glasses, Louisa nowhere to be seen. He sat next to Joseph and poured the drinks. "I told your mother to give us a few minutes."

Tomas nodded, threw back his drink, and slumped against the back of the booth. The alcohol burned on the way down, and slowly he felt the tension ease from his shoulders. He poured himself another while Joseph and Carlos discussed the merits of the Mariners' pitching coach. "How do you two know each other?"

"Your parents bought this building off us a few years back." Joseph inclined his head toward Carlos. "And we're both interested in Woodbine Automotive."

Tomas forgot about his own issues and focused on Joseph. "I thought it's been sold. Didn't a restaurant chain buy it?"

"They have the highest bid. So far," Joseph answered, then went on, "HFH owns the property to the north of the shop. Another commercial real estate firm owns the property to the south. Carlos and I are talking about partnering to buy out Ernest Gardiner and keeping the automotive shop. Carlos will run it. HFH will be a silent partner. Keeney is growing and attracting attention from large real estate firms. They don't necessarily care about Keeney itself, just making a profit. Locally owned businesses are good for the community, so it makes sense for us to work together." Joseph indicated Carlos with a head tilt.

Working together was something Tomas understood. Teaming up with Vincent in prison was one of the best decisions he'd ever made, because he wouldn't have been able to complete the contracting program or find a job once he'd been released without Vincent's help.

Tomas had been dragged, kicking and screaming, into the Keeney Builds program. A year later, he saw the wisdom and appreciated the efforts of small business owners working to improve the community. He was pleased that his mother and stepfather were an integral part of it.

"Enough about that. Let's talk about you." Carlos picked up his glass and pointed it in Tomas's direction before taking a drink.

Tomas sighed. It was one thing to talk to Joseph about Fiona, but Carlos? The two men across from him appeared to be enjoying this way too much.

"You want to marry Fiona. Good. So what's stopping you?" Carlos didn't beat around the bush. "You think she's too good for you."

Joseph jumped in. "And you think you've got nothing to offer."

"I feel like I'm being double-teamed," Tomas grumbled, rubbing a tired hand over his face. The expectant faces were not going away, so he tried to find the words. "Both of those things. Fiona's been pushed around most of her life, with her mother and that asshat" —he couldn't bring himself to say Eddie's name aloud— "telling her what to do. I want to look after her. Protect her. Take away all her problems. But if I tell her that…."

"You'll overwhelm her, and she won't want anything to do with you." Carlos threw back his drink and set the glass down on the table. "At least that's what your mother did." He smirked at the dumbstruck expression on Tomas's face. "Yeah. Your mother thought I was too slick. All fast cars and partying. You were nine when I met Louisa, but she didn't introduce me to you for a long time."

Two lines formed between his eyebrows as Tomas tried to remember meeting Carlos. "It was at a family picnic. You showed up in this cherry red low rider. My cousins were all jealous when you took Mom and me for a ride in it."

Carlos nodded. "She was pissed at me."

Joseph twisted in his seat to see Carlos clearly. "Why?"

"Trying to impress her kid but not bothering to get to know her kid. And she was right. I was all about Louisa the woman, not Louisa the mother. I didn't pay much attention to you, couldn't see that you two were a package deal. It took a long time to get my head out of my ass."

"I'll say." Louisa stood next to the table with bowls of chips and guacamole. She placed them down, then poured glasses of water for each man. "He was an idiot, but he figured it out." She kissed Tomas's forehead, then Carlos on the lips, and left to go back to the kitchen.

Carlos smiled after her before continuing, "The point is, don't make assumptions. Fiona may not be ready now. She's got a new relationship with you. Issues with her mother, a full plate at her job, and this new project of yours. If you go all caveman on her, she may kick you to the curb."

Joseph tossed his two cents in. "Ask her what she wants. You can give her some suggestions. Just don't make decisions for her."

"And remember what I said, you *are* worthy of her," Carlos said.

"Okay." Tomas let out a breath he felt like he'd been holding for hours. "I think I can do that."

CHAPTER 24

"*C*rap!"

"What? Did you hurt yourself?" Tomas was immediately beside her, looking for blood.

"I'm fine. I just realized I need to answer an email, but I'll get to it later." They were making dinner together, something she'd only ever done with her family; she and Joseph following her mother's orders.

Being with Tomas like this, working together to prepare a meal, was a pleasant experience she was quickly getting used to.

After eating, Tomas rose from the table and started to clear it. Fiona pushed her chair back to join him.

"I'll take care of this," he said. "You go do your work."

"You sure? It can wait a little longer."

He turned her toward her home office and gave her a gentle push. "Go. I've got this."

Gratefully, Fiona retreated to her office and opened up her laptop. She didn't raise her head until almost an hour later. Realizing the time, she hurried out of the room with an apology on her lips and found Tomas on the back deck, hunched over a sketchbook with gridded paper. Beside him was a ruler, an eraser, and a few pencils. He looked up at her arrival, a welcoming smile on his face.

"Oh my God! I'm so sorry to keep you waiting. I didn't think it would take so long," she rattled on, wringing her hands in worry.

Rising from his seat, he held his hands out in a calming gesture. "It's fine. There's been an idea floating around my head, and I was able to get it down on paper. I didn't notice the time."

"You're not mad?" Her heart was still pounding.

Shaking his head, he stepped closer and drew her into his arms. "Of course not. But I think this is something we need to talk about."

"Okay."

He chuckled as he looked down at her widened eyes. "Don't panic. It's nothing bad," he assured her, taking her hand. He led her back inside and over to the couch, drawing her down beside him. He shifted, placing one arm on the back of the couch, and faced her, still holding her hand.

"We haven't been together very long, and when we do have time alone, we're normally in bed."

"Yeah," it came out as more of a question.

Leaning in, Tomas's lips formed into a panty-melting smile. "Don't get me wrong. I like sex, especially with you." He kissed her softly, then pulled back. "Do you bring work home a lot?"

That was a question she hadn't been expecting. "I don't *need* to. It's more of a habit I got into. Eddie and I didn't spend a lot of time together. If he was home, he'd be in his office, and I'd be working in the dining room. Then I was alone, and work was a good diversion." She thought about the nights she'd spent beating herself up for not realizing Eddie married her only for what she represented: an "in" to her family's business. Work was something she could control, and it chased away the inadequacy that plagued her.

"So me being here each night isn't keeping you from getting stuff done?"

"No! In fact, it's made me stop being a hermit. I like having you here."

"Good. But if you have shit to take care of, or you want to be by yourself, let me know. My feelings aren't gonna be hurt."

She held up a hand like a Girl Scout. "Promise. And, well, the same goes for you. Feel free to go and be with your friends or—" she waved a hand in the air "—whatever it is you'd rather do."

"Good to know," he replied, pulling her into his lap, "but if you're good with me being here, this is where I want to be."

He circled her back with his big hands until the tension faded away to be replaced by a warm feeling, and she relaxed against him.

That night, he made love to her, slowly, attentively, as if the entire evening was all for her.

A couple days later, Fiona pulled into the parking lot of the apartment complex where Tomas lived. She would be seeing his place for the first time and was curious to see what it revealed about him. Sitting in her car, she looked over the grounds of the complex. There were three buildings in a U-shaped formation, each with three floors of apartments. In the center of the U was a grassy area and a swimming pool. The place was quiet, clean, and well-kept. It seemed very much like Tomas himself.

Fiona tugged down the visor, giving herself the once-over. Deciding to refresh her lipstick, she reached into her tote bag, touching the panties and nightie she'd placed in it before leaving the house. She wanted to stay the night, and hoped he wanted her to as well. In the time they'd been sleeping together, she could count on one hand the number of times he hadn't spent the night. She was nervous, unsure what the change in their routine meant. But she wasn't going to find any answers sitting in the car. She swiped on a layer of lipstick, fluffed her hair, climbed out of the car, and made her way to Tomas's unit.

The door was open, and he leaned against the jamb, watching her approach. It was all she could do not to lick her lips as she took in his snug-fitting jeans, equally snug-fitting T-shirt, and hot gaze directed at her.

"Hey," she said. Fresh from the shower, his hair stood up in spikes, and underneath the smell of his soap, his distinctive scent hovered around her, and she sighed.

He drew her in with a hand around the back of her neck and touched his lips to hers. "I'm glad you're here."

"Me too." She took his other hand and allowed him to pull her inside. The single-bedroom apartment was bright with late afternoon sun. To her right was a bathroom, and to her left was a kitchen with a peninsula separating the kitchen from the living area. She followed Tomas, looking around and studying his private space as if looking for clues. Two high-backed stools were pushed in against the peninsula. The counter itself was bare and clean. The kitchen counters were relatively bare as well. A tea towel was folded neatly over the oven door handle, a pot of something simmered on the stove, and a wooden spoon and an open bottle of beer rested next to it. The aroma of garlic, butter, and onion filled the air, and Fiona's stomach growled in anticipation.

Tomas grinned. "Supper should be ready soon. Want a glass of wine?" At her nod, he opened the fridge, pulled out a bottle, and turned to pour some into a glass sitting on the counter. Fiona took the glass and continued her examination.

"How long have you lived here?" she inquired, taking in

the small dining room table pushed up against the wall, with three chairs pushed in around it. The table was set with plain white dinnerware on woven bamboo placemats. Navy blue napkins were folded and placed on the plates.

Tomas moved past her to the distressed leather loveseat, settling in with his bare feet up on the trunk that served as a coffee table. It faced a credenza with a flat-screen TV resting on it and was flanked by two bookshelves.

"A year ago, September." He watched as she perused the books on the shelves, then moved over to the drafting table beside the window. She hopped up on the stool and swiveled to face him.

"It's nice."

"My sisters chose the furniture. I gave them a budget and the cash. They had a blast going through flea markets and secondhand stores."

"I'll bet." Fiona caught his eye and grinned. The furniture may have been secondhand, but it was of good quality.

"I drew the line at the bed. I wanted one that no one else had slept in."

"Perfectly understandable," she agreed with a laugh.

"How's Little One?"

Fiona rolled her eyes. "She had quite the busy day. She unrolled the toilet paper and dragged it all around the apartment. When I opened the door, she was standing on the table, a stream of toilet paper behind her and the end in her mouth. She looked at me, like, 'Go about your business, there's nothing going on here.' She was most annoyed when I cleaned it up."

Tomas threw his head back and laughed. "Did you take pictures?"

"Yes, I'll send them to you." Giggling, she looked at a closed sketchpad on the drafting table and asked, "May I look?"

He rose from the couch and stepped closer, turning her chair to face the drafting table. Reaching around behind her, he pulled the sketchpad closer and opened it. She studied the page, taking in long rectangular boxes. "These look like…."

"Shipping containers. Some cities are re-purposing them into dwellings. I'm not sure how cost-efficient they are, but I like the challenge of working with found materials."

"I've seen photos. Even apartment blocks are made out of them. Are you thinking of building something here in Keeney?"

He stepped back, and she twisted around to face him. He was rubbing the back of his neck, looking out the window, and gave a diffident shrug. "I don't know yet. There are so many possibilities. I was actually thinking about using containers to build a house for myself." He looked back at her, seeming a little vulnerable, which warmed her heart even more. Then he cleared his throat and moved to the kitchen. "Dinner's ready. Have a seat and I'll bring it in."

Dutifully, she headed to the table and took a seat, watching while Tomas brought over a pot of white bean chili, then went back for a plate of warm cornbread. "Yum." She smiled. "I could get used to this."

As tempting as the food was, she couldn't eat more than a few bites of the cornbread and forced herself to swallow a few spoonfuls of chili. Tomas ate with his usual gusto, and she waited until his bowl was empty before pushing hers away.

"Something wrong? You don't like it?" he asked.

"It's great. It's just…I have to tell you something."

"Okay."

She took a deep breath and released a torrent of words. "My mother gave the information about Woodbine Automotive being for sale to the restaurant chain who then outbid Carlos for it."

The delicious cornbread turned to a leaden lump in her

belly as she watched confusion turn to comprehension in Tomas's eyes. It had been ages since she'd seen such a hard expression on his face.

"Your mother screwed over Carlos?"

She nodded, unable to speak for the lump in her throat.

"What the fuck? What the actual fuck?" he spat out, shaking his head. "Is Joseph part of this? Is he partnering with Carlos to squeeze more money out of him? Or is he stringing Carlos along, building up his hopes only to back out later on?" His glittering gaze bore a hole through her.

"What? No. Joseph said he has a plan to fix it. He's just as angry as I am and doesn't want your family to be screwed over."

"Really?" Tomas snorted. "How long have you known about this?"

She cursed herself for giving in to Joseph. Tomas's hard glare let her know he wasn't going to be happy with her answer.

Once, when she was very small, she'd been playing in her father's greenhouse and knocked over a flowerpot, crushing the plant under the broken terra cotta. Knowing she wasn't supposed to have been there by herself, she'd cleaned up as best she could but didn't think about the vacancy left behind on the shelf. When asked, she said she knew nothing about it. Her mother didn't believe her and pressed until Fiona confessed, tears running down her face. Her mother's scolding had hurt, but her father's disappointed look hurt even more. Now, facing Tomas's thunderous expression, not telling him the truth didn't occur to her.

"Joseph told me last week," she admitted, trying to keep the tremble out of her voice.

"A week?"

"Yes. He asked—"

He didn't give her a chance to finish. He pushed his chair back, gathered the dishes, and strode to the kitchen. A plate smashed and cutlery clattered when he threw them in the sink. Then silence.

Tomas stood with back to her, gripping the edge of the counter. "I think you should leave," he said in a cold, flat voice.

Wordlessly, she fled, tears blurring her vision.

CHAPTER 25

$\mathcal{A}$ndy Tran turned off all but the lights over the entryway, closed and locked the church doors, and sighed. "Other duties as assigned," he muttered.

Seminary school hadn't prepared him to fix a broken pipe, but Andy hustled to the church to help with the cleanup when the custodian called. They'd turned off the water, mopped up the mess, and called a plumber. Not much else could be done this late at night.

Trudging up the stairs to the parking lot, he spotted a man walking aimlessly in the shadows, and slowed. The church had had a rash of prowlers lately. After being smashed to smithereens, the original mailbox was replaced with one that locked. That one was vandalized as well, and now the church admin stopped at the Keeney post office every day to pick up the mail.

Cellphone in hand to call 911 if necessary, Andy made his presence known. "Hey," he said, walking toward his car.

The man squinted in Andy's direction and replied, "Hey." He was sweaty and disheveled, wearing baggy shorts and a stained T-shirt soaked with sweat. Broad and muscular, when he moved to stand under the streetlamp, the light caught on thick dark eyebrows and a strong nose, casting the rest of his face in shadow.

Andy beeped his car open and stood next to the driver's door, ready to duck inside if the man made a move. "Can I help you with something?" Yes, he was alone in a dark parking lot, but he was a pastor. Help needed to be offered.

"I doubt it," the man answered in a voice that sounded familiar.

Andy squinted into the dark. "Tomas? Is that you?"

The man came closer. "Andy?"

"What the hell?" Andy moved away from his car. "Are you okay? You look exhausted?"

Tomas wiped his face with his sleeve. "I was running."

"Why? Was a bear chasing you?"

His lips curled up in a slight smile, otherwise Tomas didn't respond to the joke.

"It's not my thing but do you run a lot?"

Tomas stared at the ground, his mouth twisted in a bitter line. "No. I just…."

Andy leaned against the hood of the car, crossed his arms, and waited. When Tomas didn't finish, he said, "Something must be wrong if you're literally running yourself ragged? Is it Fiona?" He didn't know Tomas well but sensed this wasn't how he normally dealt with things.

Releasing a frustrated sigh, Tomas began to pace across the cracked asphalt. "Not Fiona but her fucking mother. Sorry about that, padre."

Andy waved off the apology. "That woman would make the Dalai Lama swear."

"Do you know what she did?"

"You'll have to be more specific," Andy drawled. "The list is probably long."

As if gathering his thoughts, Tomas stared into the darkness before answering, "I get that she doesn't like me, and I get that she blames me for Fiona standing up to her, but to mess with my parents? That's just...."

"Mean? Petty? Vindictive? Machiavellian?" Andy counted adjectives on his fingers. "I could go on."

"Yeah, you could." He slumped next to Andy, resting against the car's hood. "Do you know about the auto parts store?"

Andy nodded. "Joseph told me when he found out."

"Fiona told me tonight."

"I see. And you were angry because she didn't tell you sooner. Hence the running?"

Tomas shot him a "no-shit" look. "Blowing up at her didn't seem like a good idea so I told her to leave. Then it was either punch a hole in the wall or go for a run."

Andy nudged his bulky shoulder. "You chose wisely."

"Yeah. Patching drywall is a pain in the ass." His humor was coming back. Good.

It was late, and he was too tired to mince words, so Andy waded in. "You're hurt she chose Joseph over you."

"What?"

"You heard me. Fiona listened to her brother and chose not to tell you right away. And it pisses you off."

Tomas shot off the car, clenching his fists. "Fucking right it pisses me off. She's known for days. All three of you knew about it and could have told me at that meeting the other night." Anger and frustration radiated off him. "She shouldn't have kept it from me. I should have been told sooner."

Andy didn't argue. He'd thought Joseph and Fiona were wrong to keep it from Tomas and had told Joseph that. "But you weren't," he said. "Did you wonder why?"

"I know why. Because she knew I'd be pissed."

"Do you think it might be something else?" His backside was getting numb, so Andy moved to stand in front of Tomas. "Assume positive intent here. Why else would Fiona not tell you right away?"

Tomas frowned.

Andy rolled his eyes. "Come on. You're not thick. Obviously they told Carlos, so why didn't they tell you?" When Tomas didn't answer, Andy asked, "Could they want to make things right? Present you with a solution rather than a problem?"

"I suppose," Tomas said petulantly, not ready to see their side.

Looking up into the darkness, Andy tried to figure out a way to get through Tomas's stubborn, thick head. "Pretend for a moment that Linh Han was your mother." He nodded at the shudder that went through Tomas. "Agreed. If that were the case, and your mother hurt someone you cared for, how would you feel?"

Tomas answered immediately, "Like shit."

"And what would you do?"

"I'd—" Tomas closed his mouth, glared at Andy, and exhaled loudly. "You're right."

"I know I am," —he made a rolling gesture with his hand — "now answer the question."

"I'd try to fix it."

"Why?" Andy pressed.

"To minimize the damage."

"Praise the Lord!" Andy shouted, raising his arms and dropping them. "He gets it."

"You're an asshole," Tomas grumbled, slumping against the side of the car.

"I can be," Andy contemplated the man beside him, then looked at the darkened church. High above the entryway was a circular window inset with a stained-glass cross. It was lit from within and glowed in the darkness. "It's weird having your mom and their mom be so active in the church. They both want the church to thrive, but for very different reasons. Linh Han likes to be associated with success. She works on projects that make the church look good in the community. And for all her self-serving ways, she's done a lot of good."

Tomas nodded. "My mom said something like that."

"Your mom," Andy continued, "looks at the people who will be impacted the most by anything the church takes on. She's exuberant and appears impulsive, ready to jump in without a lifejacket, but she's really rather deliberate. She doesn't like people getting hurt, and tries to prevent that from happening."

He shifted to look directly at Tomas. "I suspect Linh Han tipped off that restaurant chain because it benefitted her. It was business, and Carlos being outbid was simply the fallout."

"I suppose," Tomas said, running a hand over his sweaty face. "It sucks that it was Fiona's mom behind it."

"Agreed." Tomas looked less like a thundercloud, and Andy asked, "You good?"

"Yeah."

Andy stood and pulled his keys out of his pocket. "Your mothers are forces of nature. If they can set aside their differences and work together on the project, it's going to be epic."

"That's a big *if*," Tomas replied.

Andy laughed. "Believe me, it's at the top of my prayer list. I really want this project to succeed because a lot of people will benefit from it."

Headlights illuminated them as a vehicle entered the parking lot. The men squinted against the bright lights of a Keeney Police car coming to a stop close by. "Shit," Andy said, giving the police car a friendly wave and his winningest smile. He looked anything but pastoral in his Deadpool for President T-shirt but hadn't anticipated needing his clerical collar to help with a plumbing issue.

"Everything all right here?" the female officer asked through her lowered car window.

He smiled big. "Just fine, officer. I'm Andy Tran, the pastor here. I can show you my ID if you want."

"Yeah, but do it slowly," she said. She shone a flashlight over his car and then over Tomas. "Show me your ID, too."

Tomas held his hands loosely by his sides, palms turned out, and told her, "I was out for a run and don't have it with me."

"This is my friend, Tomas Alvarado," Andy told the cop as he gave her his driver's license and business card. "We were just finishing up a conversation."

"Yeah?" she asked.

He stood still while she compared his photo to his face. Seeming satisfied, she handed his ID back then studied Tomas. "Where do you live?"

Tomas rattled off an address that made the cop's eyebrows shoot up. "Really," she replied. "What do you do?"

His posture relaxed, and he jutted his chin in a proud gesture. "I'm a contractor at Keeney Building Supply, and I teach construction classes at the college."

"Really," she said again before flicking her flashlight off. "Were you the guy auctioned off at the senior center last year? My mom bid five hundred bucks on him and lost out to her bridge partner. She's still sore about it."

Tomas shook his head, smiling slightly. "No, ma'am. That was my partner, Vincent Ortiz."

"Are you being auctioned off this year?" she asked.

"Not if I can help it."

Andy butted in, grinning broadly, "But he will be teaching a class for seniors at KBS this weekend. You could bring your mom to that."

"Yeah?"

Andy ignored Tomas's growl and carried on, "Information is available on the KBS website, and there's a link on the church's website, too. What will they be doing, Tomas?"

Tomas crossed his arms, shifting slightly so that Andy

could see his raised middle finger, but the officer couldn't see him and said, "It's about how to install a grab bar in a bathroom."

The cop looked interested. "I'll look into it. And, Tomas, get the pastor to drive you home. Running after dark without your ID isn't a good idea."

Watching the car pull out of the parking lot, Tomas grumbled, "Why the hell did you have to tell her that? And how do you know in the first place."

Andy slapped his shoulder. "I'd be a shitty pastor if I didn't know what was going on in my community. I hear there's a waiting list."

*L*ittle One's insistent meows roused Fiona from her lethargy. "I'm coming," she said, rising from the couch. The cat had completely recovered from being spayed and was no longer under house arrest. It was dark outside, and she wanted to hunt.

Fiona trudged toward the door. "Remember what we talked about? Do not follow strangers into the woods, no matter what they offer you."

The cat flicked her tail as if reminding Fiona she'd been born on the streets and nothing in Iris's backyard could scare her.

The cool night washed over Fiona as Little One sidled past her. She was about to close the door when Iris's determined voice came to her. "Are you going to make her cry?"

Fiona slipped out the door and stood to the side in the shadows, where she was able to see what was happening but invisible to anyone below.

"Excuse me?" Tomas rumbled, towering over the smaller woman.

Iris stood in front of the stairs, clutching her cardigan

over her chest. "You heard me. Are you going to make her cry? She's been pacing for hours, and I don't like it. She's had enough, so if you're going to make her cry, you can turn around, get in your truck, and go home."

Guilt sliced through Fiona. She hadn't meant to bother Iris.

Tomas stared down at the woman who signed his paycheck and sighed. "No," he said, "I'm hoping she'll accept my apology."

"Why? What did you do to that girl?"

Fiona's heart warmed that her former mother-in-law cared enough about her wellbeing to challenge a man who could bench-press her with one arm tied behind his back.

"I screwed up," he answered simply. Like spilling his guts to the owner of Keeney Building Supply was an everyday occurrence.

"Obviously," Iris snapped.

He rubbed a tired hand over his face and looked past Iris to the darkness, saying, "I got mad because I thought she should have told me something a while ago. If I had given her a chance to explain, I'd have realized she was trying to fix things. If I had listened, I wouldn't have reacted so badly, and I need to apologize for that."

Iris's loud sniff covered the sniff Fiona couldn't hold back. She'd spent the last few hours alternately berating her mother, Joseph, and Tomas for this mess, and finally, herself for not having a stronger backbone.

"Good." Iris stepped toward him and patted his arm. "I regret all the time when I thought Fiona was cold and calculating and keeping Eddie away from me. Her heart is so big, I know she didn't intend to hurt you." She moved aside and jerked her head toward the stairs. "You're good for her. Now go."

Fiona shrank back, tears streaming down her face.

Having a fierce, loyal friend like Iris was worth the pain Eddie had put her through.

Below her, Tomas took a few steps forward, then turned back to kiss Iris on the cheek. "You're good for her, too," he murmured, then climbed the stairs two at a time.

Fiona met him at the top, wiping her nose on her shirt-sleeve. "I'm sorry," she whispered.

"You have nothing to apologize for," he replied, moving to cup the back of her head.

Mascara running, eyes swollen, hair a tangled mess hanging around her face, she knew she was a mess, yet Tomas didn't bat an eye. He drew her unresisting form close until she nuzzled into his chest with a sigh.

"I should have—"

He cut her off. "Maybe. But I should have, too. I wish you *had* told me sooner, but I know why you didn't."

Sniffling, she looked up at him to ask, "You do?"

"Andy helped me figure it out. You were upset that your mother's actions impacted my family, and Joseph wanted to fix it."

Her mother's cutthroat approach to life was disturbing. Success was all that was important to her. "Yeah. What she did was terrible, and I wanted to tell you sooner but…."

"Andy told me that, too. He's really good at explaining shit."

She frowned. "Did you go to Andy for pastoral counseling?"

"Sort of. I went for a run and met him in the church parking lot, and he helped me get my head out of my ass." She laughed, which apparently was what he intended. "I am really sorry for reacting so badly and for not letting you explain."

"I know," she said, standing on her toes to kiss his jaw. "I heard what you said to Iris, and I accept your apology."

"Thank God," he murmured, burying his face in her hair.

CHAPTER 26

n IUD reduced the frequency of Fiona's periods and diminished most of her PMS, but sometimes, an aching back, tension headache, and cramping brought her to tears. When that happened, a dark room and a hot water bottle were her best friends. Eddie hadn't been sympathetic. So she'd learned to down ibuprofen, paint on a smile, and suffer silently.

Around noon, she felt the familiar heaviness in her lower abdomen. Unfortunately, she was out of Advil with no time to buy more before going into a meeting. By the time she got home it was all she could do to drag herself up the stairs to her apartment. She popped some pills and collapsed on the couch, pulling the afghan over her. An hour later, she awoke to see Tomas perched on the ottoman, stroking her shoulder, his heavy eyebrows stitched together with concern.

Remembering it was her turn to make dinner, she popped up like a jack-in-the-box. "Oh crap! Sorry, sorry, sorry. I'll have dinner ready soon." She pushed back the afghan and swung her legs to the floor, stifling a groan.

"Take it easy. You look like hell. Did you hurt yourself?"

She shook her head but stopped when it aggravated the pounding in her head. "It's nothing. Just a little headache."

"Doesn't look little to me. Are you expecting your period? Is it PMS?"

Heat rose into her face as she nodded. This man had been intimate with every part of her body, so why was it so hard to talk about a natural part of her life?

Tomas gusted out a sigh, wincing at the evidence of her pain. "Babe, I have two sisters and a mother who talk about their cycles all the damn time. So, how can I help? Make you something to eat? Help you to bed?"

Her eyes welled up at his thoughtfulness. "There's an orange box of tea in the cupboard. A cup of that would be great."

He was on his feet before she finished her sentence. Filling the kettle in the kitchen, he called out, "You haven't been like this before. When you have bad PMS, how long does it normally last?"

"A day or so." Her answer was almost a question. In truth, she didn't know. When life was really stressful, it could last up to four days. And then the bleeding would start, which meant no sex for up to ten days. She hoped he wouldn't mind.

"The kettle's on the stove. Don't move. I'll be back before it boils."

Before she could respond, he was out the door. So she sank back into the cushions, allowing the misery to wash over her.

Minutes later, he was back with Iris in tow. Tomas veered off to take care of the tea while Iris approached, her mouth turned down in sympathy. "Hey, honey," she said softly. "Don't get up. I've got your calendar with me. Let's see if we can reschedule things for you."

Tomas was beside her with a steaming mug of tea before she could protest. "If I was flat on my back with pain, you'd want me to take a day off, right?" Receiving a nod and a narrow-eyed look, he continued, "Let your assistant help you. Please?"

No one had ever treated her with such care. Tears leaked out of the corner of her eyes. Tomas leaned in to brush them away and stroked her cheek. "I know you're strong and very capable, but would you do this for me?" How could she refuse when he looked so earnest?

Smiling shakily, she sat up and took the mug of tea, warming her hands on the thick ceramic. Tomas shifted to sit at the end of the couch, taking her feet in his lap to massage them gently.

"Right." Iris smiled and opened her planner. "Let's make you some breathing room."

After Iris left, Tomas made scrambled eggs and buttered toast and brought them to Fiona. "I'm not an invalid," she groused.

"No, but stay there if you're comfortable on the couch." He sat in the armchair and started in on his own plate of food, finishing off the entire contents in a few quick bites.

Switching her glance between his empty plate and the clock on the mantel, she realized how late it was. "I'm so sorry. You must have been starved, and then you made your own dinner. Here finish—" Feeling guilty as hell, she thrust out her plate.

"Stop apologizing. I'm a grown-ass man and can feed myself. Finish eating, unless it's hard on your stomach."

"You're sure?" At his scowl, she smiled meekly and tucked into the delicious eggs. When she was done, she handed the plate to his outstretched hand. "That was perfect. Thank you."

He grunted in satisfaction and took the empty plates into the kitchen. Hearing running water and the clatter of dishes, she rose from the couch and folded the afghan. She picked up her empty mug and brought it over to where

Tomas stood elbow-deep in dishwater. "I'm going to have a bath."

"Here, let me help you."

"I'm fine. But thanks." She patted his arm reassuringly and made her way toward the bedroom. The tea and the ibuprofen were kicking in, and she was beginning to perk up. Knowing she had no work commitments the next day was even better. She started the water running in the tub, took off her clothes, and tossed them into the laundry basket in the closet. She removed her jewelry and dropped it into a ceramic tray on the top of her dresser, then padded naked into the bathroom to climb into the tub. Settling back, she closed her eyes and let the heat of the water envelop her.

"Scoot forward so I can get in behind you."

Her eyes flew open to find a naked Tomas standing in the bathroom. He made shooing gestures with his hands, and she hurried to comply. The water sloshed dangerously close to the lip of the tub as he eased in behind her. Not knowing what was expected of her, she made herself as small as possible, drawing her knees up and wrapping her arms around them.

Tomas's hands came up and rested on her shoulders, the thumbs pressing up the column of her neck. "I thought the purpose of a bath was to relax."

"I'm just…making room for you." She shivered as his deep voice rumbled through her.

"I appreciate that, but I can't rub away your aches if you're all hunched up. Unless you don't want me to?"

His hands were doing amazing things to her tight shoulders. Of their own accord, her arms relaxed and drifted over to rest on the hard thighs holding her in place. "Okay. That would be…nice."

He didn't speak, just continued massaging her neck and shoulders until she was a limp noodle and drifted in the heat of the water and the warmth of his touch. If he wanted to know her deepest, darkest secrets and get access to her bank account, now would be the time to ask. She'd give it to him in a heartbeat.

"You're almost asleep. Are you ready to get out now?" Grunting in response, she rose to her feet and climbed out of the tub to wrap herself in a towel. She turned to hand one to Tomas, and froze.

Water streamed off his fully erect penis as he rose from the tub. Fiona's eyebrows came together as she lifted her gaze to meet his.

He smirked.

She blushed.

Grabbing the towel, he wrapped it around his waist and stepped out of the tub. "You were naked and in my arms. It's a natural reaction." He kissed her lightly on the forehead. "I'll be fine."

Fiona's gaze darted around the room as she thought about options. "I could…."

"No, babe. Sex with you is awesome, but I can live without it. I waited years for you. A week or so is not going to bother me. Let's get you to bed." He turned her toward the doorway. "Go find your pajamas and climb in."

Fiona headed to her closet to retrieve the pajamas hanging behind the door. When she emerged, Tomas stood by the bed, fully dressed.

"Oh. Are you going home?" She'd been looking forward to snuggling against him but steeled herself not to show her disappointment.

Hands in his pockets, Tomas shrugged. "I don't want to, but this is new for us, and I thought you might want some space. Do you?"

"Not at all. In fact, I got something for you." She twisted to retrieve a small gift bag from the closet, then placed it on the bed. Tomas approached the bag, looking curious. He tossed aside the tissue paper, then reached in and pulled out a length of silky black fabric. Raising one eyebrow, he laughed in delight.

"You bought me pajamas!"

"Technically, they're called sleep pants. And, well, I thought I'd empty out a drawer and you can keep some things here so you don't have to carry stuff back and forth to your place every day. Not that you're here *every* day, but the nights that you do spend here you'll have something to put on. I mean, I like you naked, but if you want something to put on…." Aware she was rambling, Fiona clamped her lips together. Her plan had been to give him the sleep pants after they'd had mind-boggling sex, not on the eve of a dry spell.

Tomas shucked off his clothes and tossed them over the armchair in the corner. He stepped into the sleep pants and pulled them up until they hung above his lean hips, show-casing the V cut of his abs. "I like these."

Gusting out a sigh, Fiona's shoulders came down from her ears. "Good. You always sleep naked so I didn't know if you wanted the matching top. I can get it for you."

He'd come closer while she was speaking and wrapped his arms around her, kissing her nose. His eyes were soft and warm when he pulled back. "Maybe when it gets cold. I'm pretty hot in bed."

"I'll say." At his knowing smirk, she stammered, "Temper-ature wise! Your body is warm. You're like my own personal heating pad."

He chuckled. "Glad to help. Are you ready for bed, or do you want to stay up for a while?"

A yawn was his answer, and she let go of him to climb into the bed. He went to his jeans to retrieve his cellphone and earbuds, and put them on his bedside table. "I'll go lock up."

Fiona snuggled down against her pillow, listening as his bare feet padded around the apartment. He returned moments later with a glass of water and the bottle of ibuprofen. She smiled at his thoughtfulness and sat up to take two pills.

He rounded the bed and eased in beside her before pulling her back against his chest and burrowing his nose in her hair. "How big is this drawer you're giving me?"

"How big does it need to be?"

"I come with a lot of baggage." There was vulnerability in his statement. A request to take him as he was. Accept his imperfections.

"I've got room for your baggage." She twisted around to lie on her back and see him better. "I've got room for your big dusty boots and tool belt. Room for your toothbrush and razor. Room for your thoughts and ideas and hopes and dreams. I've got room for you."

Propped up on his elbow, his eyes gleaming in the dark, a shudder ran through his body as he pulled her closer with an arm around her waist. His hand drifted down over her lower abdomen, moving in slow circles. The heat of it felt like heaven, and she sighed. "Can you do that all night?"

"Yeah, but it will cost you."

"Name your price."

"My drafting table in your office."

If possible, Fiona's heart softened even further. "I'd love that."

CHAPTER 27

*H*ilary and Marcia had jumped on the idea of teaching home repair classes to seniors. To Tomas's relief, they agreed not to record the first class on video. He was consulted as to what was needed for the demonstration, and he looked over the infographic hand-out of instructions, but other than that, the women took care of the planning and preparation.

The first class would be taught at KBS rather than the senior center because it meant less schlepping stuff around and more room to work. An area used for seasonal products —Christmas decorations, gardening supplies, and the like— was emptied out. Workbenches and stools were brought in, a demonstration table was set up at the front of the room, and Keeney Builds students constructed walls six feet high and four feet wide. The temporary walls were made from two-by-four studs and covered with drywall so the class attendees could try installing grab bars themselves.

The class was capped at twelve, three per workbench because Tomas didn't think he could provide adequate instruction to more than that many people. Within an hour of the class being posted on the KBS website, every seat was filled, and there was a waiting list. Who knew that many people in Keeney were interested in learning how to install grab bars.

After much pleading from Marcia, he agreed to double the class size provided he had help. So Carl was brought on board, and since Vincent wasn't available, Tomas's sister Sylvie stepped in.

The compartments of Sylvie's leather toolbelt were filled with her own pink handled tools, pink work gloves, cell-phone, and she'd stitched on an elastic holster for her lip gloss. She was comfortable with all things building related and handled the tools with easy familiarity.

Sweat trickling down his spine, Tomas paced in front of the improvised classroom while Carl and Sylvie set out tools and supplies on the workbenches. He'd been teaching students on the job site for over a year and couldn't figure out why he was so nervous. He'd gone through the demo in front of Iris and Marcia, and they, in turn, installed a grab bar while he watched, and it had gone fine. It would be fine, he told himself for the 100th time.

"Are you ready?" Marcia called. Everyone gave her a thumbs-up, and she opened the door with a game show flourish. "Come on down!"

Ernest Gardiner was the first to enter, then...nobody.

Marcia stuck her head out the door, then turned back, looking shocked and dismayed. "Let me figure this out," she muttered and hurried away.

"This is it?" the old man sneered, pushing his walker into the big, bright, empty space. "This place is supposed to be filled with hot babes. Where is everybody?" Spotting Sylvie, he smiled wide. "Here's the eye candy. How ya doin' sweetheart?"

Sylvie rolled her eyes at her brother and stomped over to

Mr. Gardiner. "The name is Sylvie, and do not refer to me as sweetheart, babe, or eye candy. Got it?"

The old man's eyes sparkled. "Got it."

Seemingly satisfied they'd reached an understanding, Sylvie softened her tone and led the old guy to a workbench in the front row. "Let's get you situated. Do you want to sit on a stool or your walker?"

He looked confused for a moment. "You're gonna teach the class just for me?"

Sylvie and Carl looked to Tomas, waiting for his answer.

Relief rolling off him in waves, Tomas replied, "Sure am."

Mr. Gardiner settled himself on a stool and pulled out a pair of smudged reading glasses to look over the tools laid out before him.

"You don't need to stick around," Tomas told Carl and Sylvie. "I've got this." He was pleased the old curmudgeon had shown up and knew they'd get along just fine.

"Nah." Sylvie shook her head, making her ponytail swing. "It will mess up Marcia's bookkeeping if I don't stay the full two hours. Besides, you'll need help putting all the stuff away."

"I'll stay, too," Carl answered quickly, eyes glued on Sylvie, who pinked up under his scrutiny.

Marcia opened the door and held it wide for two women to enter. Both were tall, with skin colors that fell somewhere closer to Sylvie and Tomas's light bronze than Carl's dark brown. One woman appeared to be in her seventies, her gray hair pulled into a tidy bun, and the other looked closer to forty. Marcia led them to the front and made introductions as they sat at the bench beside Mr. Gardiner. "This is Emily Leota and her daughter Megan. Carl and Sylvie are assisting Tomas today."

The older woman, Emily, murmured hello to everyone while Megan grinned at Tomas. "Nice to see you again," she said.

Frowning, Tomas shook his head. "I'm sorry, I don't remember meeting you."

"That's okay," Megan said. "It was dark, and I was in uniform."

"Oh! You're the cop." He ignored Sylvie and Carl's interested looks. "Glad you were able to come."

"I called the activity coordinator at the senior center to find out what happened to everyone else. She told me that their bus broke down and they don't have a way to get people here. Everyone is very disappointed to miss the class, so I told her we'd reschedule it." Marica gave Tomas a hopeful look when she finished her explanation.

He nodded and looked at the others. "Let's get started. You can each have your own workbench, and Carl and Sylvie will assist if necessary."

Carl went to stand beside Emily Leota while Sylvie moved closer to Mr. Gardiner. He picked up an electronic stud finder and opened his mouth to say something, but Sylvie got there first.

"No jokes or I'll take it away from you," she warned, waving a finger at him.

Chuckling, the old man put it down. "Yes, ma'am," he said.

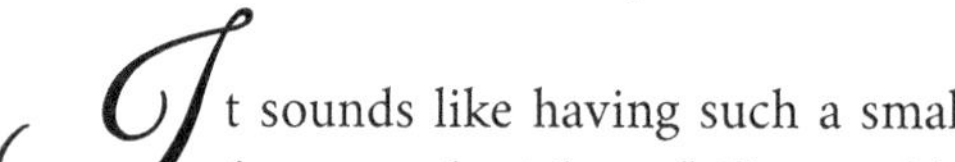

"It sounds like having such a small turnout made for a good trial run," Fiona said, dishing up the Thai food she'd picked up on the way home. "I wish I could have been there."

"That's okay. Apparently, I'm doing another one for the people who couldn't make it this time." Tomas plucked the cat off a dining chair and deposited her on the couch before sitting at the table.

"Any big takeaways from the day?" Fiona asked, handing him a plate.

"Yeah, keep Carl away from my sister."

Fiona laughed. "Why? What did he do?"

His eyebrows beetled together, Tomas poked at his food, not saying anything. Fiona hid her smile behind her water glass. Protective big brother was a side she hadn't seen before, and it was pretty darn cute. "Was he showing her how to handle a tool?" She blinked innocently at Tomas's scowl and giggled. "Seriously, was he being a jerk? Because that doesn't seem like Carl." The youngest of KBS's contractors reminded her of a Labrador puppy, friendly, eager, and ready to try anything.

"No…." Tomas drew out his answer, still frowning. "I was supposed to ask you to talk to Sylvie about career counseling, but I forgot. Mom and Carlos are worried that she can't seem to settle and doesn't have a clear path."

"Okay, but what does that have to do with Carl?"

"I don't have a problem with Carl. I just don't want her to…." He flicked a glance at Fiona before staring down at his plate. "I want her to figure shit out sooner than I did, and not drift from job to job."

Fiona forked up some noodles, thinking about what he'd said. "And you think dating Carl would distract her from figuring things out?"

Little One strolled over to rub against Tomas's leg and stared up at him. As much as the cat lived at Fiona's house, Tomas was clearly her person. He reached down to scratch her ears before answering Fiona's question. "Maybe?"

"And maybe Carl could be a good influence on her. You've told me he's a good worker."

Tomas nodded. "Oh yeah. The kid's come a long way, and I don't expect him to stick around KBS much longer. Customers like him and I know big building firms are trying to poach him. He's got a great future ahead of him."

"So would it be so bad if Sylvie spent time with him?" Fiona prodded.

"I suppose not," he said grudgingly before finally eating his dinner.

She wasn't going to say anything else, but Fiona suspected that if Tomas tried to interfere with Sylvie's love life, he'd get an earful. Part of her wanted to be a fly on the wall for that conversation.

Seeming more relaxed, Tomas finished his meal and pushed the plate away to rest his elbows on the table. "We've never talked about the future."

Fiona toyed with her fork, wondering where he was going with that comment. "Not really."

"You haven't been divorced that long. Do you think you want to marry again?"

"I hadn't thought about marrying again. That is, not until Mother invited Pastor Andy to dinner."

Tomas caught her eye, lips quirked up. "That worked out for Joseph, though."

"Yeah. They're a cute couple and if Joseph doesn't screw it up, this might work."

"Have you heard from your mother?"

Frowning, she shook her head. It hurt that her mother's pride was more important to her than her daughter's happiness. Her mother did not apologize; Fiona had always acquiesced. But this was too big, and she wasn't going to back down. "What she said was wrong. Even if you weren't in a relationship with me, she has no excuse for saying that."

"I've heard it before."

Fiona lifted her head and met his bitter gaze. "Still, that doesn't make it right. I don't know when I'll hear from her."

"How is that going to affect our project?"

"That's business, and I know my father likes the idea. It shouldn't be hard to convince the other family members, and with Joseph beside me, I think it will be fine." Yeah, her mother would jump at the chance to lead a venture that brought a lot of positive attention her way.

Tomas didn't push. Just accepted her answer and changed the subject.

"So, marriage. If you met a guy who had a record, worked with his hands, was a bit overprotective, and shit with words, would you consider marrying him?"

Mouth suddenly dry, Fiona fortified herself with a sip of water. Having seen her at her worst and knowing all her ugly secrets, he should be the one having reservations about marrying *her*. "Yes. I'd consider it."

The tightness around Tomas's eyes relaxed. "I won't push you. We've got time, and when you're ready, we'll talk about it. But I want you to know that I'm all in. You're it for me."

"You're it for me, too," she replied softly as warmth flooded through her.

As far as proposals went, it wasn't the most romantic. Eddie had gotten down on one knee in a high-end restaurant to present her with an ostentatious engagement ring. And look how well that went. She could see Tomas in her future, but as a husband? The thought scared and excited her at the same time. However, there was something she needed to know. "Do you want children?"

"Yeah. But I'm not in a hurry. You?"

"I don't know." If this was a deal breaker, they may as well face it now. She searched his eyes for a reaction. He didn't flinch; he didn't pull back. Simply nodded. "My childhood was fine, but my mother was cold. I don't want to be—"

Tomas cut her off. "You aren't your mother. And if you choose, I think you would be a great mother. Again, we've got time."

"You can father children for the next forty years. But if we wait too long, or I can't have children…" she trailed off. After realizing Eddie had married her as a business arrangement, she'd put children firmly out of her mind. He'd be a crappy father, and Fiona wouldn't allow children to be used as pawns.

Her father would probably love grandchildren. Her mother would be more interested in continuing the family business. Having seen the closeness of Tomas's family, the generous, loving heart of Louisa, and the quiet acceptance of Carlos, she knew they would be awesome grandparents. The kind who wanted to be involved and could be counted on when needed.

Tomas reached across the table to take her hand, guiding her out of her seat and around to his lap. He pulled her down and held her loosely, looking into her worried eyes with a warm, loving gaze. "My father took off when I was so young I don't remember him. I had uncles and cousins and grandfathers to take his place. I was a little shit, and I made his life miserable, but Carlos *is* my dad. Not by blood; by choice.

"I want to be with *you,* with or without kids. I won't pressure you to get pregnant. If we do decide, and we can't have kids of our own, I'm happy to adopt and raise a child with you."

"Yeah?" For the first time ever, raising a family—especially if it was with Tomas, held her interest. With the way he treated her, she knew any children they had would be loved unconditionally.

"Yeah. In fact, if you want to practice, my cousin Johnny has twins. We can borrow them."

"You can't borrow kids!"

"Sure, you can. Johnny says they're exhausting, and he and his wife Esme would love to get rid of them for a while. They'd probably pay us."

Fiona's eyes narrowed at his grin. "I think that's called babysitting."

"Whatever." Tomas shrugged in dismissal. "Just say the word and we can be practice parents for a few hours. We can also practice *making* babies." He leaned closer, gliding his nose along hers, then across her cheek to her ear. His low voice sent delightful shivers through her body. "That's probably more fun."

"I like practicing. In fact, we can practice all night if you want."

He rose from the chair with her in his arms, and in a few short strides, they were in the bedroom. They took care of the dishes much, much later.

CHAPTER 28

The original office for Han Family Holdings was above the first nail salon her parents ever opened. It had fake wood paneling, stained carpets, and fluorescent lights that buzzed. Fiona remembered doing her homework at a chipped Formica table that also held a photocopier and coffee maker. HFH was now located in a sleek, freestanding building with meticulously trimmed shrubbery surrounding it. It was bland, cold, and professional—much like her mother.

Joseph was getting out of his car as Fiona pulled into the parking lot. Scanning the lot, she saw both her parents' cars as well. Even though they lived together and worked together, her parents took separate vehicles because of their differing work habits.

Scrolling through his phone, Joseph waited for Fiona, shooting her a wry grin as she drew closer. "You're wearing jeans. And your hair is down. Wow. Mother's going to blow a gasket."

"You should talk." She removed her sunglasses as her gaze traveled over him, taking in the khaki slacks, unbuttoned and untucked shirt with the sleeves rolled up, and topsider shoes without socks. Joseph was much more relaxed since he'd started dating Andy, and she was happy for him.

"They're expecting me. I'm updating them about the automotive shop purchase. I didn't say you were joining me."

"Good. It'll probably piss Mother off, but Dad won't mind."

Turning as one, they walked the short distance to the entrance. Joseph opened the door, and Fiona entered first, waved at the receptionist, and proceeded to her mother's office. She stopped just short of the open door, her palms sweating. She hadn't seen or spoken to her mother in three weeks, while calls and visits from her father had increased. It was as if her mother's outburst had broken down a wall between them. A wall that neither Fiona nor her father could see but had felt for years. Taking a breath, she looked into Joseph's eyes, seeing the same determination she felt. He cocked his head toward the door with a tight smile, moved past her, and walked into the room, Fiona right behind him.

Her mother's office was similar to her mother herself. It was a place of business. Clean, organized, with bare walls and expensive, functional furniture, lacking personality. A large desk dominated the space, with two straight-backed armless chairs in front of it. To the right was a conference table surrounded by similar chairs. A flowering plant sat on the table, looking out of place. It was from her father's greenhouse, the only indication that her mother had a life outside her office.

Seated at the head of the table, her mother didn't look up when they entered but did so when her father gasped. Nostrils flaring, back straightening, Linh Han's cold glance swept over her children.

David moved around the table and took Fiona's hand. "It's good to see you," he said with a smile that crinkled his eyes.

Fiona returned his smile. "You too, Dad." She looked past him and met her mother's gaze. "Hello, Mother."

"Why are you here? I wasn't expecting you." She turned accusing eyes toward Joseph.

He ignored their mother. Instead, with a hand on Fiona's back, he ushered her to the conference table, where they each took a seat. Their father returned to his chair across from Fiona and Joseph and pushed aside the papers in front of him, looking curious.

"We want to propose something to the company. An opportunity to assist the community while promoting HFH." They'd decided Joseph would speak first as Fiona was no longer part of the day-to-day operations of the family's business.

"Did you know about this?" Linh Han shot an accusing glare at her husband.

"No. But I think we should listen." He gave Fiona a barely perceptible wink. Apparently, he didn't share everything with his wife.

She huffed. "Very well. Continue."

Fiona and Joseph tag-teamed their parents for the next thirty minutes, setting out how the venture would benefit HFH and Keeney.

"Remember the fire that broke out after the fourth of July three years ago?" Joseph drew their attention to an event still haunting the community. A dry spring led to a tinder-like summer. That, combined with illegal fireworks, caused a fire that ended in three deaths. Pointed fingers and lawsuits meant that the five houses in the cul-de-sac where the fire occurred were never rebuilt. They stood scarred and empty, a blight in an otherwise attractive neighborhood. The burned-out buildings drew the attention of vandals and squatters, causing headaches for the police.

"I've spoken with the city manager. The city bought the houses and is willing to sell them to HFH for our project.

They like the idea of Keeney Builds working with low-income families, and using sweat equity to create homes. With the houses being close to the high school and walking distance to an elementary school, families will jump at this."

Fiona watched her parents exchange glances. Her father was openly interested, smiling slightly. Linh Han's expression was harder to read, but she was definitely paying attention.

She spoke while looking directly at her mother. "With support from Keeney Building Supply, Tomas will be working with the families. Acting as the general contractor, being on-site to supervise the work, and providing instruction where necessary. The families will work together until all five houses are habitable."

"Tomas? What nationalities will these families be?" Her mother's lips curled into a sneer.

Fiona's eyes flashed, but it was Joseph who answered. "Does it matter? Andy will be working with other churches and non-profit agencies to find families willing to do the work and are in the position to be able to put money into it."

"A down payment?" Her father was scratching numbers on a tablet of paper. "Isn't that the sticking point for most people, coming up with a down payment?"

"Yeah, which is why we're going to eliminate that. Secure promissory notes with low, fixed interest rates that won't skyrocket in the future and cripple families. With the amount of attention this will draw, I don't think reneging on a loan will be a problem."

"We won't make any money that way," Linh Han protested.

"This isn't about making money. We will recoup our costs over time, but the more important thing is that Keeney families benefit, and the whole community benefits," Fiona said. "That's more important."

Her mother ignored her. "They should be citizens."

"Why?" Fiona challenged her. "You and Dad weren't citizens when you bought your first house."

"We didn't need a handout. We did—"

David Han put a hand over his wife's arm, drawing her attention. "It is a good idea." He spoke directly to her. "You've been looking for a legacy. This will be it. Supporting families to work together and build a community while building homes. This is how we give back to a community that's supported us. Yes?" At her reluctant nod he turned to Fiona and Joseph, and smiled. "We will convene a board meeting for you to make a presentation. Bring Tomas and Andy. The other family members will no doubt have questions and will want to meet them."

Her mother muttered under her breath while her father rose and walked around the table. He placed a hand on each of his children's shoulders. "I'm proud of you. This is a great idea."

Joseph and Fiona grinned at each other. They gathered their things, said goodbye to their mother, and followed their father out to the reception area. "Well done," he said, putting his hands together in silent applause. "This is exactly what a legacy should be. Improving lives for others is so much better than a stone monument."

"It was Tomas's idea—not the legacy part, but the idea of working beside people who need help getting into homes. When he shared it with me, I knew it was worthwhile pursuing. I'm glad you think so, too." Fiona smiled up at her father.

"Your young man is exceptional. I really need to make time to work with him. Maybe he'll let me use one of those nail guns." Their father looked between Fiona and Joseph, smiling broadly. "I'm glad you each found someone worthy of you." Kissing Fiona on the forehead, he grasped Joseph's shoulder and then returned to his wife's office.

"Wow. That was—"

"Almost way too easy." Joseph opened the door and stood back for Fiona to precede him out of the building.

"Mother's not happy," she said.

"Yeah. She has me worried. But Dad's firmly on our side, and that's a big deal."

They made plans to meet up soon, both heading for their cars to get on with their days. Beeping the lock to open her car door, Fiona hoped and prayed that the tingling nerves were a letdown from the meeting, not a premonition of things to come.

"*H*ave you set a date?"

Tomas sputtered into his coffee and glared at Ali. "What?"

"A wedding date," Ali spoke as if addressing a young child.

"We're not there yet," Tomas growled, wiping coffee off his shirt. They'd just started exploring the idea. Talking about dates was way in the future.

"What's taking so long?"

"Asks the guy who's never been married." Vincent strolled into the KBS break room with a shit-eating grin on his face. "And are you ever gonna make an honest woman out of my mother?"

A dull red blush stole up Ali's cheeks and colored his bald head. He muttered something about invoices and beat a hasty retreat, the sound of Vincent's laughter trailing behind him.

Vincent cocked his head in the direction of KBS's chief operating officer's speedy departure. "I love messing with him."

Tomas smirked in acknowledgment, going to his locker to retrieve a clean shirt. He turned back to find Vincent leaning against the counter, studying him over a steaming cup of coffee, a warm smile on his face.

"What?"

"Proud of you, bro. I've heard about this idea of yours, and it is really gonna make a difference for families in Keeney."

Feigning indifference, Tomas shrugged. "Fiona's done all the heavy lifting. Her and her brother, Joseph."

"Uh-uh. She's crediting you with the idea. From you, it extends to Keeney Builds and KBS. *We* look good because of your forward thinking." Vincent raised his coffee mug in salute.

"Thanks, but we're not out of the woods yet. The board of HFH has to sign off on it before we can get the funding. When that happens, it's go time." Tomas stepped past Vincent to rinse out his coffee mug and leave it on the draining board. He was pleased and excited while at the same time feeling like he was an unarmed gladiator about to enter the Coliseum, afraid to be chewed up and spit out. Fiona said that the meeting with her parents had gone well and that it was just a matter of convincing the other board members. It was strange to think that his idea had stirred such excitement.

"Not that long ago, you and I were lining up with metal trays in a prison dining hall. Now you're making corporate presentations." Vincent elbowed him.

"Don't remind me," Tomas muttered. "I hate this shit."

"I hear ya." Vincent and Tomas had made the presentation that brought Keeney Builds to life. They'd sweat bullets that day, and it hadn't gotten any easier. "Ma told me your mother is helping select the families for the homes."

Tomas leaned against the counter beside Vincent, staring absently out the window overlooking the floor of KBS. "Yeah, she's thrilled."

"You don't sound happy. You don't think she should do it?"

Tomas shook his head. "No. That part's fine. She'd be

great at it. Knows lots of people, has lots of connections. It's just…." He turned to face Vincent fully. "You heard what Fiona's mother said about me. If she treats my mother like shit, I'm gonna lose it." He didn't need to say any more. Vincent's mother was Native American, and his father had Mexican heritage. He'd experienced similar racist comments and was fiercely protective of his own mother. "And if that happens, what does it mean for Fiona and me? We're both tight with our families, so if things fall apart…."

"Now you're buying trouble. I don't know Fiona's mother, but I hear she's a savvy businesswoman. Her reputation means a lot to her, so I doubt she's gonna make waves. What does your mom think?"

"She's more forgiving than I am, expects Linh Han to apologize, and hopes I'll accept it."

"And will you?"

"Maybe. For Fiona's sake, I might." It would need to be more than an apology. It would need to be stepping back from trying to control Fiona's life. If she couldn't do that, she might lose Fiona forever. He didn't want her to lose her mother, but if Linh Han continued to be toxic, Fiona stepping away from her might be the healthiest thing for her.

Her father had stepped forward, and Fiona had accepted his apology. He was also keenly interested in the tiny house builds and seemed to accept Tomas for exactly who he was. This made Fiona happy, and that's all Tomas cared about.

The deal Carlos and Joseph worked out to buy Woodbine Automotive was going smoothly, which was good. Tomas hadn't seen it, but was assured that the contract was solid, and that Carlos would not be screwed over. HFH were investors, but Carlos would run the shop the way he wanted.

He drifted over to the window and stood watching the hive of activity that was KBS on a Tuesday afternoon. He'd been an employee for a little over a year and a half and marveled at the changes. Recognizing that older people preferred face-to-face interactions rather than looking things up online or talking on the phone, Hilary had installed a kiosk in one corner of the store specifically for people wanting to hire a contractor, and it was a success. Staffed by students going through the Keeney Builds program, it brought energy to the store.

She'd also installed monitors above the cash registers. Customers standing in line were treated to a loop of how-to videos featuring Keeney Builds students working with women and senior citizens. These stemmed from the conversation Tomas, Fiona, and Iris had had. Next to the checkout counters were free laminated cards detailing the tools required to finish each job and the QR code needed to access the video on their own. Pride swelled in Tomas's chest, knowing he'd been a part of these changes.

Vincent joined him at the window. Without looking at him, Tomas said, "I remember Eddie telling me there wasn't a job here for me. I wasn't surprised. I didn't believe you'd found a place for us that easily. Guys like us, we're not supposed to have it good." Feeling Vincent stiffen beside him, he shot him a side eye. "That's what I thought *then*. I've got it good; work I love, a supportive family, a chance to do good, and a woman who wants me. I'm glad you chased me down and dragged me back here. I'm glad you forced me to get my head out of my ass."

"Damn straight." Vincent nudged him with a shoulder, and they watched the floor, lost in their own thoughts.

Down below, a pretty young woman entered, looking around as if seeking someone. As if drawn by his gaze, she looked up to the window. Tomas knew she couldn't see him but waved anyway.

"Who's that?"

"My sister Sylvie. She's here for a job interview."

"Yeah? On the floor?"

"No. An assistant for Hilary, Ali, and Marcia." Tomas was

proud and nervous at the same time. "It's a second interview. She impressed Marcia when she assisted me with the class. Sylvie thought they were just talking and didn't realize it was an interview."

"Ma's sneaky that way," Vincent said with a grin. "She ferrets out information better than the FBI."

"I believe it. Now Sylvie's here to meet Hilary."

Vincent clapped Tomas on the shoulder and went over to the sink to dump his coffee. "I hope it works out. That would mean my wife won't be working so hard." He waggled his eyebrows. "Seriously, you're gonna rock that presentation. And I hope things work out with Fiona's mother."

The churning in Tomas's gut was back. He told himself Linh Han loved her daughter and wanted Fiona to be happy. If only that really were the case.

CHAPTER 29

"Seriously? Is this how you prepare for big meetings?" Hands on his hips, Joseph glared at Andy holding aloft a bottle of tequila.

Fiona and Tomas, Joseph and Andy stood in the parking lot outside of HFH minutes before they were due to make their presentation to the board. Fiona didn't know about the others, but her nerves were jangling, and the calming effects of morning sex with Tomas were a distant memory.

She'd presented to organizations and spoken before audiences big and small without breaking a sweat. This one was different. Personal. As much as she wanted the project for the community, she wanted it for Tomas. He wasn't smooth and polished, but his heart was in the right place. Hopefully, the board would be able to see that. As if sensing her unease, he stepped closer, his big hand circling her back with calming strokes.

"Only when the bishop is present." Shooting an impish grin at Joseph, Andy produced four shot glasses, poured, and passed around the fiery liquid. They each held up their glasses. "Working with each of you these past weeks has been a bright spot in my day. When businesses, non-profits, and faith communities work together, magic can happen. So let's make it happen. To magic!"

"To magic!" The others joined in and tossed back the shots.

Eyes watering, Fiona coughed. Tomas took the empty shot glass from her hand and replaced it with a water bottle. She smiled at him gratefully. The warmth in his eyes, combined with the warmth of the alcohol, moved through her, and her heart rate decreased slightly. What had she done to deserve him?

Waking to find his large form beside her was quickly becoming her favorite part of the day. The nights he didn't sleep with her were few and far between, and when that happened, they'd talk on the phone until they were both yawning, and she'd awaken to find sweet text messages waiting for her. When she'd signed the divorce papers a few months ago, the idea of marrying again was furthest from her mind. But Tomas was making her reconsider.

He asked her opinion. He listened to her concerns without leaping up to fix them. He suggested but didn't demand. He was generous without expecting anything in return.

She pinched his arm. "Ow! What was that for?"

She gave him her most innocent smile. "Just checking if you're real."

"O-kay…." He looked at her like she'd lost her mind.

And maybe she had. A presentation to HFH's board was not how she'd expected to introduce her future husband to her family. And while the question hadn't been officially asked and answered, Fiona knew it would happen.

"What kind of questions are you anticipating?" Andy looked at Joseph while adjusting his clerical collar. She'd gotten so used to thinking of him as a friend and Joseph's boyfriend that she had forgotten he was a pastor.

When Joseph failed to respond, Andy elbowed him in the

ribs. "Hmm? Sorry. Can't tell you. I just know it will be unlike any other HFH board meeting." He shot them each a tight smile before turning and heading toward the building, dropping his empty plastic shot glass into a trash can beside the entry.

The worry was back in Fiona's belly. Exchanging questioning looks with the other men, she followed her brother into the building.

$\mathcal{A}$ sense of unease crawled up the back of Tomas's neck as he watched Fiona and her brother.

"Where is everyone?" she asked.

Fiona clearly expected to see her parents and eight cousins, but the conference room was empty. The big table was bare, and all sixteen padded chairs were pushed in. She looked at Joseph, eyebrows raised in question. "Did the time get changed?"

A muscle ticked in Joseph's jaw, but before he could answer, the rear door of the room opened, and their mother walked in.

"You're here." She nodded at her children, smiled politely at Andy, and ignored Tomas completely.

So this was how it was gonna be. He remained stoic as he moved to stand right behind Fiona, putting himself in Linh Han's sightline.

"Yes. Where is the rest of the family?" Fiona dropped her tote bag into a chair and sorted through it, pulling out file folders for each person in attendance. "Did you tell them a later time so we can get set up?"

With a condescending smile, Linh Han moved closer, stopping behind the chair at the end of the table, and draping her hands over the padded leather top. "That won't be necessary. The presentation has been canceled." She turned to Andy. "Sorry for the inconvenience."

"What do you mean, canceled?" Fiona straightened, clutching the folders to her chest.

"Exactly that. HFH isn't interested in your proposal so there was no point in meeting."

"You can't do that. Joseph and I are board members. Decisions can't be made without us."

A satisfied smile formed on Linh Han's face. "Oh, but I can. Joseph's idea of buying that cul-de-sac of burned-out homes is excellent. I have a friend on the Keeney planning board, so I was able to secure the property at a great price. That neighborhood is attractive, and HFH will have no problem finding buyers for the two luxury houses we will build."

"But that doesn't help the community. Our idea was to help lower-income families get into their own homes." Anger now radiated off Fiona. Tomas placed a big hand on her shoulder in reassurance.

Linh Han caught the gesture and looked at him for the first time, her lip curled in derision. "HFH wants to support families who will add something to Keeney, not be a burden on its resources."

"I don't understand how you can do that!" Fiona clutched the folders with white-knuckled hands.

Joseph spoke for the first time. "She bought their shares."

Fiona gasped.

Linh Han smiled. "That's right. The cousins were happy to sell their shares to me. I now have a controlling interest, so luxury homes it will be. Pastor Andy, when they've been sold, I will make a sizable donation to the church. You can use it to do a feeding program or maybe education. Something for the unfortunate in the community."

"Don't make promises you can't keep, my dear. You don't, in fact, own controlling interest."

Heads turned at the quiet words from David Han. He stepped forward, approaching Andy first to shake his hand, then turning his attention to Tomas.

Tomas looked down at the older man. Iron gray hair brushed back, he stood erect, dressed in neatly pressed khaki pants and a button-down shirt. "Hello, sir. It's good to see you again."

"David. Please call me David." His dark eyes, so much like Fiona's, roved over Tomas's face. "My daughter tells me that it was your idea to rebuild these houses as a community project. I'm looking forward to hearing more."

"Yes sir, I mean David." Tomas returned his smile, wondering why he appeared so relaxed.

David moved to stand beside Joseph, patting his arm in lieu of a handshake.

Tomas didn't know Linh Han well enough to be able to decipher her expression. But she sure as hell didn't look happy.

"What do you mean, David? I secured those shares yesterday." Her manicured hands clutched the back of the chair, the knuckles whitening with her grip.

"Actually, you didn't. Not all of them. As the CFO, your cousin Reggie called me and asked if he could receive payment sooner. Needless to say, I was confused. When I understood what he was talking about, I raised your offer. The money should be going into his account…." David looked at his wristwatch. "My mistake. The transfer occurred thirty minutes ago."

Her eyes shooting daggers at her husband, Linh Han hissed. "That's not enough, though. I have fifty-five percent of the company. HFH will not fund housing for dirty Mexicans." She focused on Tomas, speaking to him directly for the first time ever. "You people make me sick. Sneaking into the country illegally, breeding like rabbits, always wanting a handout. Your mother has the ear of my pastor. Your father is stealing my son from the business. And my daughter is allowing you, a convict, to sleep in her bed, put your dirty hands all over her!"

"Enough!" Five voices roared in unison.

Chest heaving, Linh Han clamped her mouth shut. Her eyes darted back and forth across the angry faces ranged in front of her. "I own fifty-five percent of the company. Your proposal will not go ahead."

David turned to face the others and bowed slightly. "I'm sorry you had to see that. My wife's words and actions are unforgivable." He moved to stand between Joseph and Fiona and put his arms around them. "After my conversation with Reggie, I conferred with Joseph. Between the two of us, we called the other cousins. They each agreed to the amounts we offered for their shares. So, no, my dear, you do not own fifty-five percent of the company." He squeezed his children. "We own eighty-five percent."

Linh Han screamed.

Fiona gasped.

Tomas snorted.

Andy high-fived Joseph. "Well played," he said.

Linh Han attempted a rally. "You can't afford that. You don't have the money."

"Yes, mother, he does." Joseph crossed his arms and looked smug. "Every year, instead of buying a new car, Dad's been investing. His portfolio is doing quite well."

Linh Han gaped at her husband. "How much…how much did you pay them."

David clasped his hands in front of him and rocked up on the balls of his feet. "When I explained what was being proposed, they each agreed to sell me their shares for one dollar more than what you offered. Except for Reggie, he insisted on two. He always drove a hard bargain." He rubbed his hands briskly and beamed around the room. "Shall we take a vote? All in favor of endorsing the proposal?"

Joseph, Fiona, and David shot their hands in the air.

"Motion carried. Now, how about I treat you all to lunch? Tomas, I've yet to try your family's restaurant." He ushered the younger people out of the conference room, turning at the door to say to his wife, "Please turn out the lights on your way out."

Tomas lifted a dazed Fiona into his truck. She barely noticed as he buckled her seat belt. She was still staring at the front of the building as he settled behind the steering wheel. "You okay?"

"I don't know. That was...." Tears started coursing down her cheeks.

Leaning over the console, Tomas cradled her head, drawing her closer. "It's okay."

"No, it's not. My mother is—"

"A shitty human being."

Fiona snorted, blowing snot bubbles. Feeling slightly relieved, Tomas opened the glove box, found some napkins, and handed them to her.

"I won't try to sugarcoat it. Not only is she racist, but she's greedy and ruthless."

"She's always been cold, but I never thought of her as heartless." After wiping her eyes, Fiona held the crumpled napkin tightly, not looking at Tomas. "So yeah, that's my family. Nice introduction, right?"

"Your dad was pretty awesome."

She turned to him, a wondering look in her eyes. "I don't know where that came from. He's always deferred to her, standing in the background. But today he was so decisive."

"She's probably never gone off the rails like that before. And you gotta know, after what she said about my family, I don't ever want to see her again." Repressed anger bubbled up to the surface. He did his best to keep it out of his voice. "I know that puts you in a tight spot but—"

Fiona shook her head vehemently. "No. I agree. I have no

desire to see her, either. But for now, I don't want to talk about her or even think about her. I'm just sorry…." She choked on a sob and leaned into his warmth.

Wrapping his arms around her, he held her until the tears subsided. Fiona was warm and loving and thoughtful, always going overboard to help others improve their lives. It had to be killing her to discover the truth about her mother. Tomas didn't get it. His own mother opened her heart to everyone she met. She held strong opinions, but at the end of the day, she believed there was room at the table for everyone. He pulled back, kissing Fiona gently on the forehead, and started the truck.

The drive to the restaurant wasn't long, and he spotted his mother standing by the door when he pulled into the parking lot. He hadn't even turned off the engine before Louisa was tugging open the passenger door and enveloping Fiona in a tight hug. He met his mother's gaze and, at her nod, got out of the truck and went into the restaurant, leaving the two women alone.

He found the others at a large table. Carlos had joined them, and Andy was animatedly giving him a blow-by-blow description of the morning. His stepfather tipped his chin up in greeting, and Joseph raised an eyebrow in question while David pulled out the chair beside him. "My mother is with Fiona," Tomas told them, settling into his chair. Joseph pushed a beer toward him and turned his head toward Andy, draping a possessive arm around the back of his chair.

"My children have each found partners who are worthy of them." David sipped his beer and glanced up at Tomas. "You've now seen our dirty laundry. I hope you aren't thrown off by it."

Tomas's smile was unamused. "Thrown off? No. But don't expect me to forgive and forget." He wondered what kind of marriage Fiona's parents had that her dad could have been so unaware of his wife's thoughts and activities.

"I wouldn't expect you to. I've been a fool," David spoke softly, but the others at the table heard him and gave him their undivided attention. "Our children were cared for, educated, and uncomplaining. So I looked past my wife's prejudices and controlling behavior in order to keep the peace. I see I should have paid more attention and spoken up long ago. It may have prevented this from happening."

"I don't know if you could have prevented it." Fiona stood at the side of the table, eyes puffy from crying but otherwise looking composed. Louisa was behind her, an arm around her waist protectively, looking like the fierce, loving mother Fiona deserved but never had. "Mother is not wired to be compassionate. She's too self-involved."

David looked like he was about to protest, but Joseph got there first. "Fiona's right. Mother had an agenda, and Tomas screwed with it."

"Actually, I think it was more that his mother screwed with it," Andy spoke up, his gaze focused on Louisa. "You're a natural-born leader. People listen to you. The congregation respects Linh Han's ability to get things done, but they don't like her. She only has time for someone if they can do something for her. I think when Fiona chose Tomas, that was fanning the flame. She can't get rid of you, Louisa, but she could destroy something that held value to you."

Tomas watched his mother, seeing her thoughts and feelings chase each other across her face. Although he'd never thought of it that way, Andy was bang-on. His mother was a leader. At the moment, she appeared troubled. "I don't know what to say. I've never had angry words with your mother. We worked together a few times, got along good, so I don't know…."

David rose to approach her. "Mrs. Santiago, I doubt you did anything but be yourself. The blame is totally on my wife."

"Okay," she said through watery eyes. "Please, call me Louisa."

Acknowledging the invitation with a slight bow, David extended his hand. "I will if you call me David. I think we should be on a first-name basis as we are going to be family."

"Dad!"

"What?"

"Tomas and I aren't there yet."

"Well, you should be. I'm not getting any younger."

Fiona glared at her father as she moved to the chair Tomas pulled out for her. "Sorry," she said quietly. "I wasn't expecting that."

Taking her hand, Tomas kissed the inside of her wrist. "No worries. You know I'm on board with the idea."

A server arrived with a tray filled with tortilla chips, salsa, and guacamole, as well as a pot of tea for Louisa and Fiona. Louisa settled into a chair between Carlos and Fiona and looked fondly at her son, clearly pleased with the idea.

Directing the conversation away from Fiona, Tomas spoke to Andy. "Are you gonna kick Linh Han out of the church?"

Andy still wore his clerical collar, not concerned about being seen having a beer. "I can't kick her out. I will ask her to step down from her leadership roles and make a public statement about not condoning racist language and behavior. It will draw attention to your families, so it's up to you. But I think I should." He ran his hand up and down Joseph's back.

Joseph leaned into him with a tired smile on his face. "That will suck but I think you should, too. Mother has to understand that her actions have consequences, and losing her status in the community is the best way for her to do that. Dad? Fiona?"

Sitting back, Tomas observed the Han family, thinking it was telling that Fiona and Joseph called their father Dad, while referring to Linh Han as Mother. Gripping his hand, Fiona leaned across him to claim her father's attention. Neither looked happy, but both were resolute and nodded at Joseph.

"And your family?" Andy glanced at Tomas before focusing on Louisa and Carlos.

"This is hard. On one hand the words 'turn the other cheek' are being whispered in my ear. But on the other...." Louisa sighed, not looking happy. She exchanged glances with Carlos before speaking directly to Tomas. "When you went to prison, I feared for your life. I *know* things happened to you that you won't tell me. I know some of those things happened because you are Latino. I couldn't do anything then. I can now." She shifted in her chair to see Andy more clearly. "I don't think of myself as a leader. I do know I *am* a role model." She waved at the restaurant. "I have staff who watch me and two daughters I hope look up to me. They would suffer if I sat back and did nothing. So, yes. Make the statement."

Tension eased out of Tomas. At the same time, he felt Fiona stiffen beside him. This was going to suck for both of them, both their families. Sensing his concern, she squeezed his hand and squared her shoulders. "HFH needs to make a statement as well. Mother should be terminated, and a letter of explanation should be sent to all tenants. I know that's going to leave a gap, but Joseph, if you and I—"

"No. It's time I step up," David spoke up, placing his elbows on the table and steepling his hands. "I've been hanging out in the greenhouse instead of working. I may need some help, but I can run this company. You should also know I will be speaking to a divorce lawyer. I don't want to talk about it right now, but you need to know that. Now, can we talk about something else? Like turning those burned-out houses into homes?"

Murmurs of agreement were heard. As the conversation started, it became clear that the process would be much smoother without having to appease Linh Han. As ideas started to flow and the conversation got animated, Tomas tugged Fiona up from the table and walked her toward a quiet corner of the restaurant. Turning her so that she was sheltered from view by his big body, he cradled her face and studied her. Color was returning to her cheeks, but she looked exhausted.

"What can I do?" he asked, drawing his thumbs across her cheekbones.

She leaned into him. "Love me."

"I already do." This tiny, determined woman with big ideas had wormed her way into his heart ages ago. Letting her know freed him.

Tears welled in her eyes. "I want us to be a family," she whispered.

He whispered back, "Just say where and when. I'll be there."

CHAPTER 30

Six Months Later....

Aware of the many eyes on her, Fiona walked slowly down the aisle. She stopped before the altar, stepped to the right, and turned to face the back of the sanctuary. A tall woman with dark hair shorn close to her head stood across from her. She nodded at Fiona and winked. Fiona's eye roll was imperceptible to the guests, but Lauren, Andy's sister, caught it. Wearing matching mint green dresses with hoop skirts and giant bows on their butts, they looked like they'd stepped out of *Gone With the Wind*.

They'd both balked, stating they weren't bridesmaids but best women. Andy was vehement. It was his wedding. He was paying for the dresses, and they would wear them. Fortunately, he'd agreed to allow them to change after the ceremony and before the reception. A sunshine yellow sundress hung in the back of Tomas's truck, along with accessories. Fiona didn't know what Lauren was going to do with her dress, but she intended to donate hers to the high school drama department. There was no way it was going home with her.

A bee had found its way into the church and hovered over her bouquet. Not interested in the white freesia or peach roses, it drifted off to the tall pillar of hydrangea behind the pastor. The sanctuary had been decorated to within an inch of its life, draped in fresh flowers and tulle. Fiona didn't think she'd ever been to a more ornate wedding in her life. While the organist played softly, Fiona searched for Tomas. Among the mostly Vietnamese guests, he wasn't difficult to find. Wearing a light gray jacket and slacks with a crisp white shirt, he drew many admiring eyes. He'd refused to wear a tie, and the open collar of his shirt exposed the golden skin of his neck. He caught her glance and smirked, then raised his phone to snap a picture. She narrowed her eyes, which only served to make him laugh outright.

The change in the music had her switch her attention to the back of the church. Joseph and her father entered first, her father smiling proudly, Joseph looking relaxed and amused. They both wore dark gray suits with tails. Behind them, Andy stood between his parents, beaming at everyone as they moved down the aisle. He wore tails as well, only his were white and, whereas the other men had mint green cummerbunds, his was peach. This was his day, and he was in his glory.

The ceremony ended, and Tomas waited his turn to file out of the church. A movement caught his eye, and he spotted Linh Han standing behind a column, out of sight of her family and the guests assembled for the wedding of her only son. A wedding to which she had not been invited. Looking around, it appeared he was the only one to notice her, so he remained in place, waiting to see if she'd cause a scene. Through the big open doors at the back of the church, Joseph and Andy could be seen holding hands and smiling. Fiona appeared, saying something that caused the two men to laugh loudly and wrap her in a hug. A stifled sob drew Tomas's attention back to Linh Han. He must have made a noise because her eyes met his, and she gasped.

Dressed neatly and expensively as always, her thin, haggard face told the story of the past few months. Served with divorce papers, terminated from HFH, stripped of her leadership roles in the church, and crucified by the press; all had taken a toll on the once-proud woman. Eyes darting around the sanctuary, she was clearly looking for an exit.

"Don't even think of going out front." Tomas jerked his head toward the door and kept talking while slowly approaching her. "You saw the ceremony. They're having a great day. Don't spoil it for them."

She reared back. "I wouldn't do that to my children."

"Forgive me if I don't believe you." He'd cleared the end of the pew and was now less than five feet away. He balanced lightly on his feet, prepared to tackle her if necessary.

"You can't stop me from seeing them."

Tomas removed his jacket and hung it over the back of a pew. Fiona had just bought it for him and would kill him if he split a seam. "Actually, I can. Don't think I won't haul your ass out of here like an unwanted gate crasher. Because that's what you are. Unwanted." He didn't care if he was in a church. He didn't care if this was Fiona's mother. She was a conniving bitch who'd gotten off easy.

"Tomas! Are you coming?"

Fiona's voice caused him to groan inwardly. She didn't need this. Without her mother around, Fiona had relaxed. Her tightly held control had slipped, and she expressed herself more freely, being more demonstrative with those she cared for.

Two months ago, he'd arrived at her apartment after

work to find that she'd moved all his clothes into her closet and dresser. So, he moved in. Other than his drafting table and favorite coffee mug, he left everything behind for his sister Sylvie, who was taking over the lease. On Fiona's hand was the engagement ring he'd given her last night. Fairly simple, a single large diamond set flush into the white gold band. They hadn't told anyone, and she wasn't showing it off because it was Joseph and Andy's day, but she wasn't hiding it, either.

Swiftly, he moved to hide Linh Han from her daughter's sight. Looking over his shoulder, he called, "Be right there."

Fiona waved, her ring sparkling in the sunlight.

Linh Han hissed. "You're engaged. How nice."

"Yeah. Your worst nightmare. Your daughter's gonna marry an uneducated Mexican. And there's not a damn thing you can do about it. Despite you, our two families are working together, making homes possible for more immigrants. So I gotta thank you. Your power play brought Fiona and me closer together, and it's making this community a better place." He reached out to take her arm and escort her to the back door when his mother's voice froze him in his tracks.

"I'll get him." The clack of high heels on the stone floor brought his mother closer. "Tomas, we're waiting to go to the reception. Fiona needs to change, and you've got the keys."

Scowling, Tomas stepped aside, allowing Linh Han to be visible to his mother and Fiona. "I was trying to get rid of her," he muttered.

"Apparently, not hard enough." Dressed in a red dress that hugged her curves, his mother looked great, although she clashed with the mint and peach wedding colors.

Glancing between the two older women, Tomas noticed differences that went beyond their choice of clothes. Louisa Santiago glowed with health and well-being. Her hair shone, her smile came easily, and she looked like a woman who was loved and was content with her life. Linh Han's features were tight and pinched. She looked brittle, like she would blow away if the slightest wind kicked up. Tomas doubted that she'd ever been happy. Satisfied, maybe, but not happy. Now, she vibrated with barely controlled fury.

"You think you've won. You, with your—"

"Enough Mother," Fiona snapped. She looked around, then asked in a quieter voice, "Why are you here?"

Tomas caught his mother's eye, and they moved to form a shield, blocking the tense conversation from the other wedding guests.

"I came to…." Linh Han darted a glance at Louisa, then back at Fiona, but didn't finish.

"To apologize?" Fiona looked so hopeful Tomas held his breath.

It took so long to happen, and Linh Han's nod was so tiny, he would have missed it if he'd blinked. The murmur of voices from outside the church drifted into the sanctuary as he, his mother, and Fiona waited for more.

"Well," Linh Han finally said, "I'll just—"

Louisa smoothly blocked her from getting past them. "I'm pretty sure you have more to say to Fiona. Don't you?"

Fiona trembled as she stared at her mother, hope slowly fading from her eyes to be replaced by disappointment. Tomas wanted to wring his future mother-in-law's scrawny neck for doing that to her. Instead, he pulled Fiona into his side, prepared to do whatever she asked of him.

Linh Han caught the movement, her gaze locking on Fiona's hand clutching his shirt before moving up to meet Tomas's eyes.

In a voice barely above a whisper, she said, "I was wrong."

Sagging against him, Fiona let out a tiny sob, and Tomas held her closer.

It was probably sunlight coming through the stained-glass window, but he thought he saw a sheen of tears in Linh

Han's eyes. Knowing they'd be waiting all day if they expected more than that for an apology, he said, "Thank you." Tension leaked from the moment like air from a balloon, and he loosened his shoulders.

Laughter rang out behind them, and Fiona's mother craned her neck, trying to look past Louisa.

Dabbing at her eyes, Fiona pulled away and gestured to the group outside. "Do you want to say hello?"

He didn't think it was a good idea, but Tomas kept his mouth shut.

Thankfully, her mother demurred. "Maybe not," she replied and turned around.

She was almost at the side exit when Joseph's voice rang out, "Mother? Is that you?" Andy close on his heels, Joseph hurried down the center aisle. "What are you doing here?" His voice was hard as his gaze flicked between his mother and sister.

Fiona stepped between them as her brother advanced. "She came to apologize," she told him.

Joseph halted in his tracks, looking dumbfounded. "Really?" His head swiveled between Fiona, Tomas, and Louisa, then back to Fiona.

"Really," she answered, "and there were witnesses."

The wind went out of Joseph's sails. "That's...that's good." He reached behind him and took Andy's hand. Wonder filled his voice as he said, "My mother is here. And she apologized."

Andy patted his arm. "I heard." He kissed his husband's cheek and smiled like his carefully orchestrated day had not been disrupted. "Would you like to join us for dinner?"

Linh Han was shaking her head before he'd finished the question. "No, thank you. I don't want to intrude."

For weeks, moaning about the guest list and where to seat everyone had been the focus of Andy's conversation. Yet he'd extended the invitation without gritting his teeth. Tomas rolled his eyes but managed to refrain from snorting. His mother gave him a look. "Behave," she muttered.

"Nonsense," Andy waved away the protest. "You're family. There's always room at the table." He took Linh Han by one arm and Joseph by the other, leading them back down the aisle. Joseph turned back and smiled at Fiona, his lips forming a silent *"Thank you."*

"Are you good?" Tomas asked, running a hand up and down her back and leading her through the pews.

Fiona sniffed and gave him a watery smile. "Yeah, but I've changed my mind," she said as they stopped to pick up her bouquet and his jacket. "I'm not going to change. It will make Andy's day if I wear this to the reception."

His mother laughed. "Honey, you won't be able to get into the truck. How are you going to get there?"

She had a point. With all the ruffles and hoops, Tomas doubted he'd be able to see out the windshield.

"I'll stand in the back and hold on to the hood," Fiona said. "Tomas can drive slowly, and I'll wave like a prom queen." She cocked her hand and gave a queenly wave, smiling through her smudged mascara.

"Uh-huh." Voice full of skepticism, Louisa led them to where Carlos waited in the bright sunlight.

"Here." Tomas tossed the truck keys to Carlos. "You drive."

"What are you doing?" Fiona hoisted her skirt and hastened to catch up as he walked to the curb.

Pulling on his suit jacket, he grinned at her. "Precious cargo." Opening up the tailgate, he picked up Fiona and deposited her in the truck bed. Jumping up, he closed the tailgate behind them and motioned her over. "Stand here." He caged her in between the truck cab and himself. "You wave, I'll hold on."

Laughter rang out as Carlos and Louisa climbed into the

truck, and they drove slowly through town, Fiona waving when people stopped and stared.

Fabulous & Flawed
(A sneak peek)

A bottle of bubbly tucked in her tote bag, Sylvie Santiago all but skipped across the parking lot and up the stairs to her apartment. She paused on a step to do a little happy dance.

The bank had approved her mortgage application and her dream of being a homeowner was close to becoming a reality. Not just a homeowner, either. The property she had her eye on was a duplex that had seen better days. She would live in one side while fixing it up, rent it out, then move into the other side and fix it up.

The blare of music from another apartment barely registered. She was busy deciding on paint colors. Yellow was her favorite, but should she go with something safer? She'd ask Dean. Sanchez Homes was his family's business. He'd know what colors brought in homebuyers.

Sylvie did a clumsy pirouette as she rounded the corner to her front door, then righted herself. The obnoxious EDM was coming from her apartment.

Digging out her keys, she quickened her pace. It was three o'clock in the afternoon. Dean shouldn't be home yet. And he sure as hell shouldn't be playing music that loud.

She pushed the door open, ready to scold her boyfriend but the words didn't come out. Takeout containers and empty bottles littered the coffee table and clothes were strewn all over the floor. The bare backside of a busty blonde bobbed up and down on Dean's spread, naked, hairy thighs.

Sylvie shrieked.

The blonde froze.

Dean poked his head around the woman. "Oh. You're home early."

"Apparently so." Sylvie stomped to the speakers and turned them off. Shock, betrayal, and anger warred inside her. She chose to go with anger. "What the hell, Dean?"

For more about this and other upcoming stories, go to www.lynnehancockpearson.com to join her newsletter. You can unsubscribe at any time.

Reviews are like a warm hug, consider leaving one to let others know you enjoyed *Perfectly Polished* and guide readers to my books.

Planners & Dreamers series

Grand Gestures

Jane will grit her teeth and smile at the snobby and suspicious CFO if it means landing the contract. But she won't put on a dress and definitely not heels.

Fraudulent Trust

How was Delia supposed to know she needed to support herself? That's what trust funds are for.

Holiday Headaches

Sid and Connie are practically strangers but they could be roommates. What could possibly go wrong?

Keeney Builds series

#HotAndHandy

Everyone in town loves the handsome handyman. Everyone except his new neighbor.

ABOUT THE AUTHOR

Lynne Hancock Pearson writes fun, flirty, feel-good fiction that simmers at a low heat. Stories of people finding their way, even if it takes a while to get there. She lives near Seattle with three finicky felines, two towering offspring, and one long-suffering husband. She is a left-handed middle child who grew up in the Great White North and is a proud member of the Métis Nation of Canada.

9 798985 352771